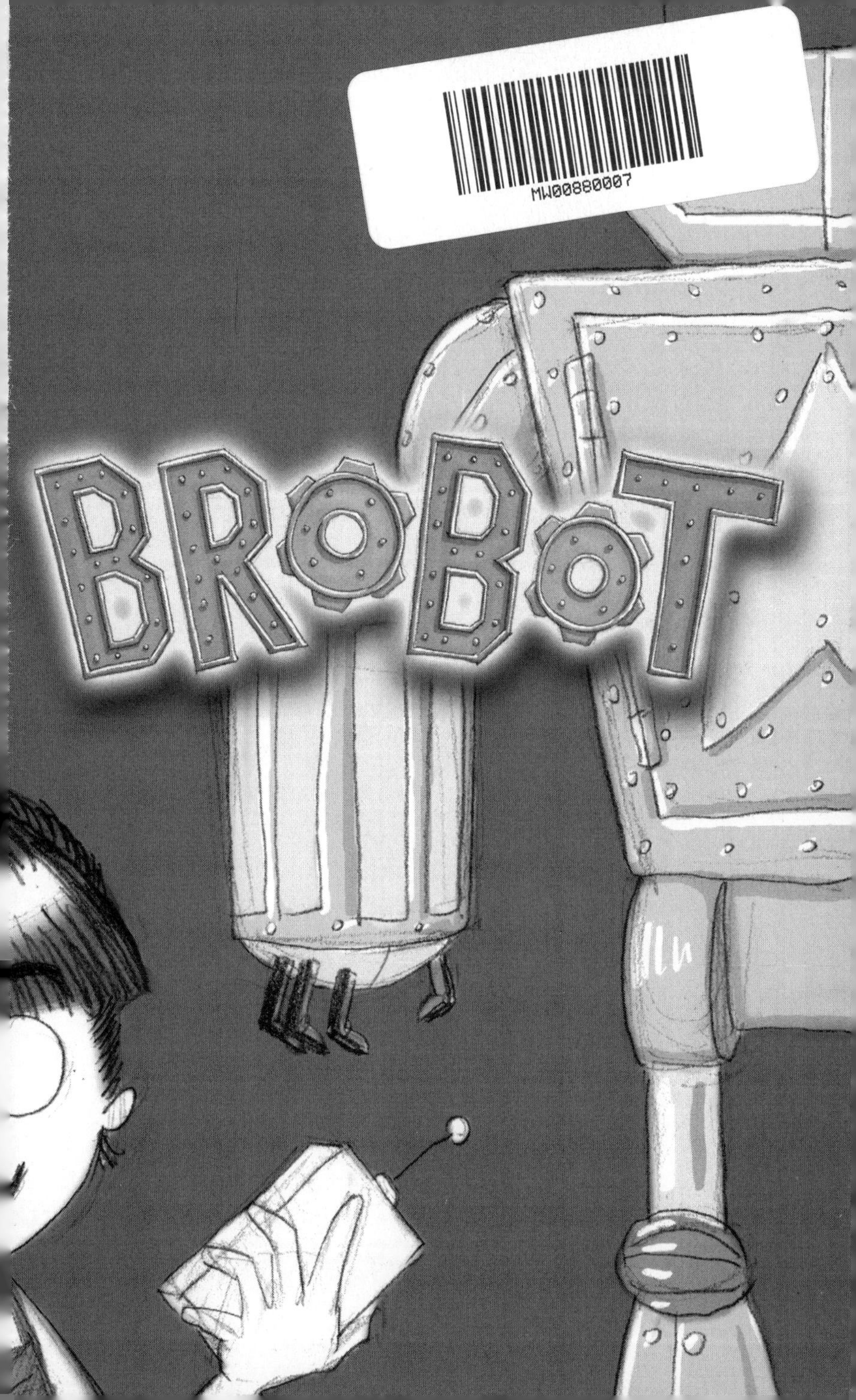
BROBOT

To Bob and Bear -
just as a brother and sister should be.
And to you, the reader - thank you!

BROBOT

James Foley

FREMANTLE PRESS

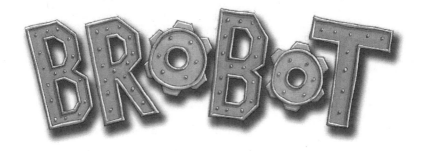

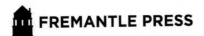

Greetings!
I'm **Sally Tinker**,
the world's foremost inventor
under the age of
twelve.

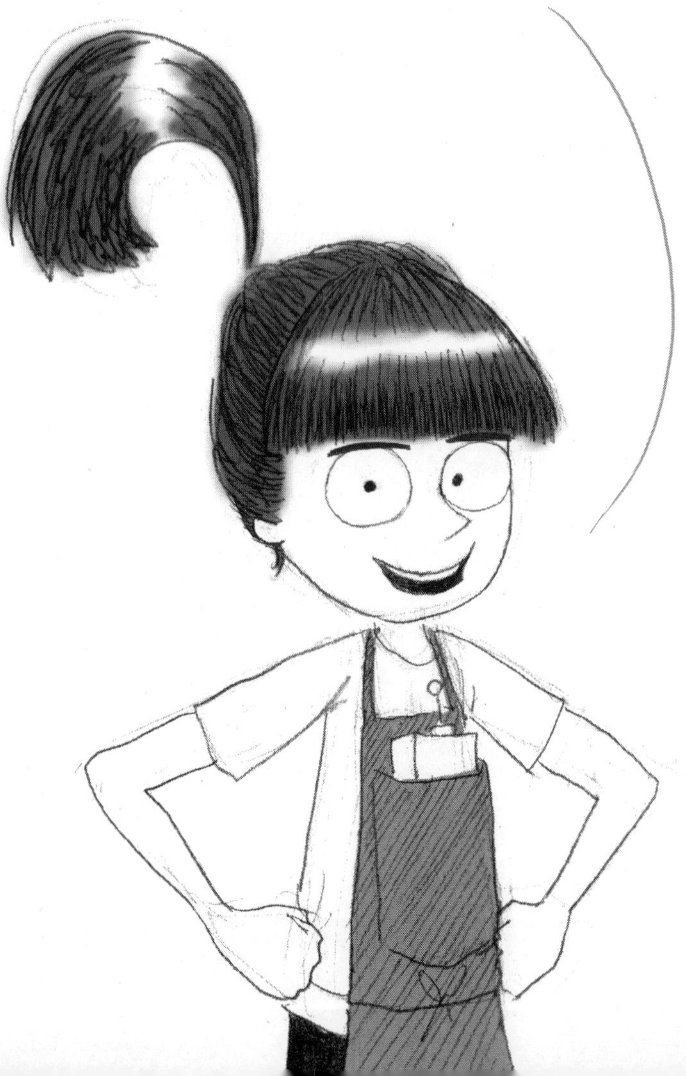

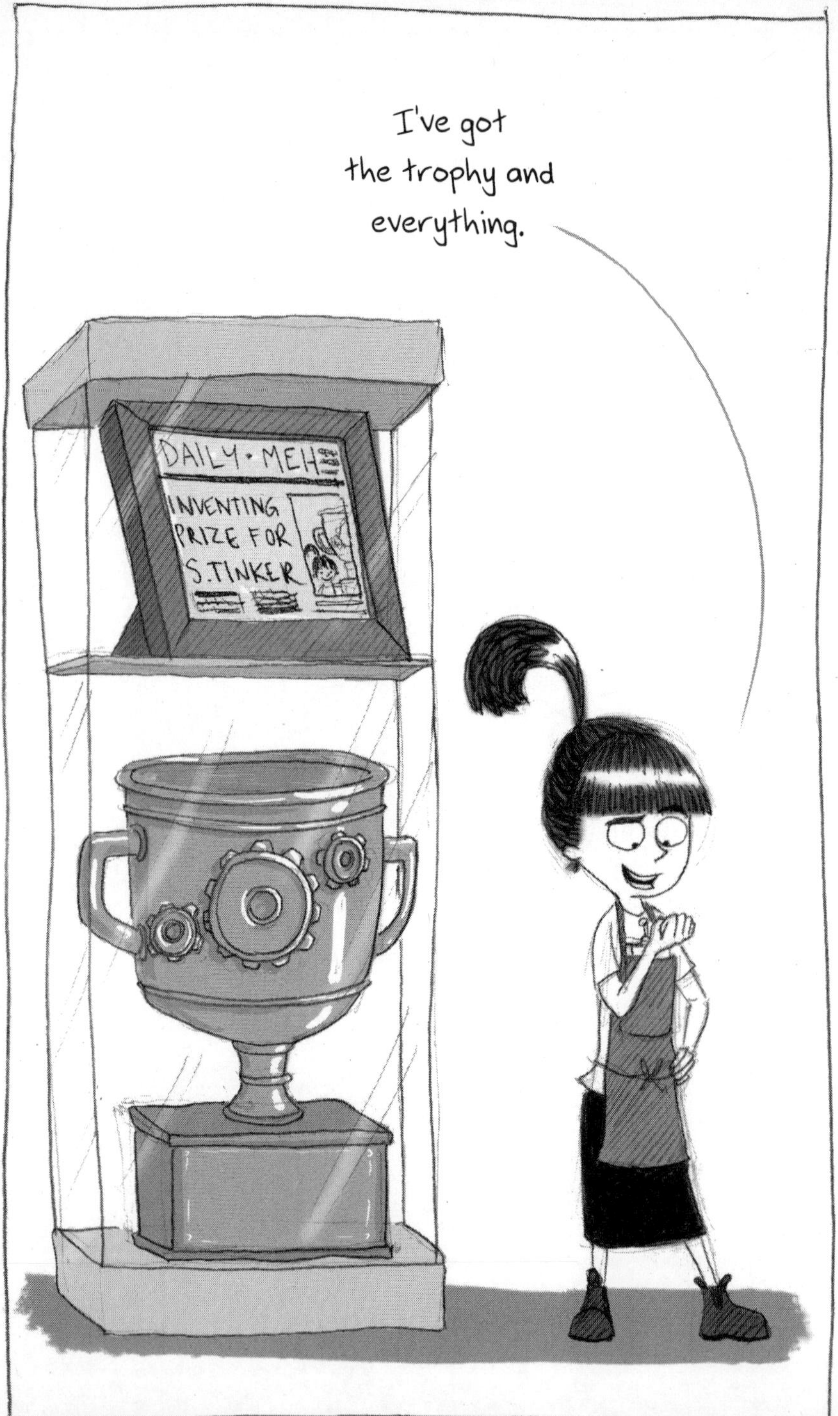
I've got the trophy and everything.
DAILY • MEH
INVENTING PRIZE FOR S.TINKER

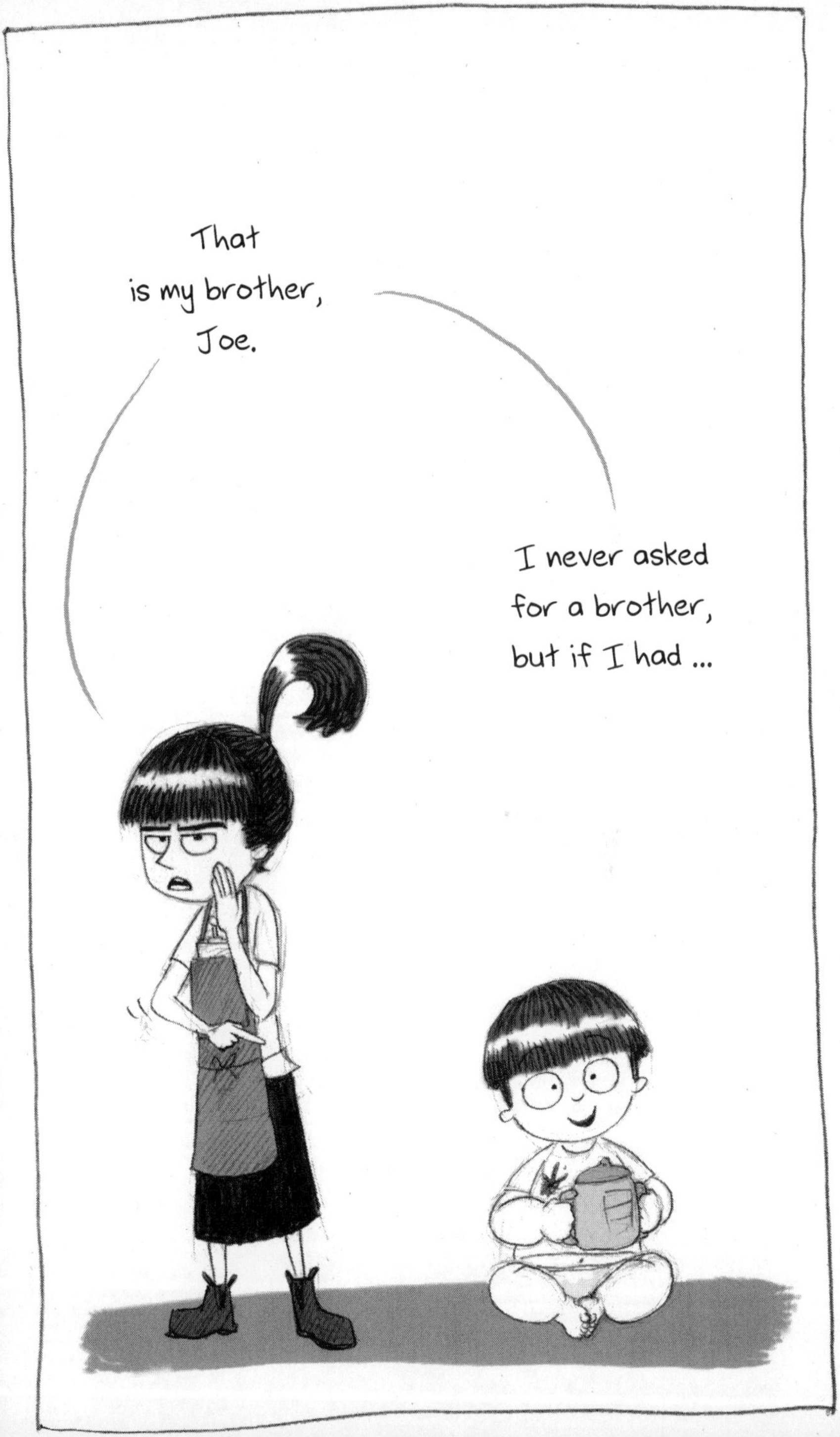
That is my brother, Joe.
I never asked for a brother, but if I had ...

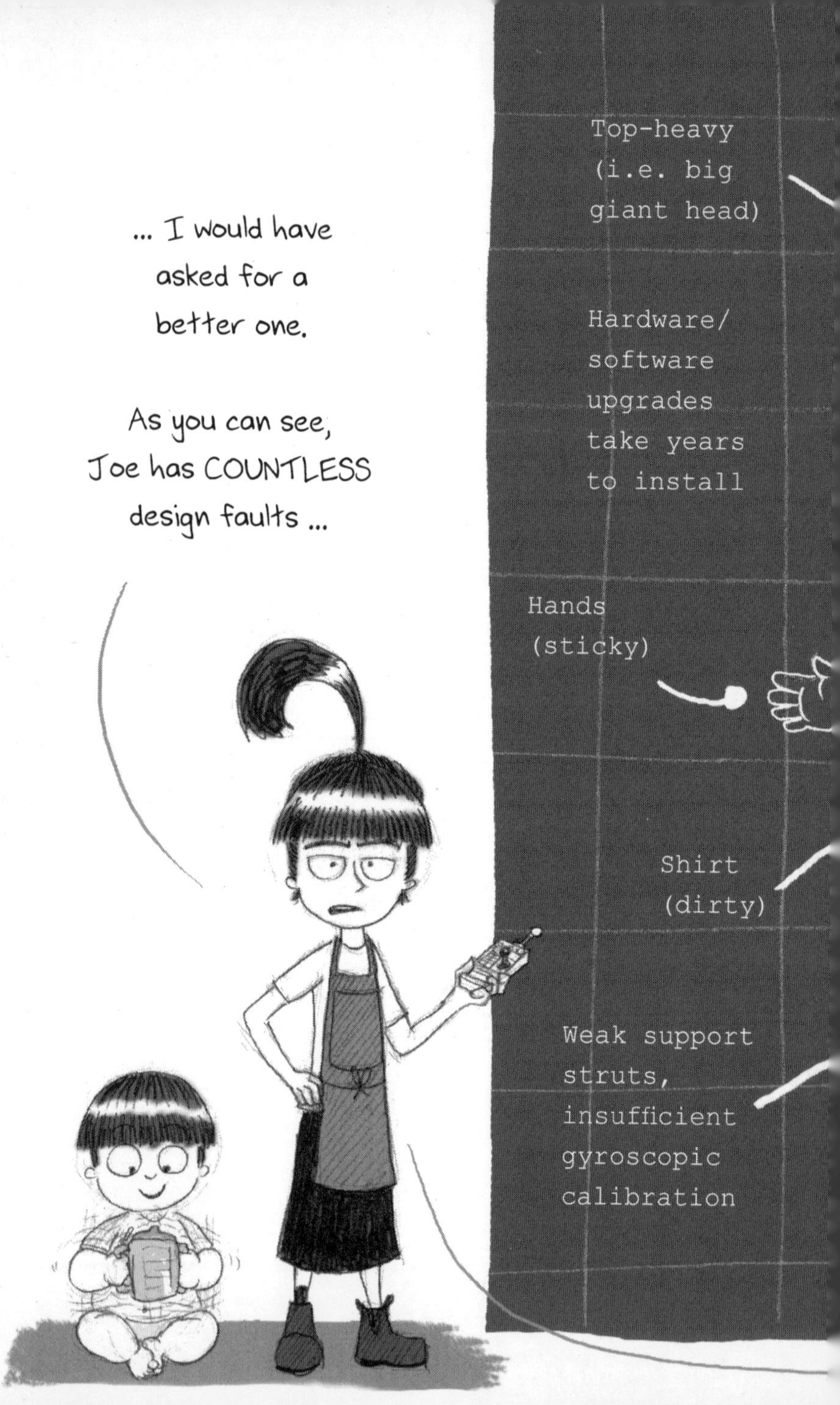
... I would have asked for a better one.
As you can see, Joe has COUNTLESS design faults ...
Top-heavy (i.e. big giant head)
Hardware/ software upgrades take years to install
Hands (sticky)
Shirt (dirty)
Weak support struts, insufficient gyroscopic calibration

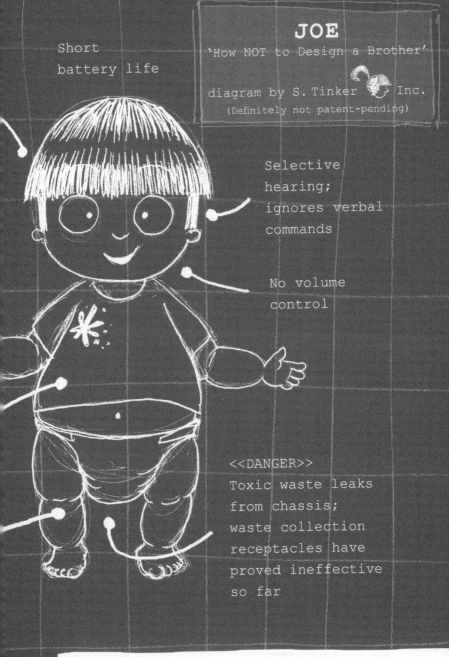

JOE

'How NOT to Design a Brother'

diagram by S. Tinker Inc.

(Definitely not patent-pending)

Short battery life

Selective hearing; ignores verbal commands

No volume control

<<DANGER>>
Toxic waste leaks from chassis; waste collection receptacles have proved ineffective so far

... but there are three problems that are particularly serious:

1. He's always making a mess.

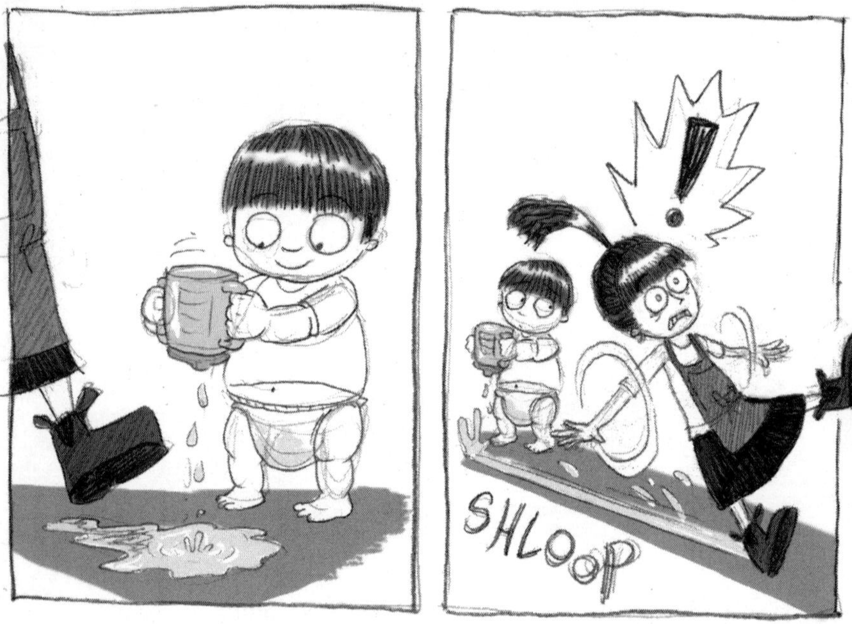
!
SHLOOP

2. He's always breaking my machines.

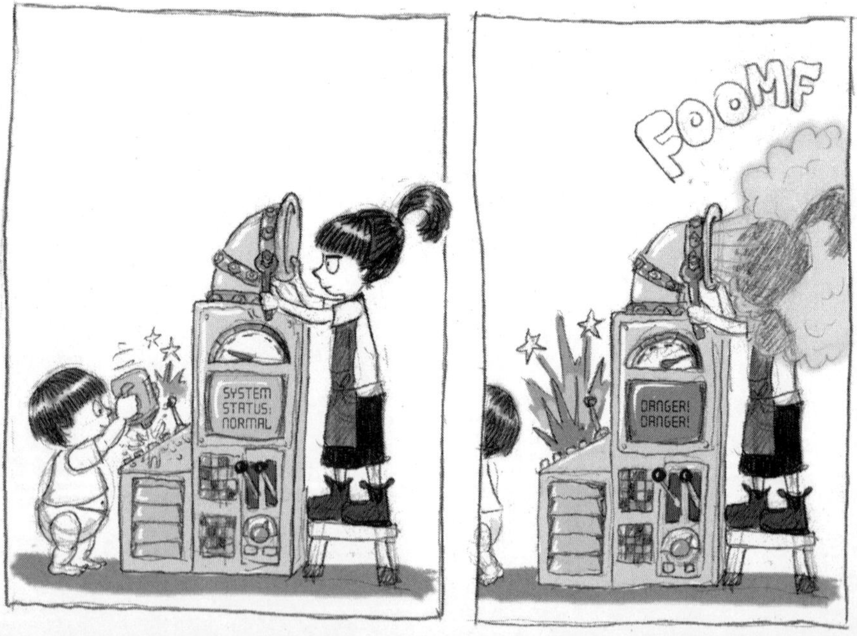
SYSTEM STATUS: NORMAL
FOOMF
DANGER! DANGER!

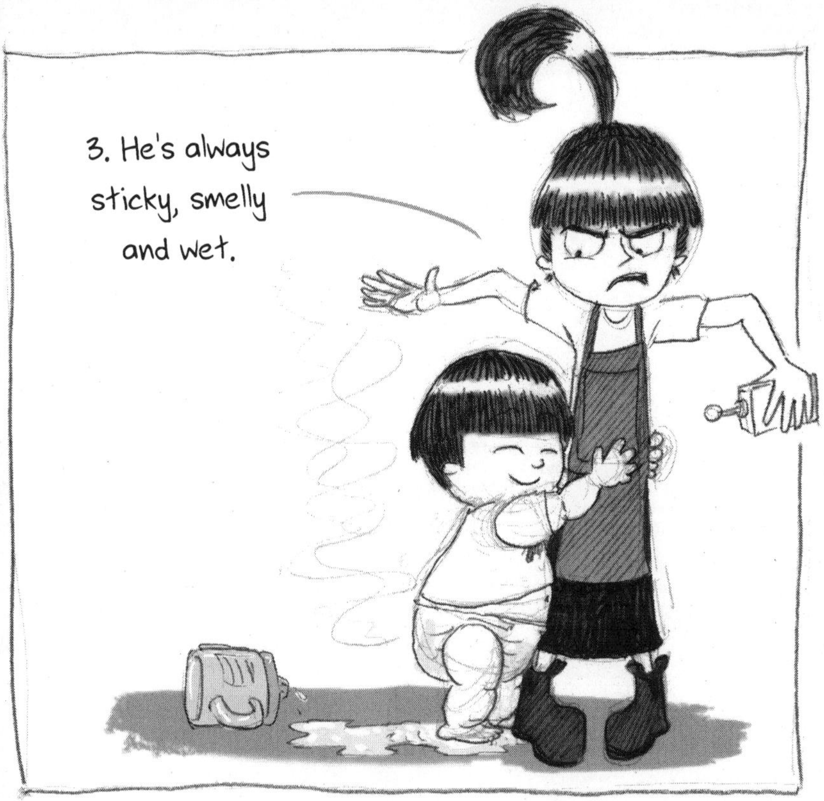
3. He's always sticky, smelly and wet.

Worst of all,
Joe is impossible to control.

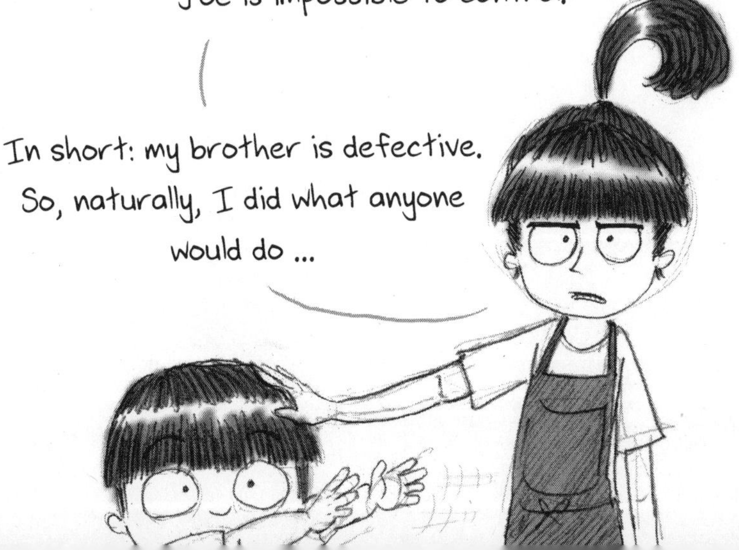
In short: my brother is defective.
So, naturally, I did what anyone would do ...

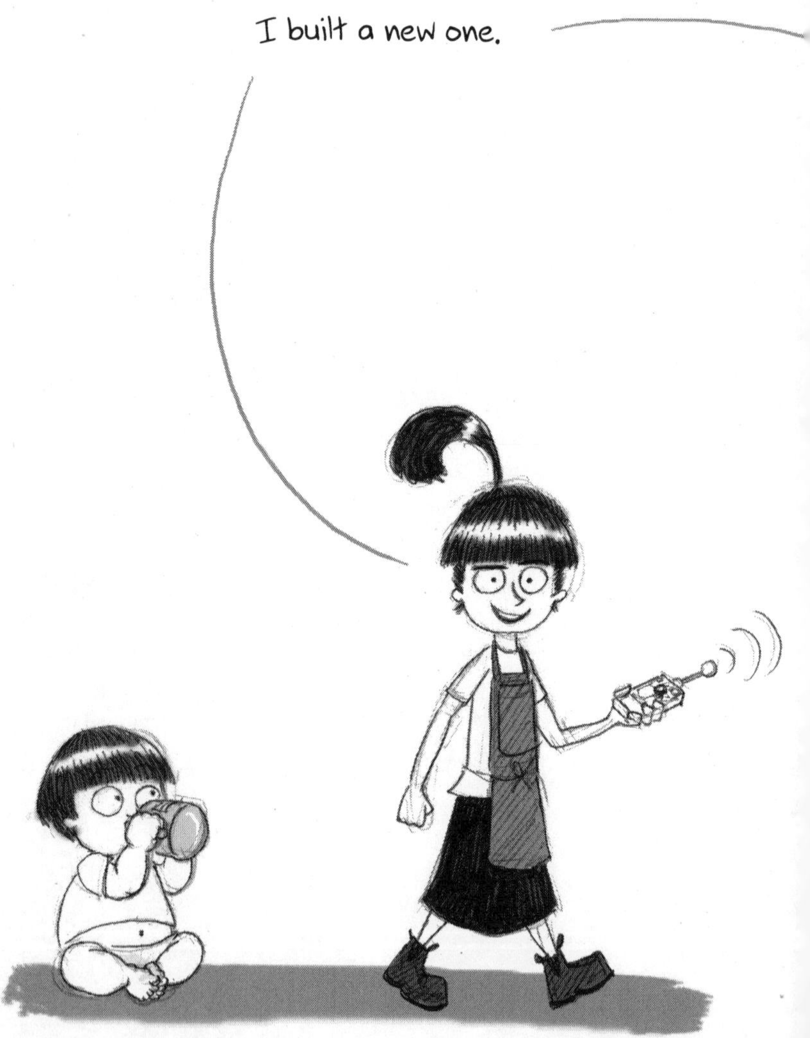
I built a new one.

BEHOLD!
My amazing,
patent-pending ...

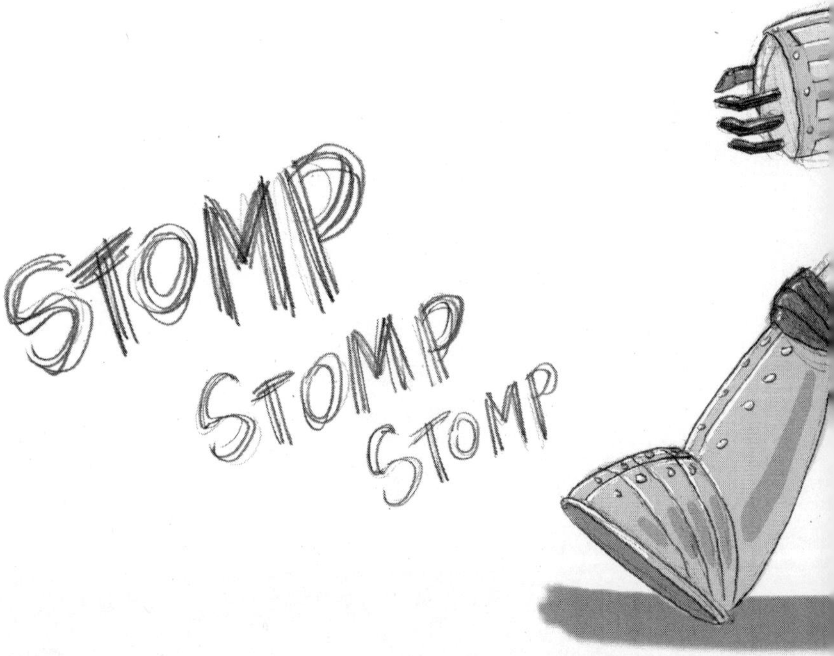
STOMP
STOMP
STOMP

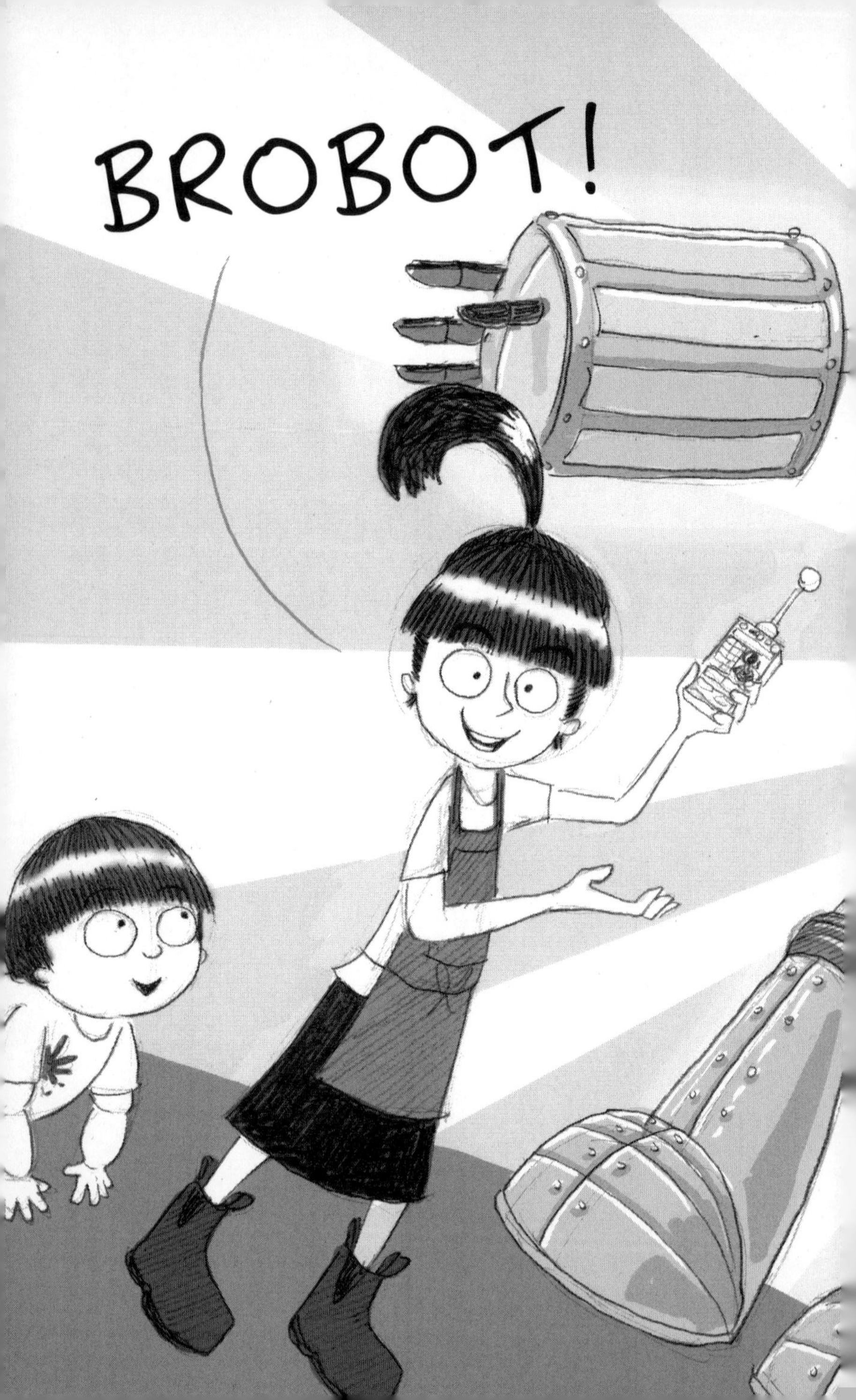
BROBOT!

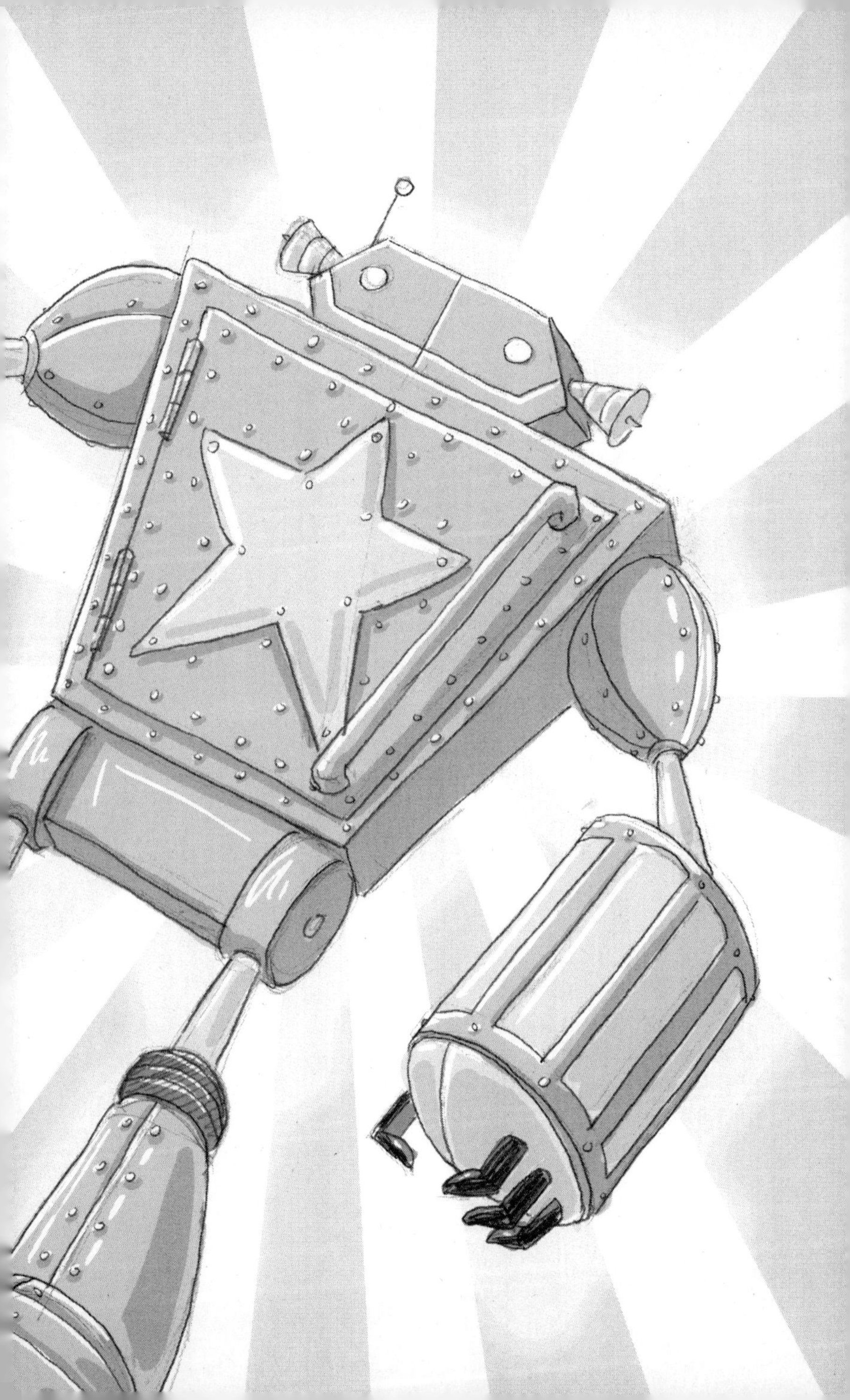

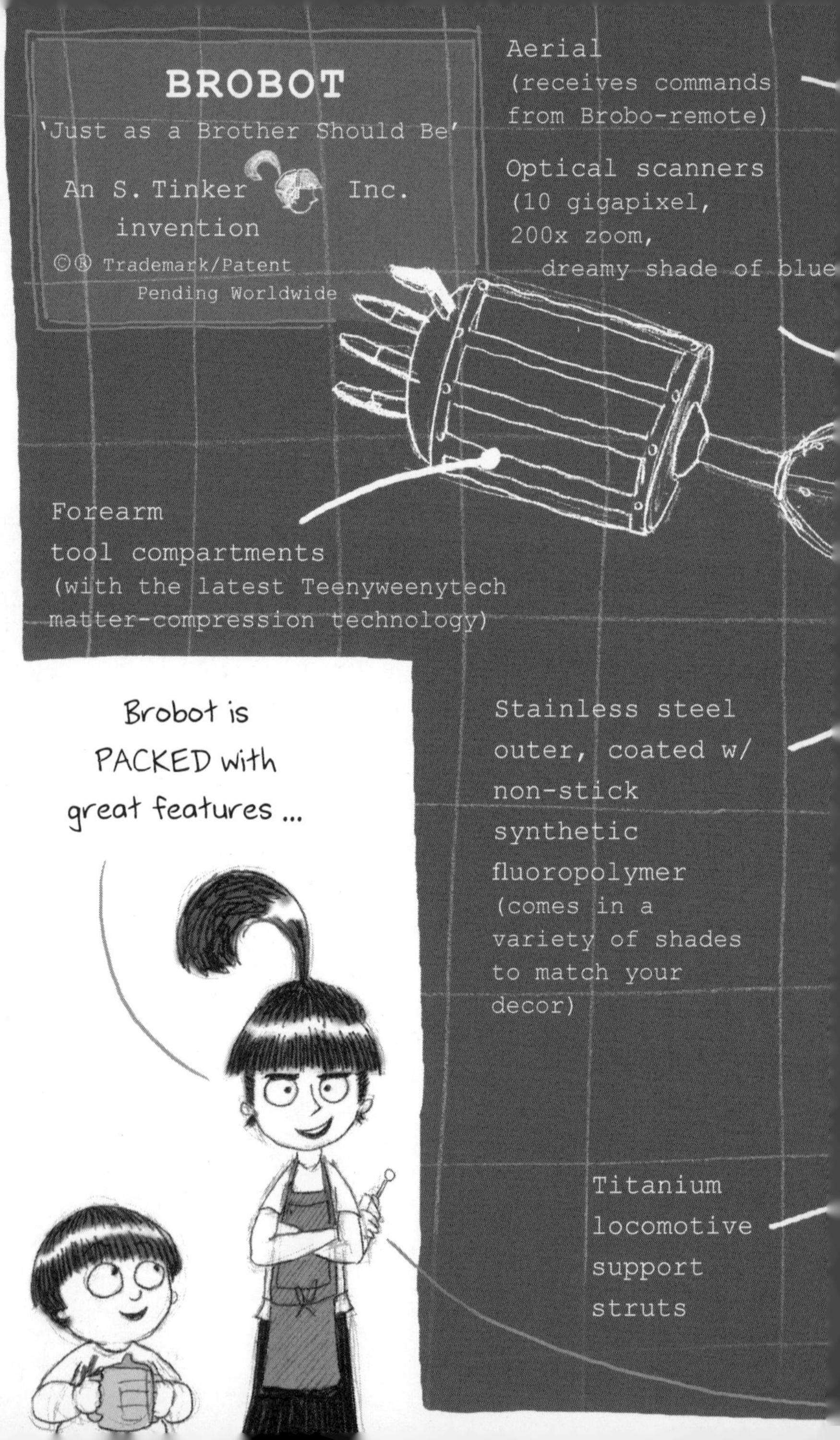
BROBOT
'Just as a Brother Should Be'
An S. Tinker Inc. invention
©® Trademark/Patent Pending Worldwide
Aerial (receives commands from Brobo-remote)
Optical scanners (10 gigapixel, 200x zoom, dreamy shade of blue
Forearm tool compartments (with the latest Teenyweenytech matter-compression technology)
Brobot is PACKED with great features ...
Stainless steel outer, coated w/ non-stick synthetic fluoropolymer (comes in a variety of shades to match your decor)
Titanium locomotive support struts

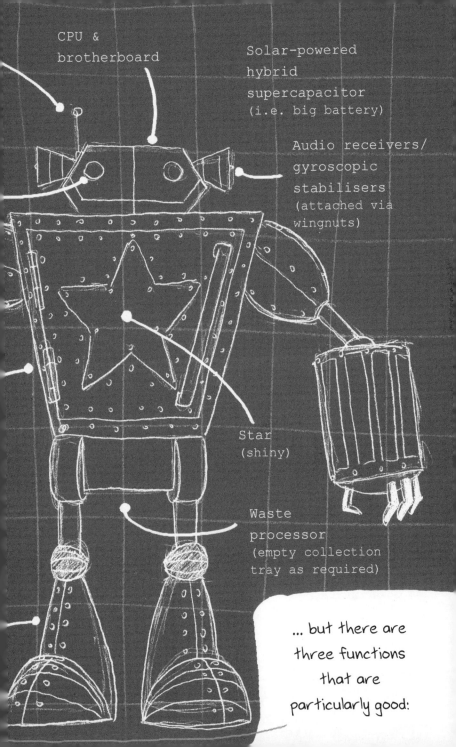

CPU &
brotherboard

Solar-powered
hybrid
supercapacitor
(i.e. big battery)

Audio receivers/
gyroscopic
stabilisers
(attached via
wingnuts)

Star
(shiny)

Waste
processor
(empty collection
tray as required)

... but there are
three functions
that are
particularly good:

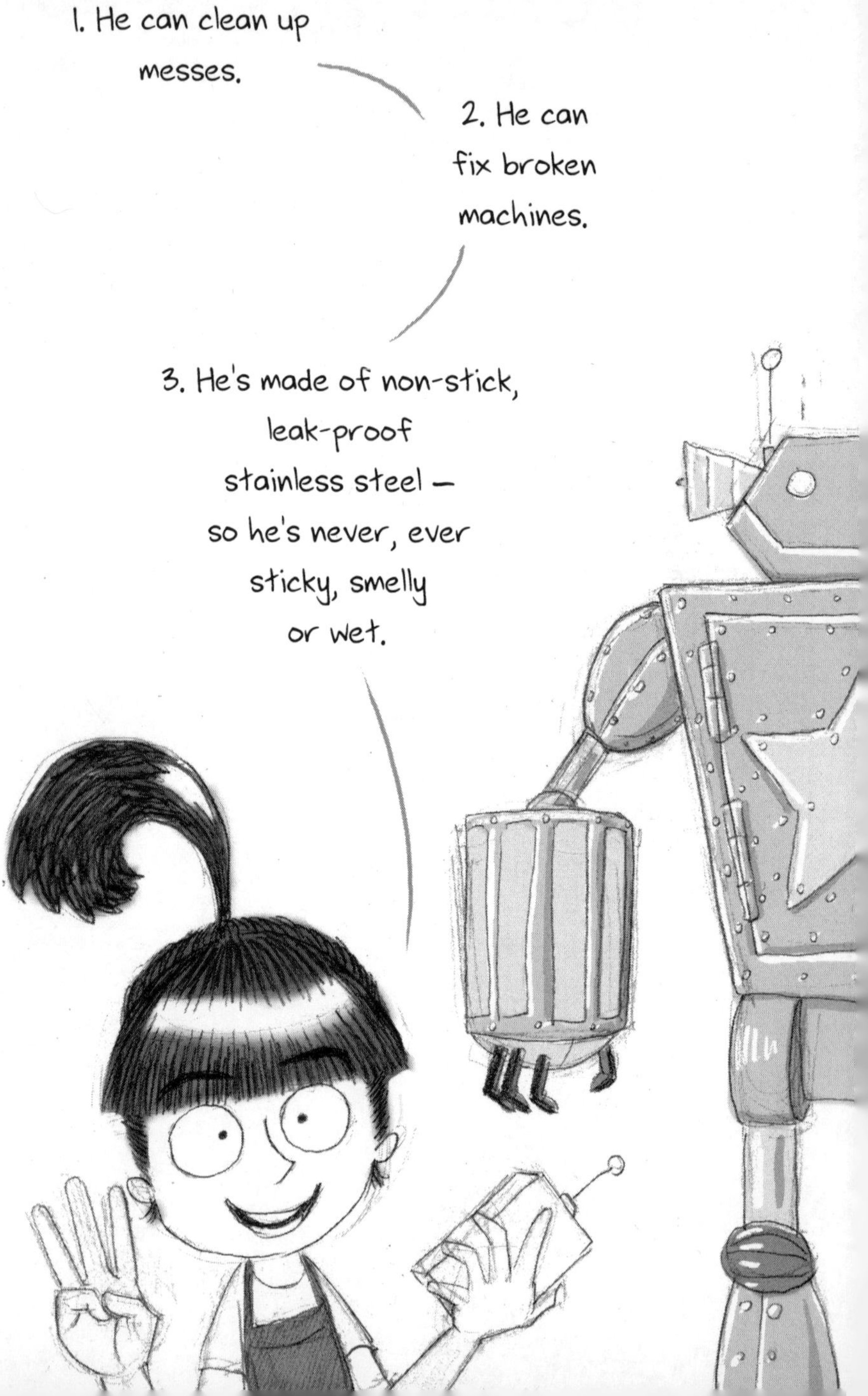
1. He can clean up messes.
2. He can fix broken machines.
3. He's made of non-stick, leak-proof stainless steel — so he's never, ever sticky, smelly or wet.

In short:
Brobot is just
as a brother should be.

As an added bonus,
Brobot has a built-in cupcake oven,
so his exhaust smells delicious.

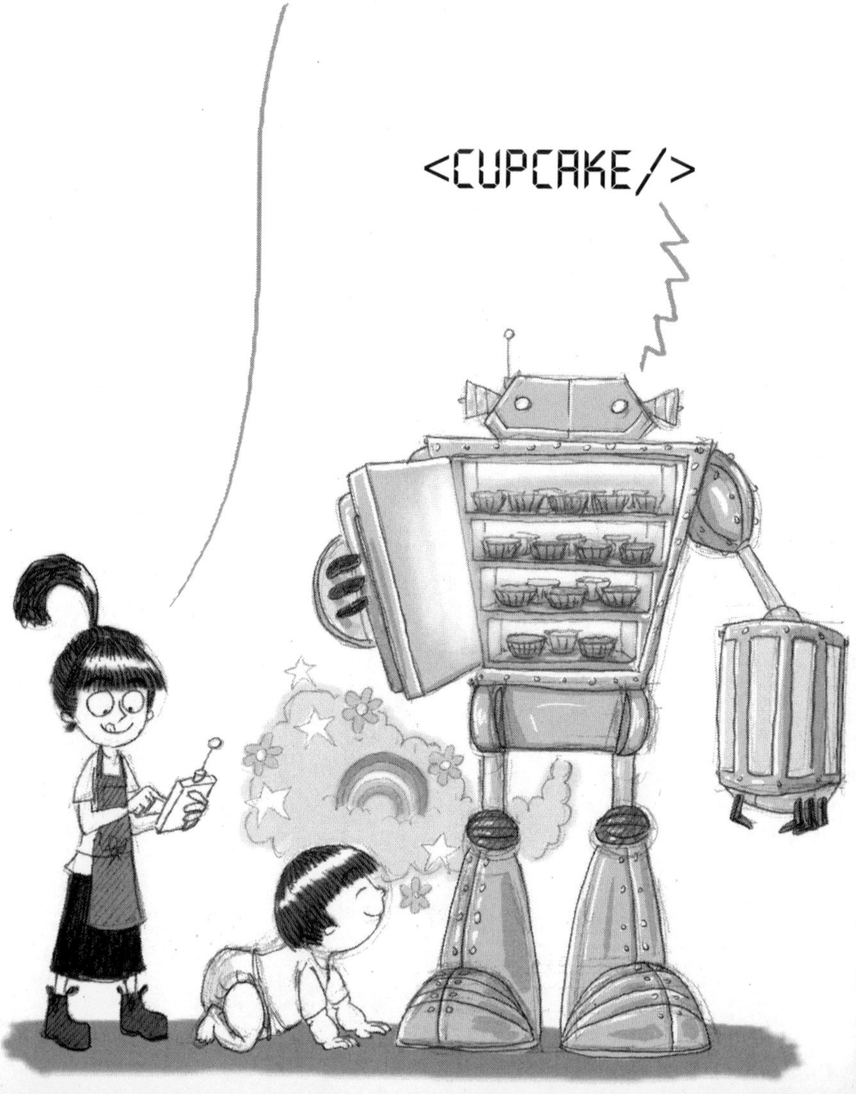
<CUPCAKE/>

And best of all,
I can control Brobot's every move
using the Brobo-remote.

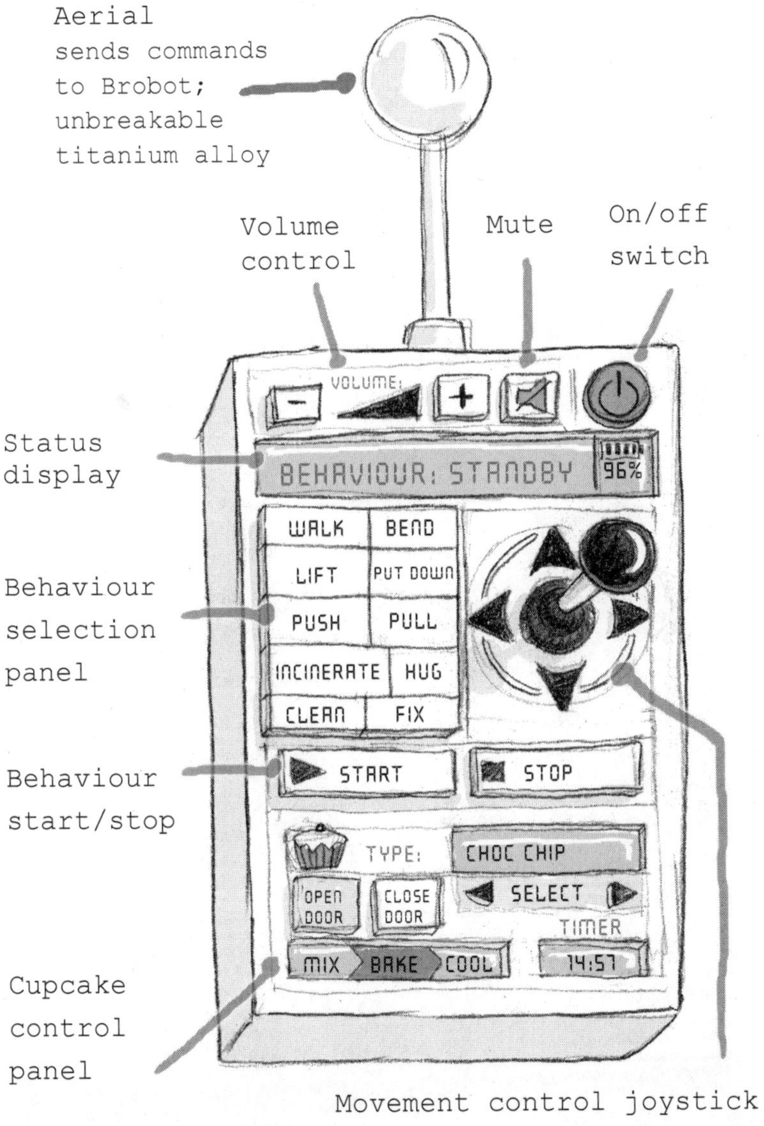
Aerial
sends commands to Brobot; unbreakable titanium alloy
Volume control
Mute
On/off switch
VOLUME:
Status display
BEHAVIOUR: STANDBY
96%
Behaviour selection panel
WALK
BEND
LIFT
PUT DOWN
PUSH
PULL
INCINERATE
HUG
CLEAN
FIX
Behaviour start/stop
START
STOP
TYPE:
CHOC CHIP
OPEN DOOR
CLOSE DOOR
SELECT
TIMER
14:57
MIX
BAKE
COOL
Cupcake control panel
Movement control joystick

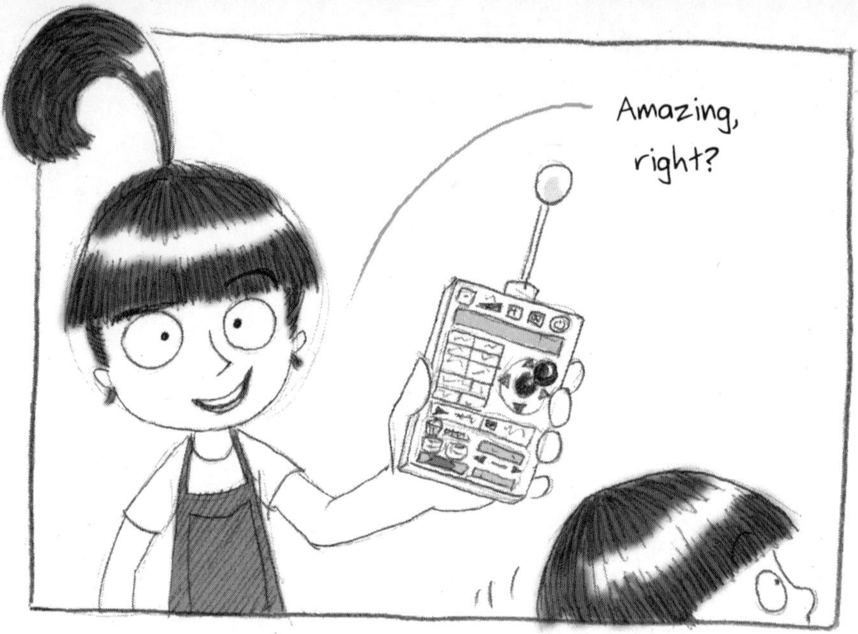
Amazing, right?

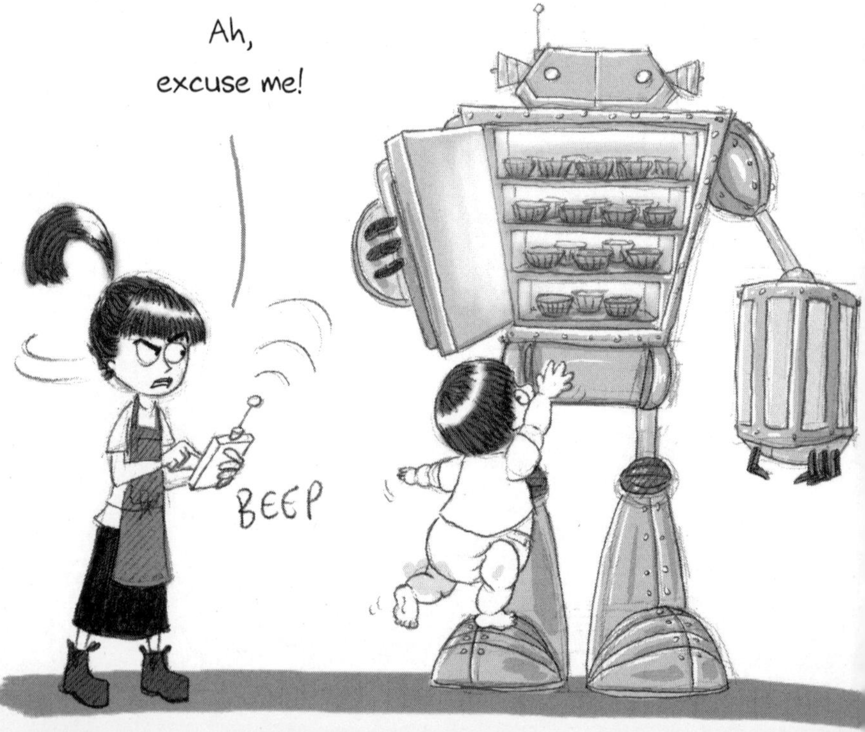
Ah, excuse me!
BEEP

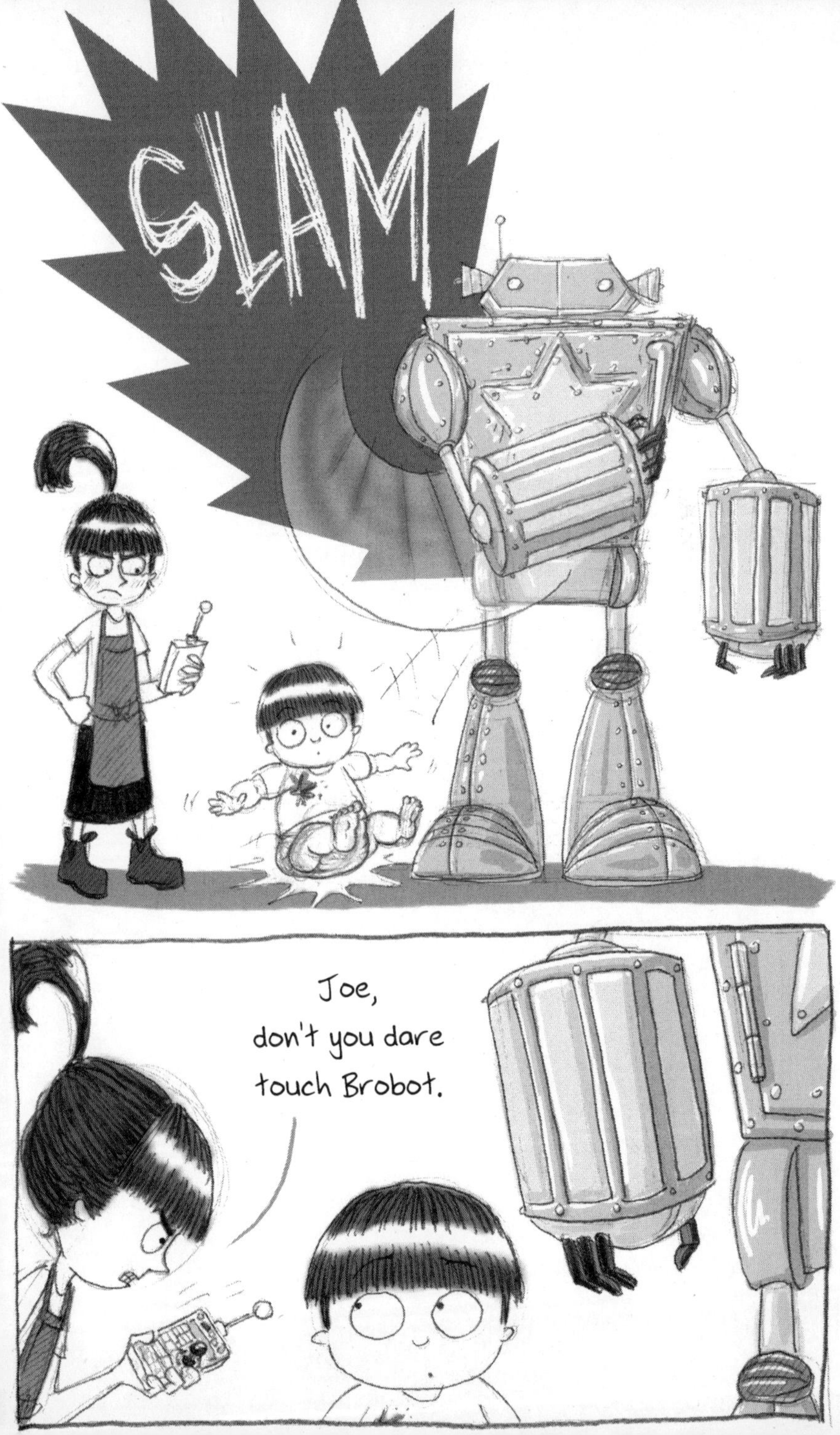
SLAM
Joe,
don't you dare
touch Brobot.

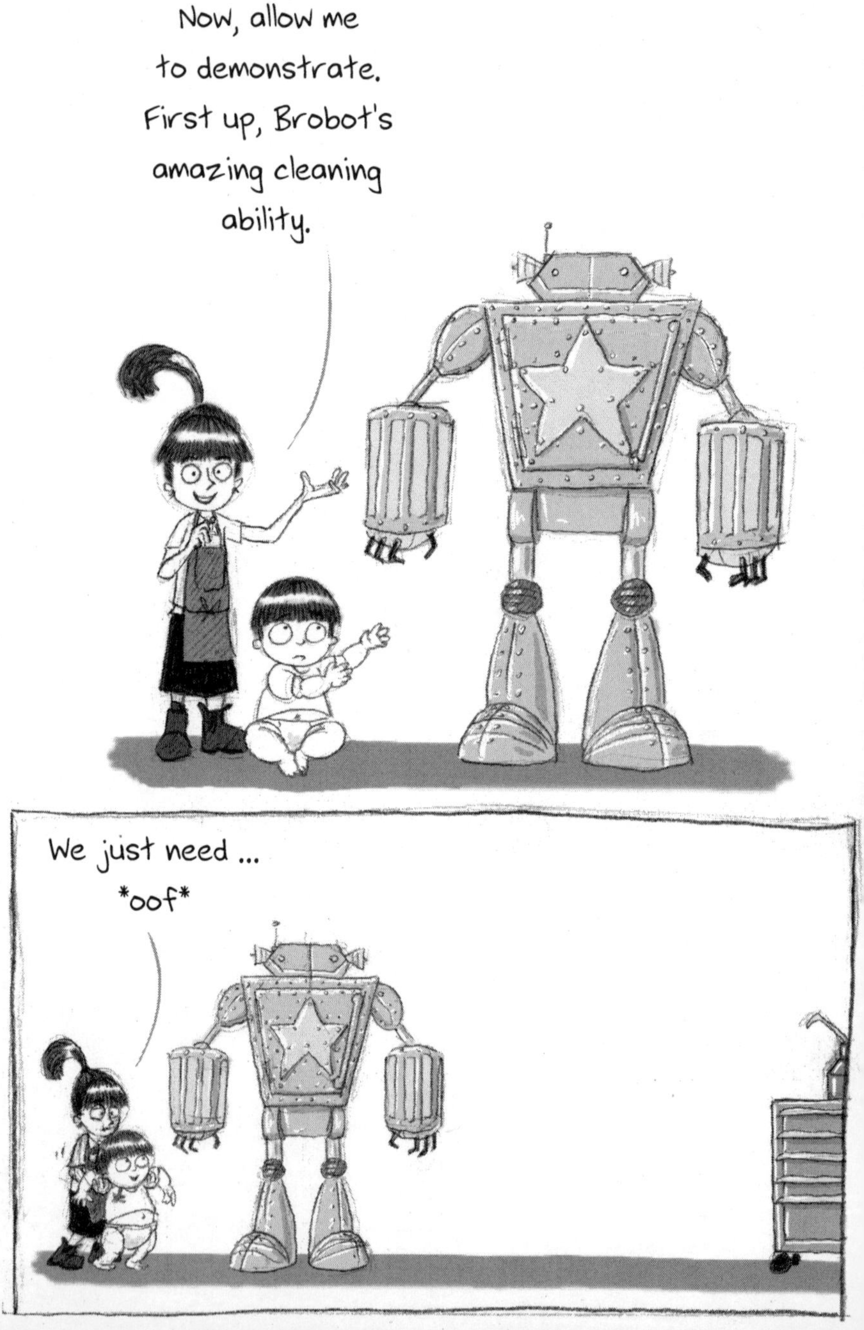
Now, allow me to demonstrate. First up, Brobot's amazing cleaning ability.
We just need ... *oof*

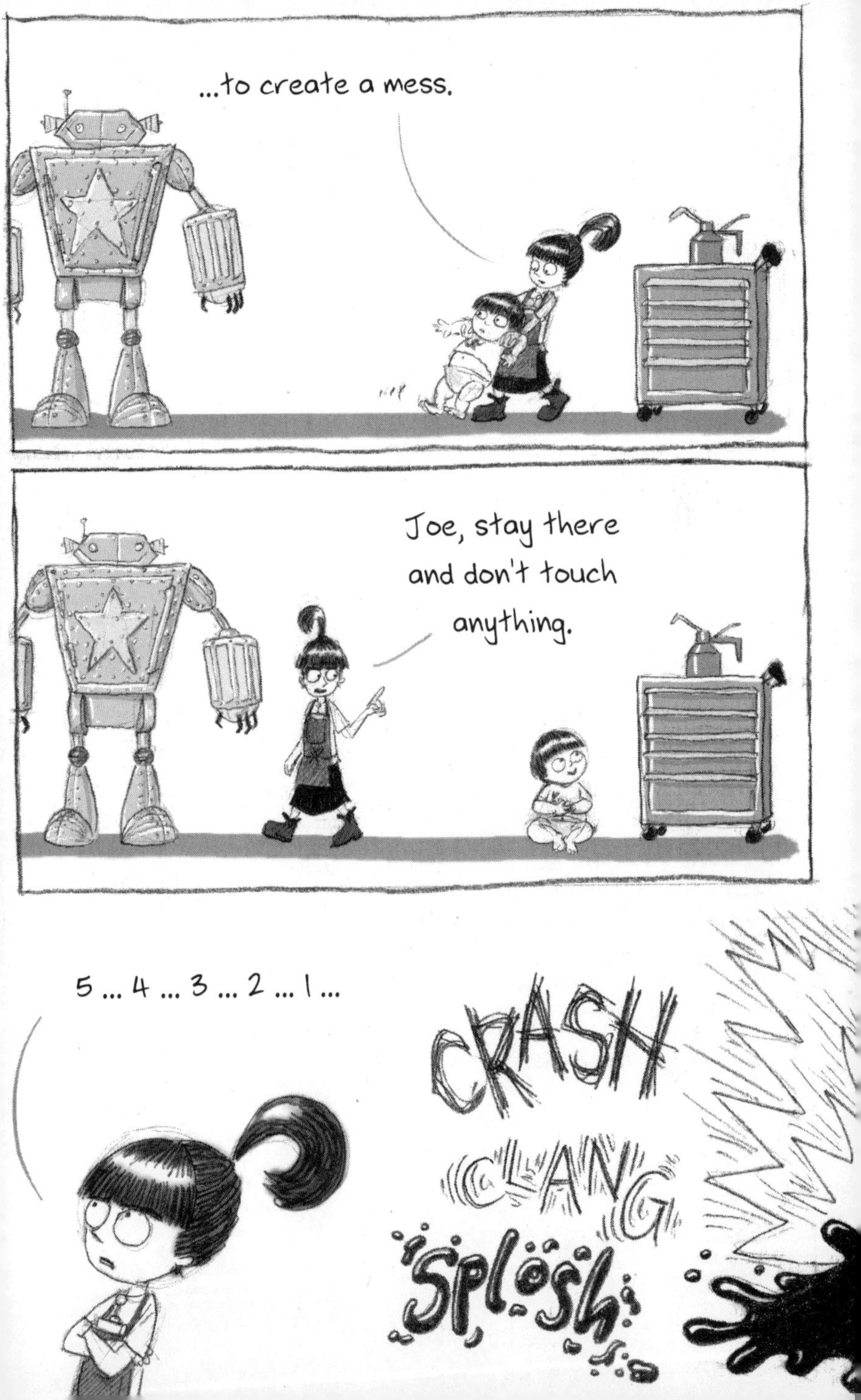
...to create a mess.
Joe, stay there and don't touch anything.
5 ... 4 ... 3 ... 2 ... 1 ...
CRASH
CLANG
Splosh

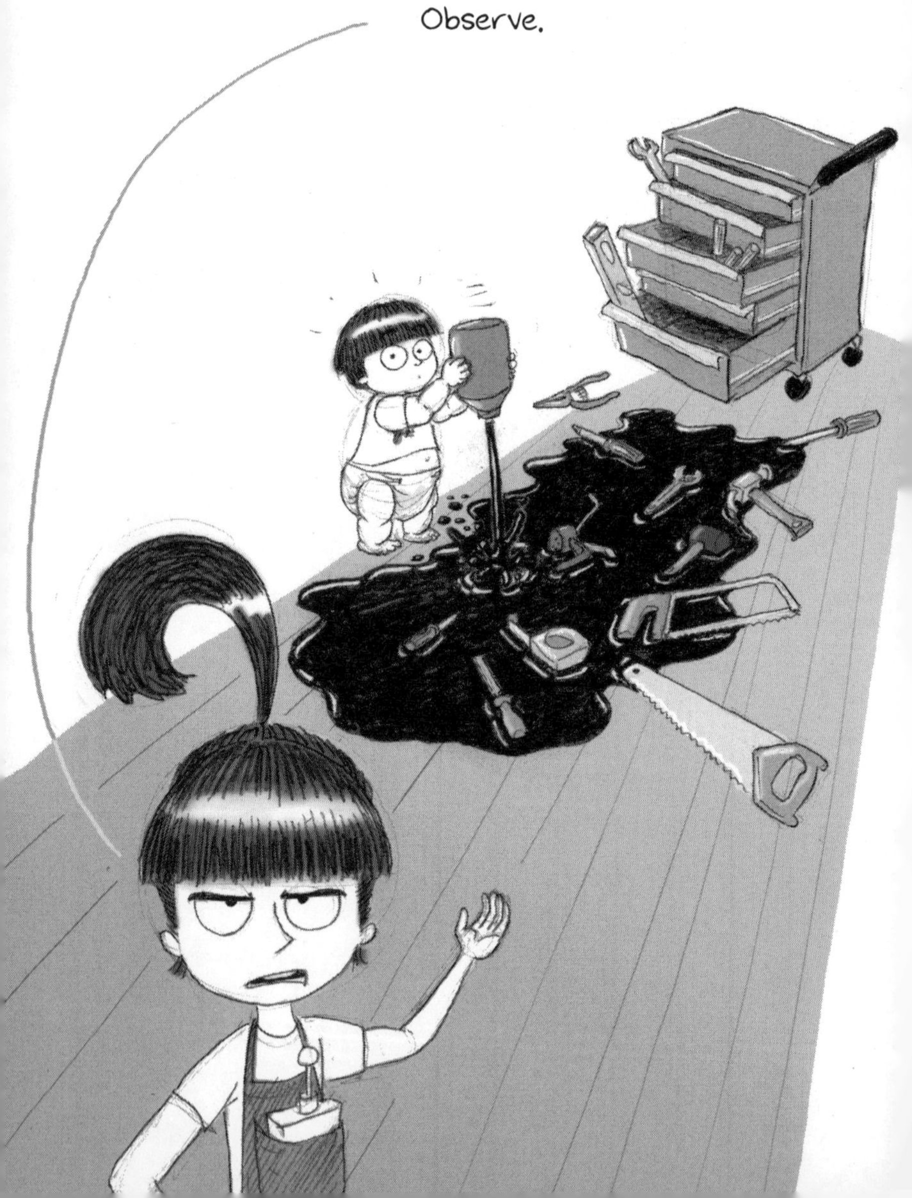
Observe.

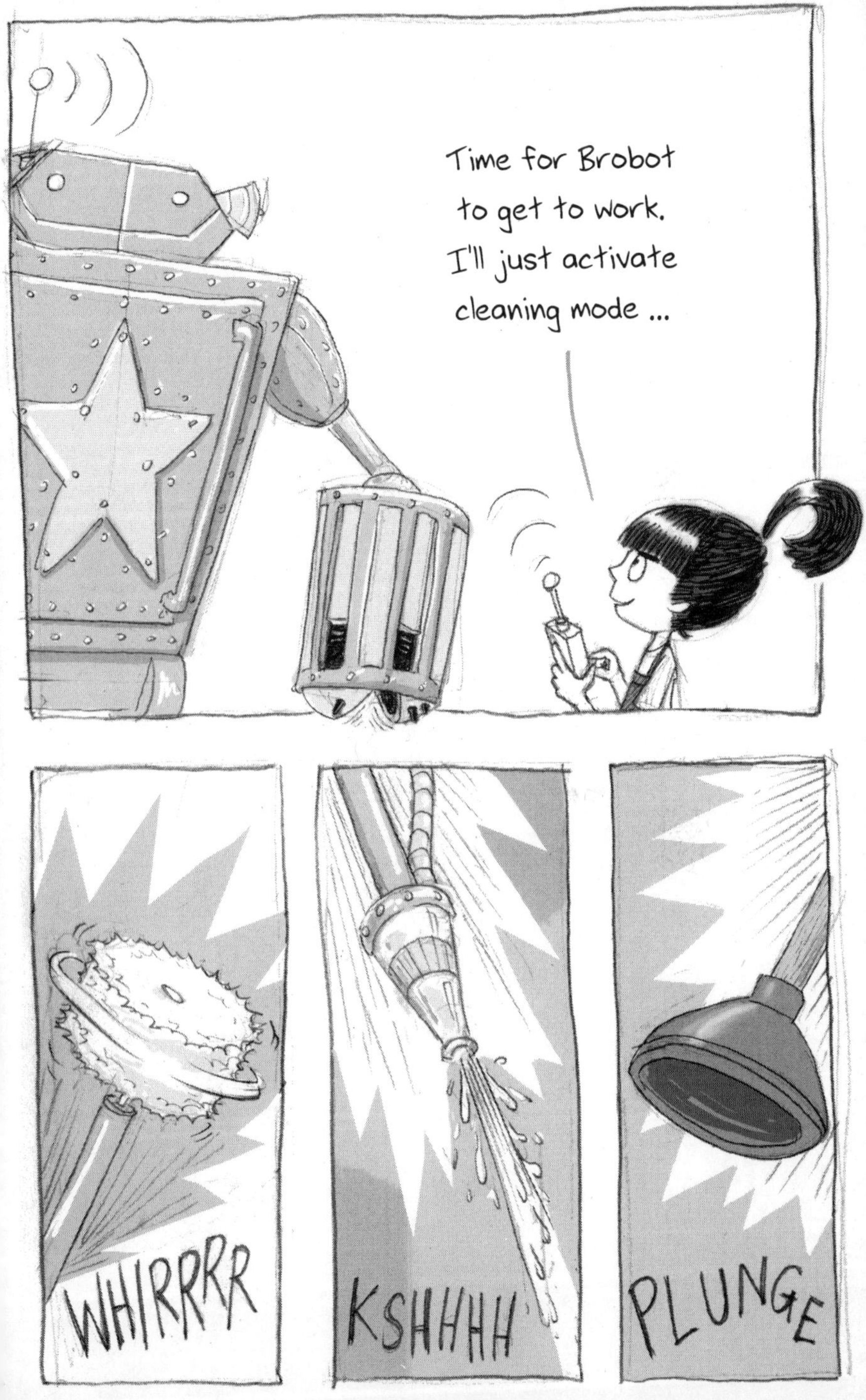
Time for Brobot to get to work. I'll just activate cleaning mode ...
WHIRRRR
KSHHHH
PLUNGE

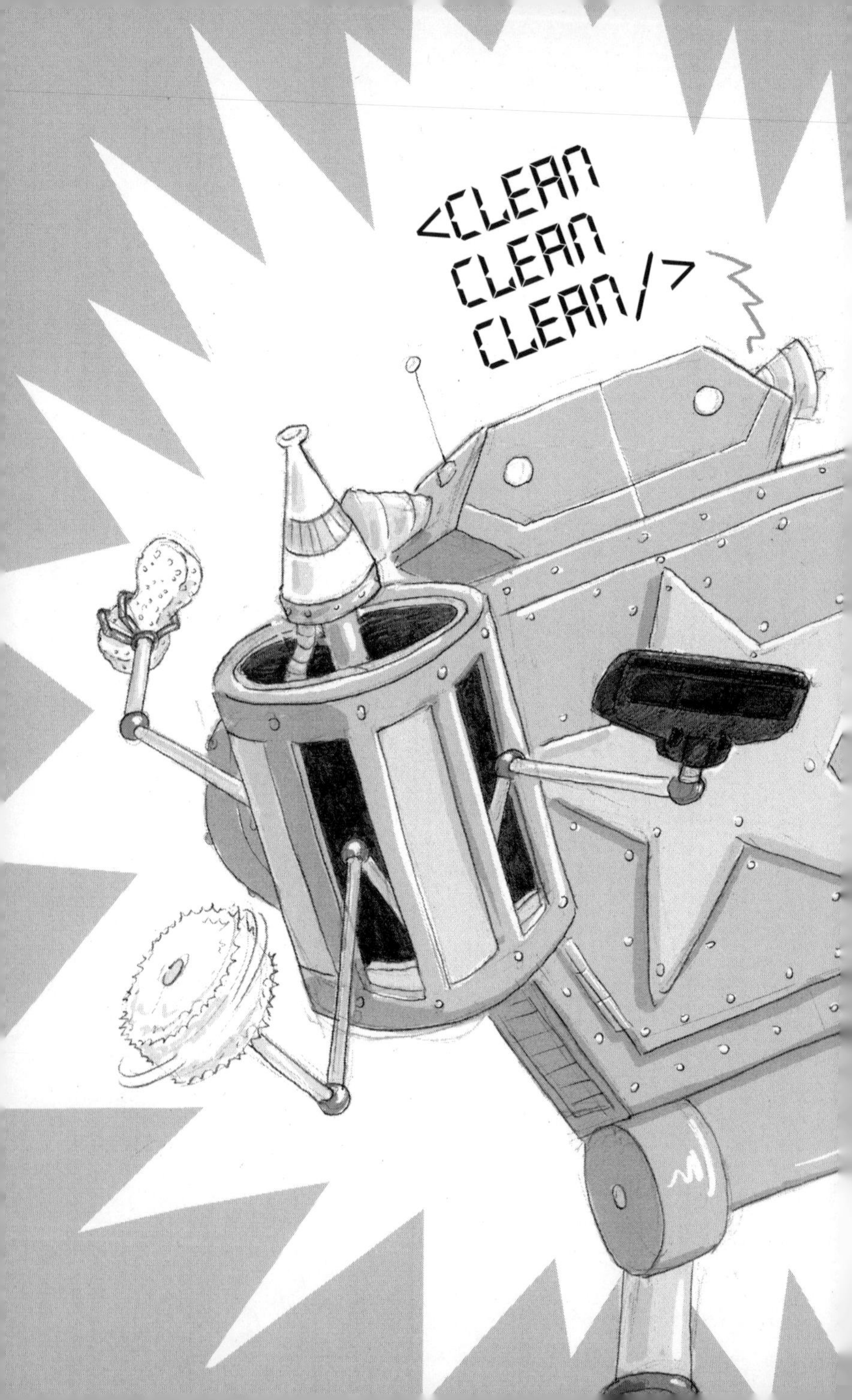
<CLEAN
CLEAN
CLEAN/>

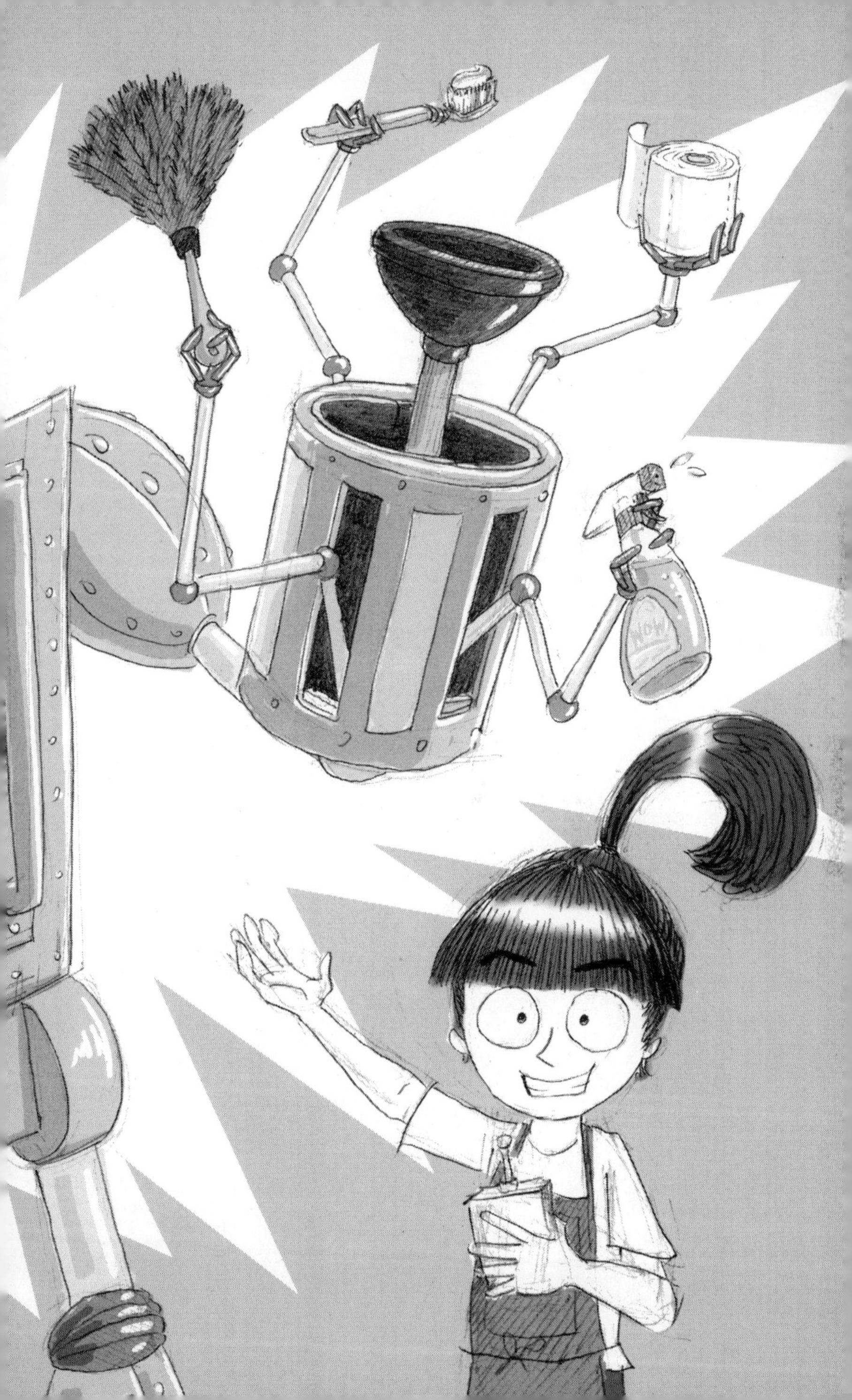

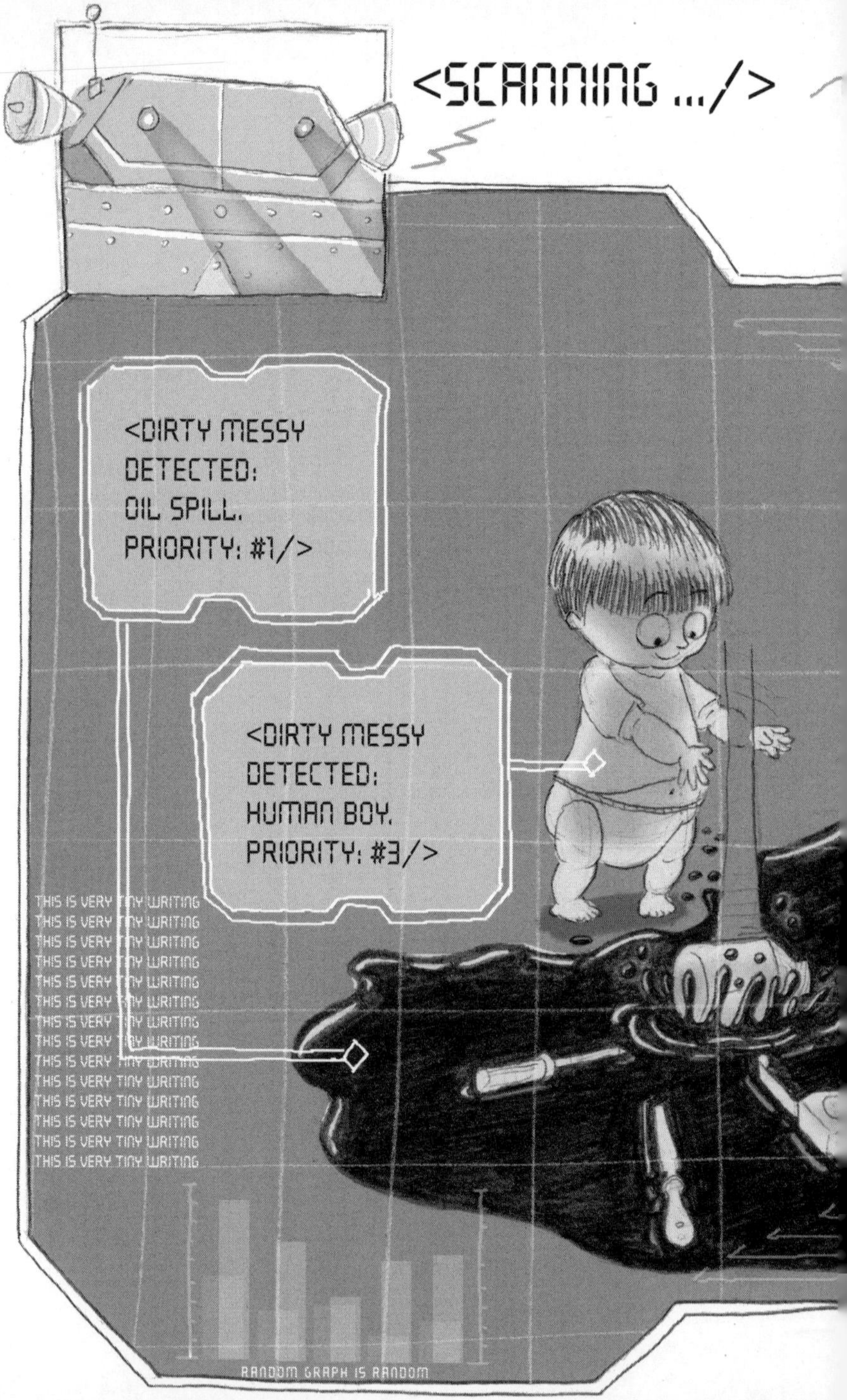
<SCANNING .../>
<DIRTY MESSY DETECTED: OIL SPILL. PRIORITY: #1/>
<DIRTY MESSY DETECTED: HUMAN BOY. PRIORITY: #3/>
THIS IS VERY TINY WRITING
THIS IS VERY TINY WRITING
THIS IS VERY TINY WRITING
THIS IS VERY TINY WRITING
THIS IS VERY TINY WRITING
THIS IS VERY TINY WRITING
THIS IS VERY TINY WRITING
THIS IS VERY TINY WRITING
THIS IS VERY TINY WRITING
THIS IS VERY TINY WRITING
THIS IS VERY TINY WRITING
THIS IS VERY TINY WRITING
THIS IS VERY TINY WRITING
THIS IS VERY TINY WRITING
RANDOM GRAPH IS RANDOM

<SCAN COMPLETE/>
<DIRTY MESSY DETECTED/>

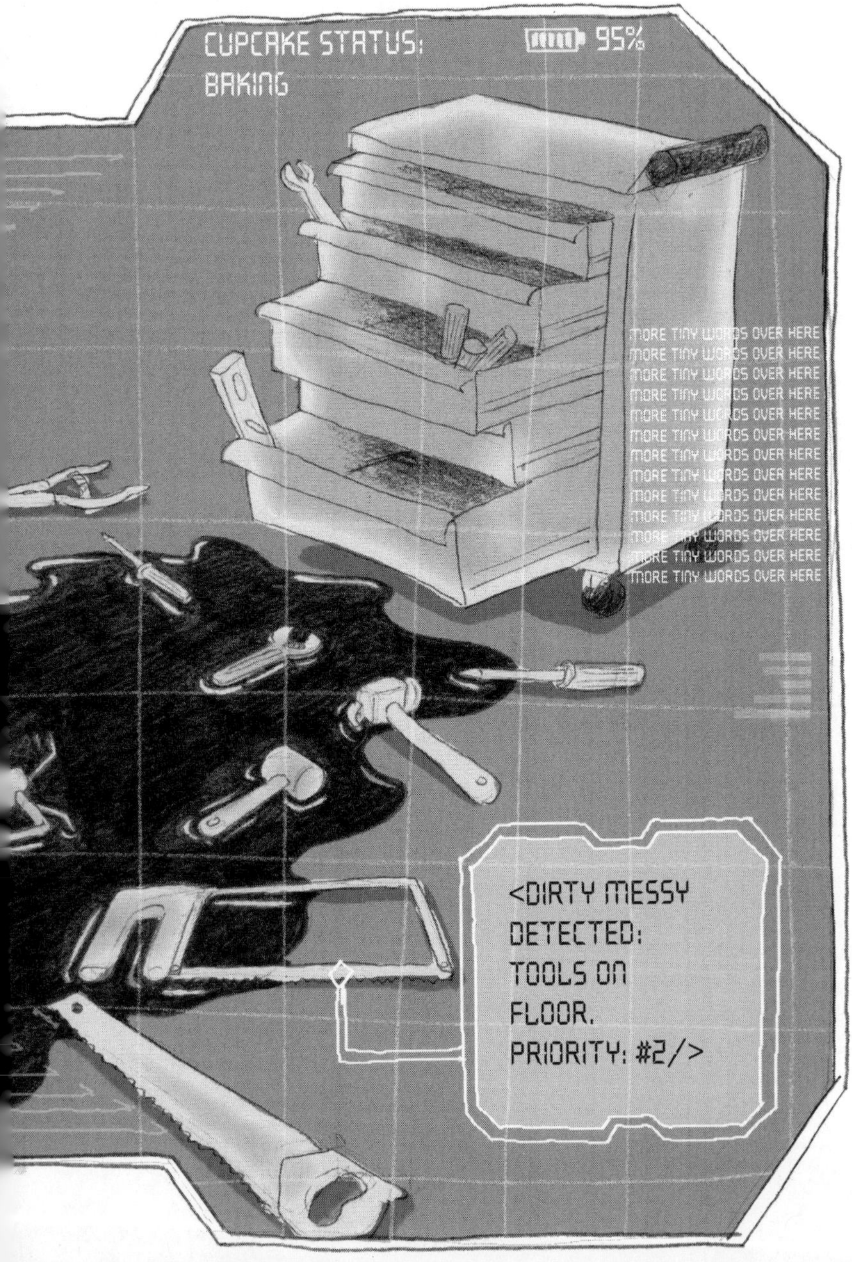
CUPCAKE STATUS:
BAKING
95%
MORE TINY WORDS OVER HERE
MORE TINY WORDS OVER HERE
MORE TINY WORDS OVER HERE
MORE TINY WORDS OVER HERE
MORE TINY WORDS OVER HERE
MORE TINY WORDS OVER HERE
MORE TINY WORDS OVER HERE
MORE TINY WORDS OVER HERE
MORE TINY WORDS OVER HERE
MORE TINY WORDS OVER HERE
MORE TINY WORDS OVER HERE
MORE TINY WORDS OVER HERE
MORE TINY WORDS OVER HERE
<DIRTY MESSY DETECTED: TOOLS ON FLOOR. PRIORITY: #2/>

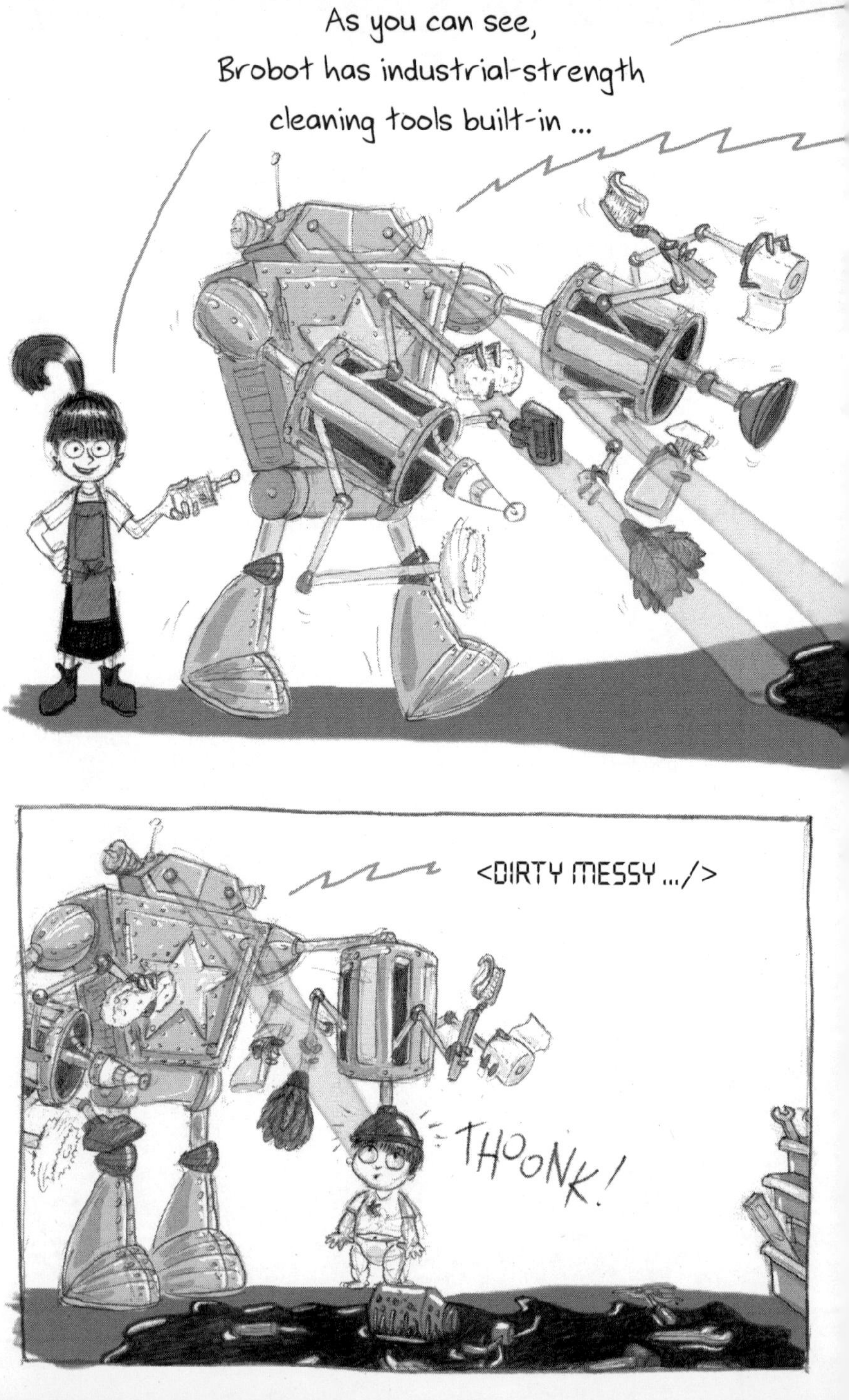
As you can see,
Brobot has industrial-strength
cleaning tools built-in ...
<DIRTY MESSY .../>
THOONK!

... so even the dirtiest messes are spotless in no time.

<DIRTY MESSY
DIRTY MESSY .../>

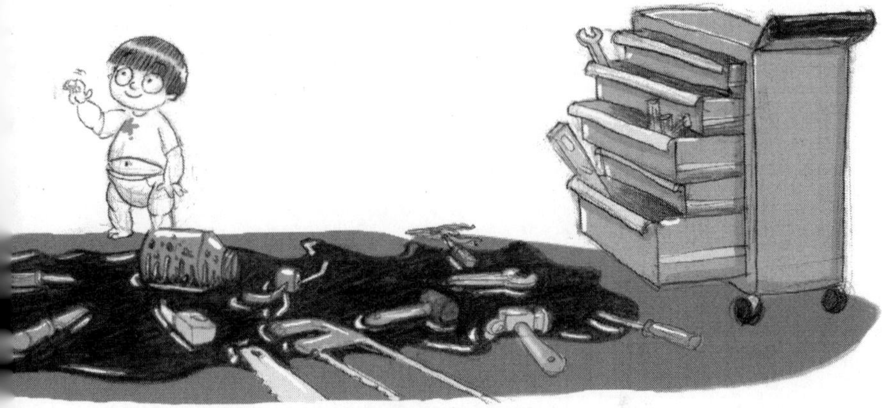

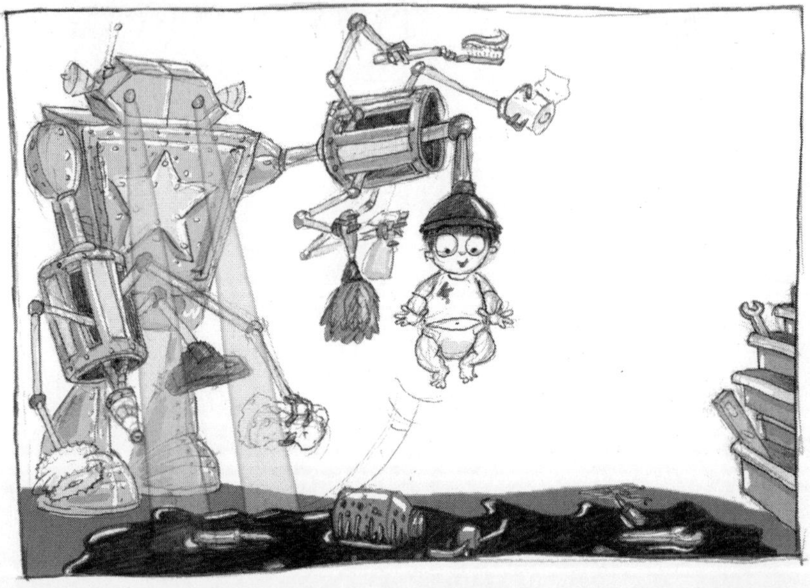

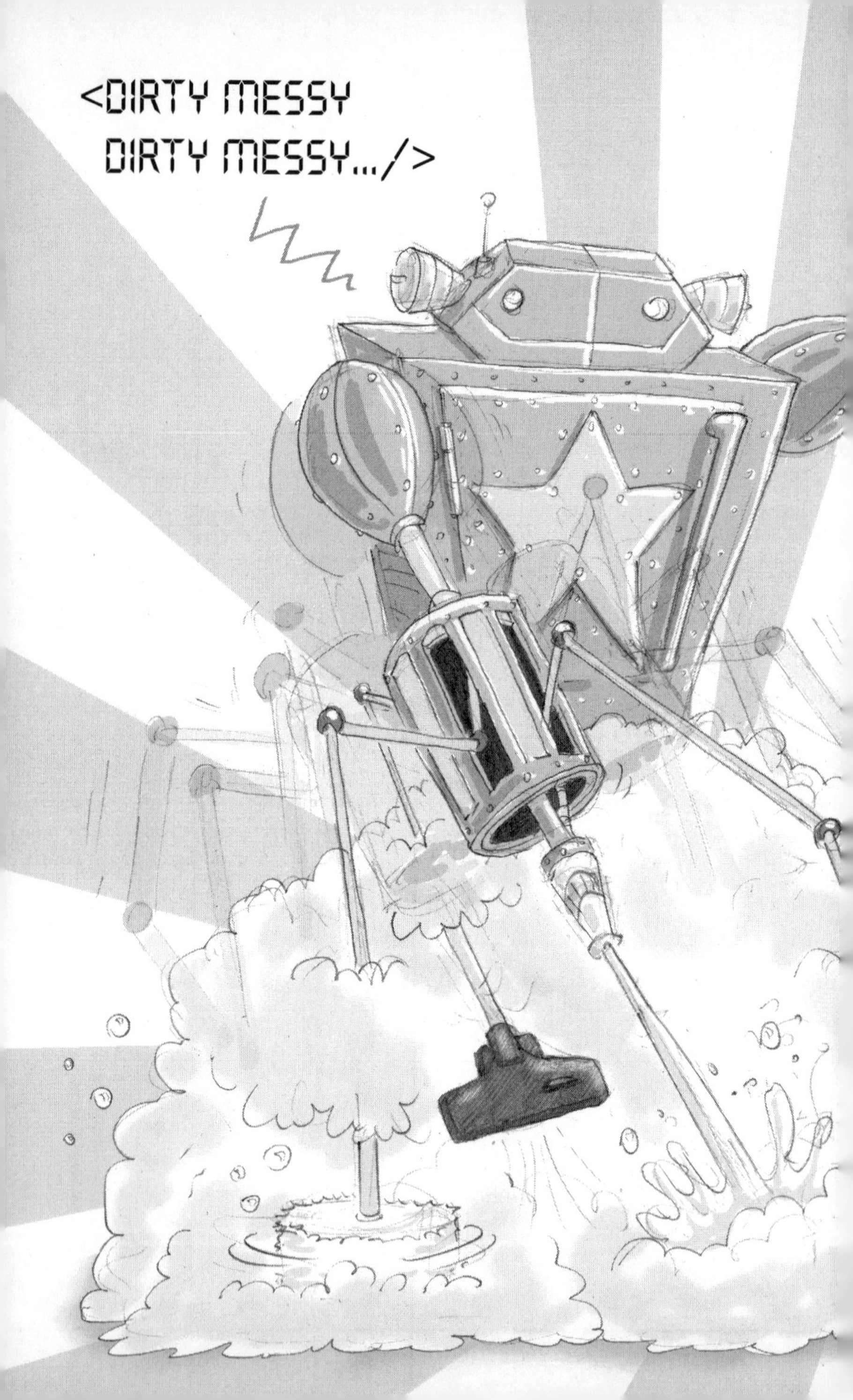
<DIRTY MESSY
DIRTY MESSY.../>

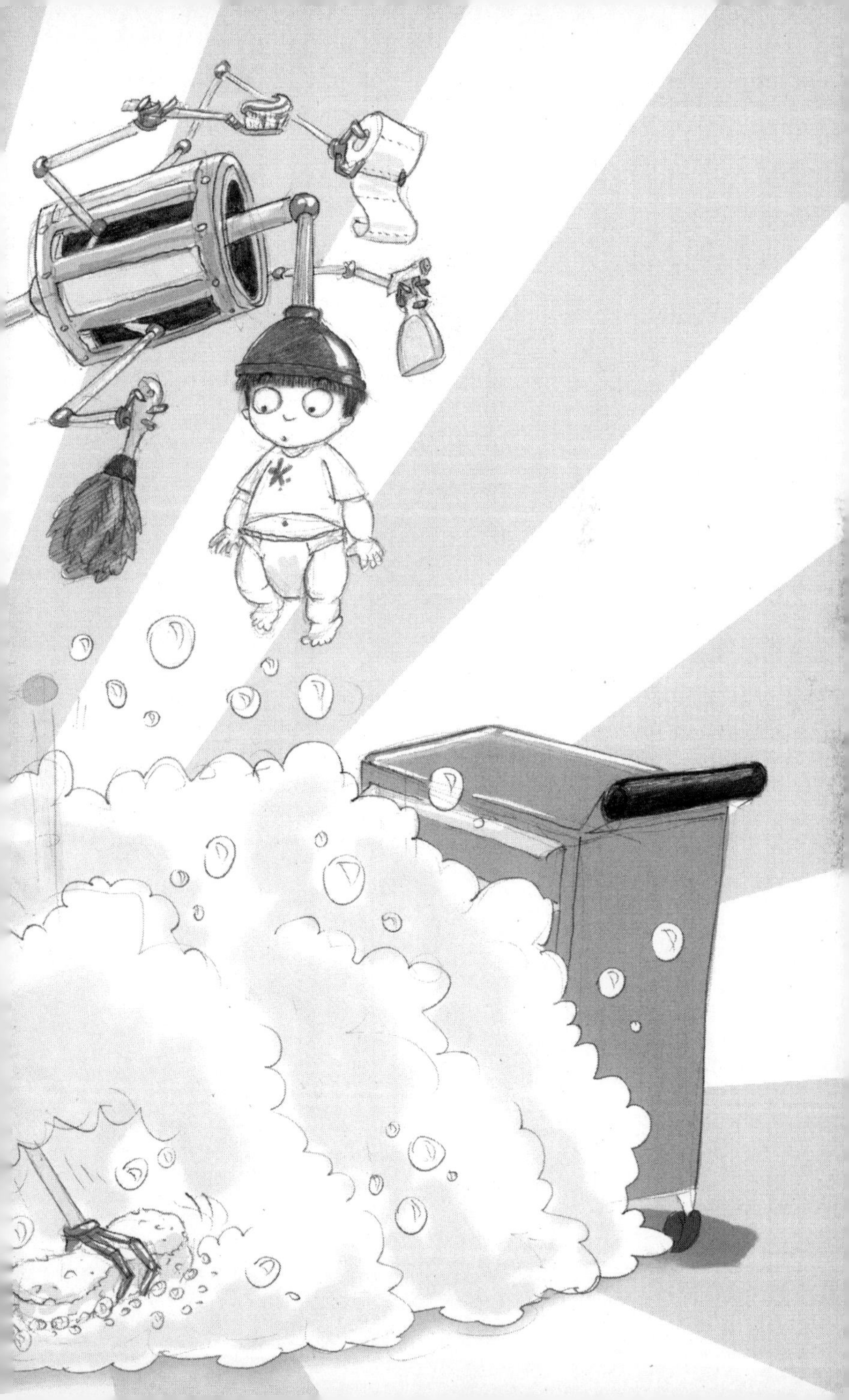

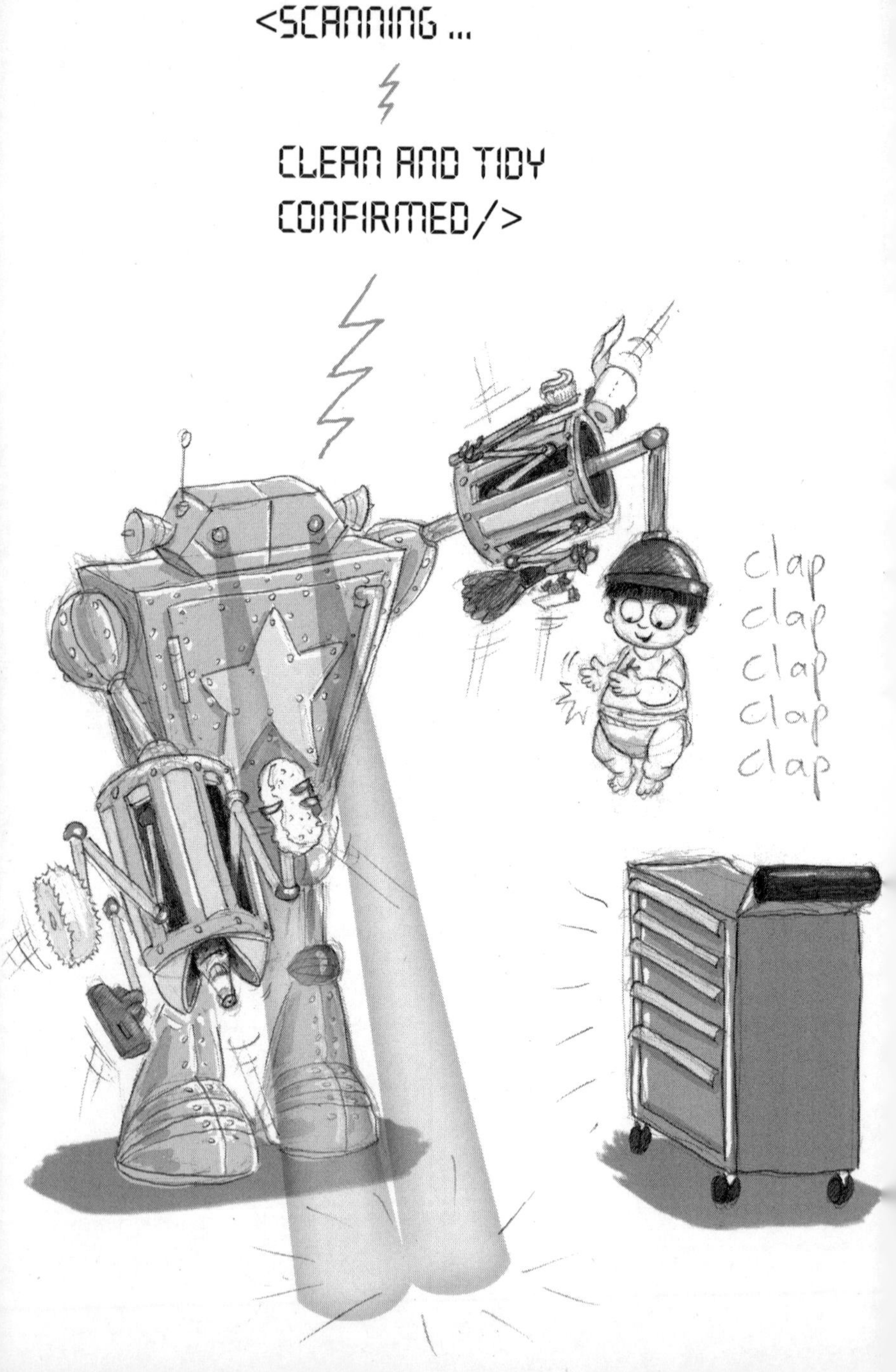
<SCANNING ...
CLEAN AND TIDY
CONFIRMED/>
clap
clap
clap
clap
clap

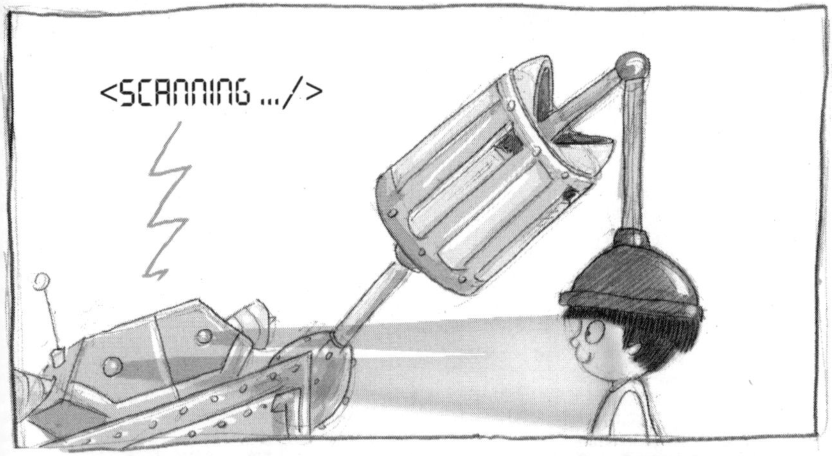
<SCANNING .../>

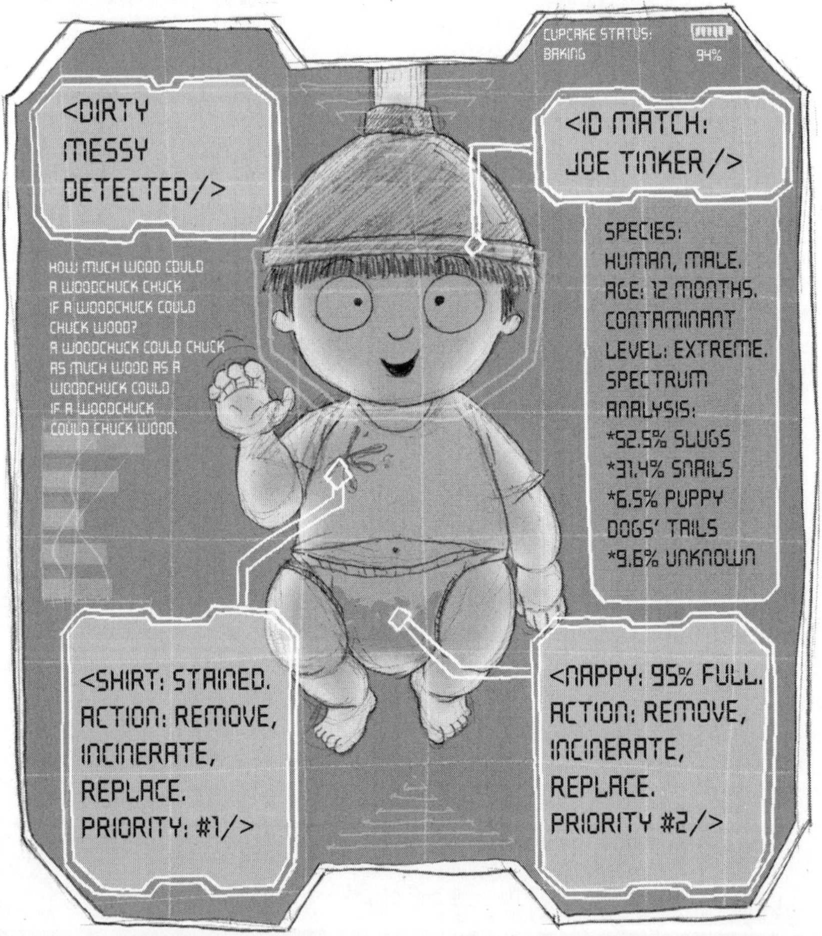
CUPCAKE STATUS:
BAKING 94%
<DIRTY MESSY DETECTED/>
<ID MATCH: JOE TINKER/>
HOW MUCH WOOD COULD A WOODCHUCK CHUCK IF A WOODCHUCK COULD CHUCK WOOD? A WOODCHUCK COULD CHUCK AS MUCH WOOD AS A WOODCHUCK COULD IF A WOODCHUCK COULD CHUCK WOOD.
SPECIES: HUMAN, MALE. AGE: 12 MONTHS. CONTAMINANT LEVEL: EXTREME. SPECTRUM ANALYSIS:
*52.5% SLUGS
*31.4% SNAILS
*6.5% PUPPY DOGS' TAILS
*9.6% UNKNOWN
<SHIRT: STAINED. ACTION: REMOVE, INCINERATE, REPLACE. PRIORITY: #1/>
<NAPPY: 95% FULL. ACTION: REMOVE, INCINERATE, REPLACE. PRIORITY #2/>

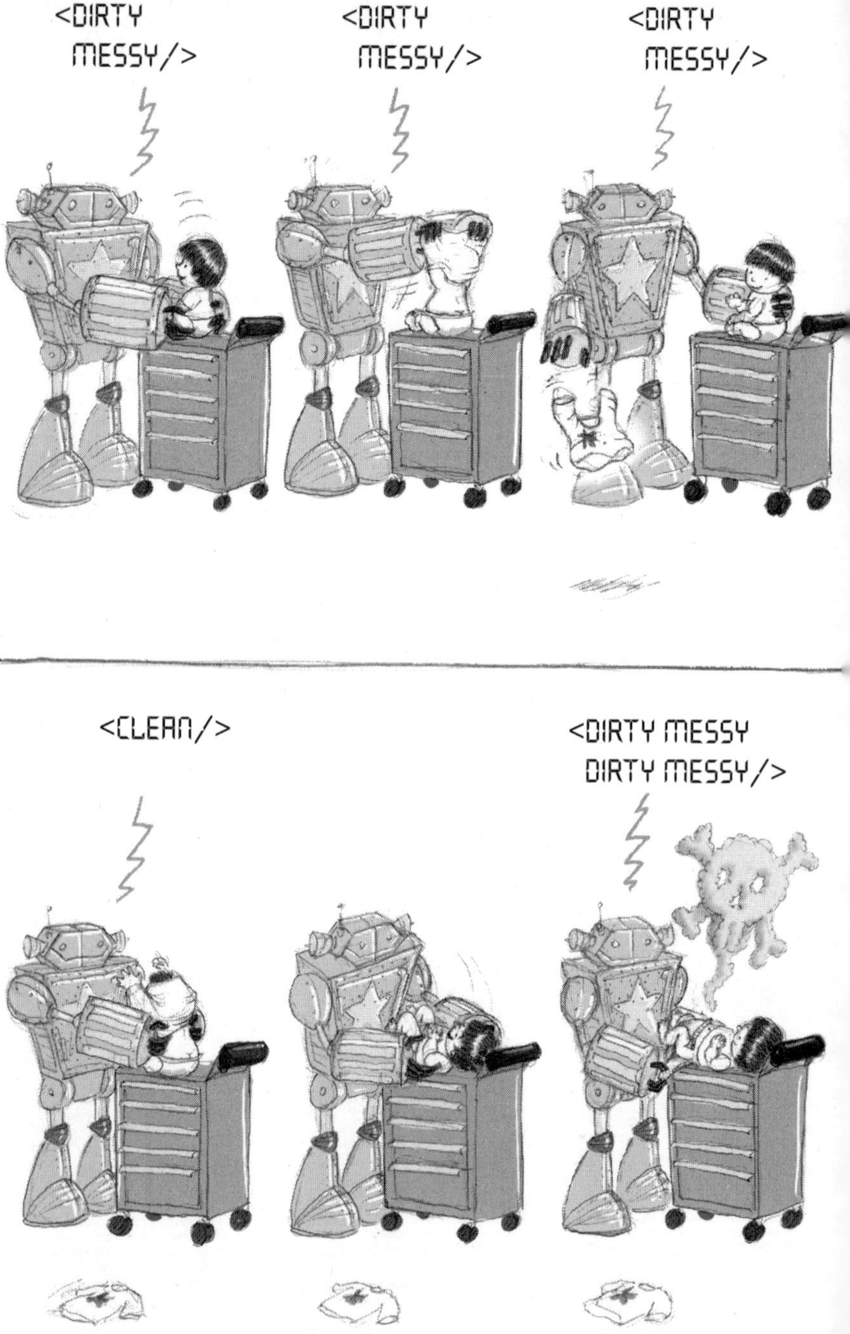

<DIRTY MESSY/>
<DIRTY MESSY/>
<DIRTY MESSY/>
<CLEAN/>
<DIRTY MESSY DIRTY MESSY/>

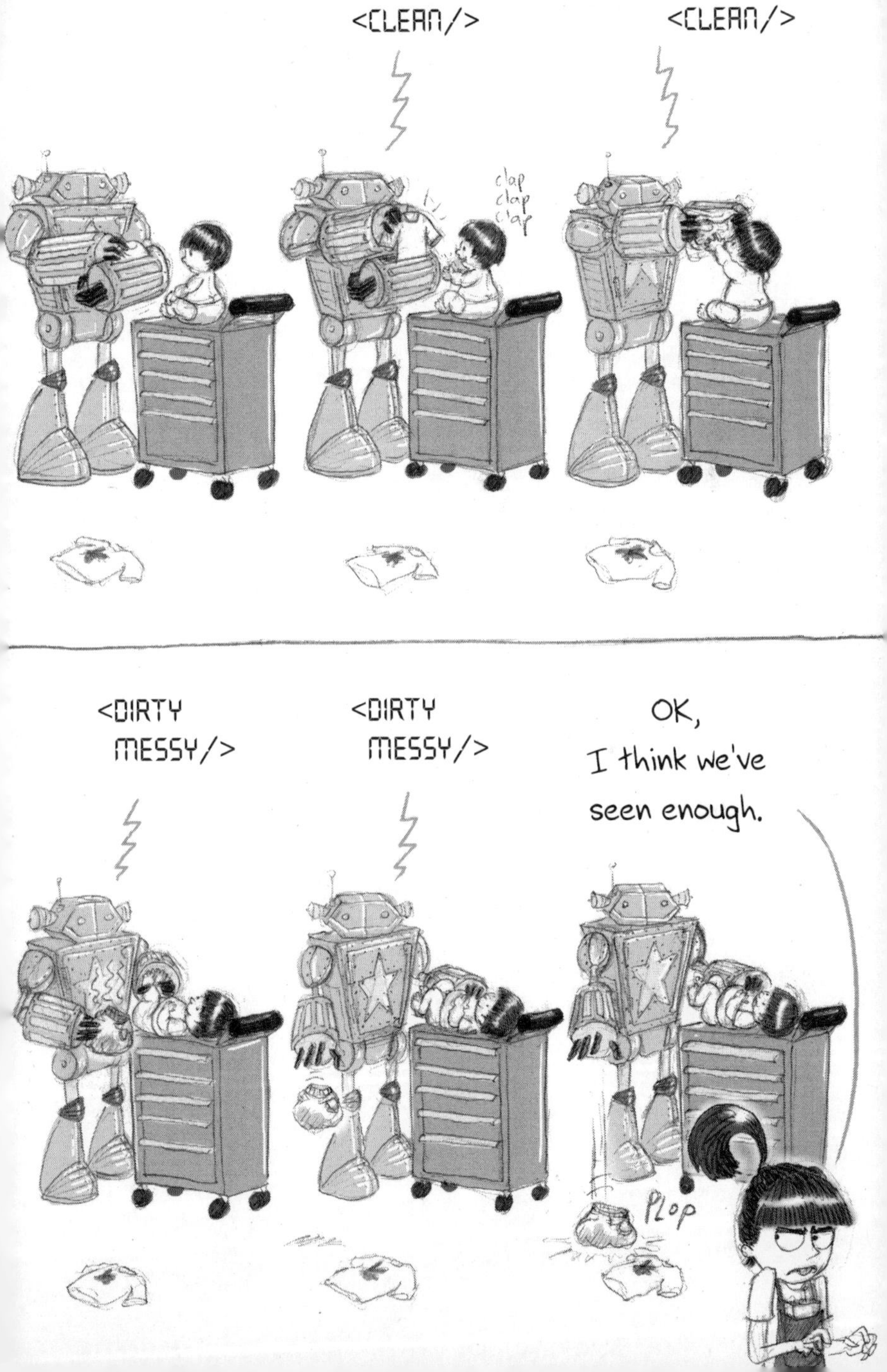
<CLEAN/>
clap clap clap
<CLEAN/>
<DIRTY MESSY/>
<DIRTY MESSY/>
OK, I think we've seen enough.
Plop

Because I am Sally Tinker
(the world's foremost inventor under
the age of twelve), I've made sure Brobot
has another brilliant feature:

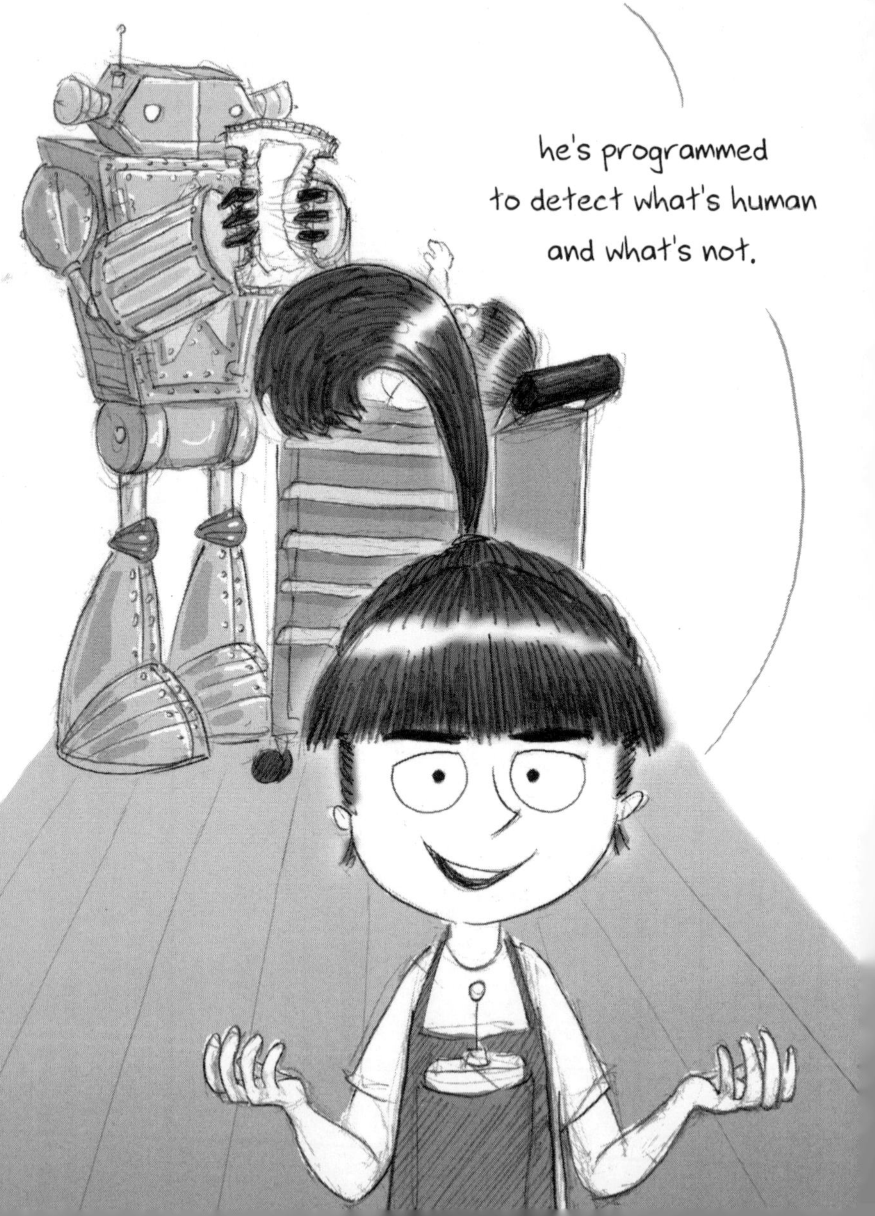
he's programmed
to detect what's human
and what's not.

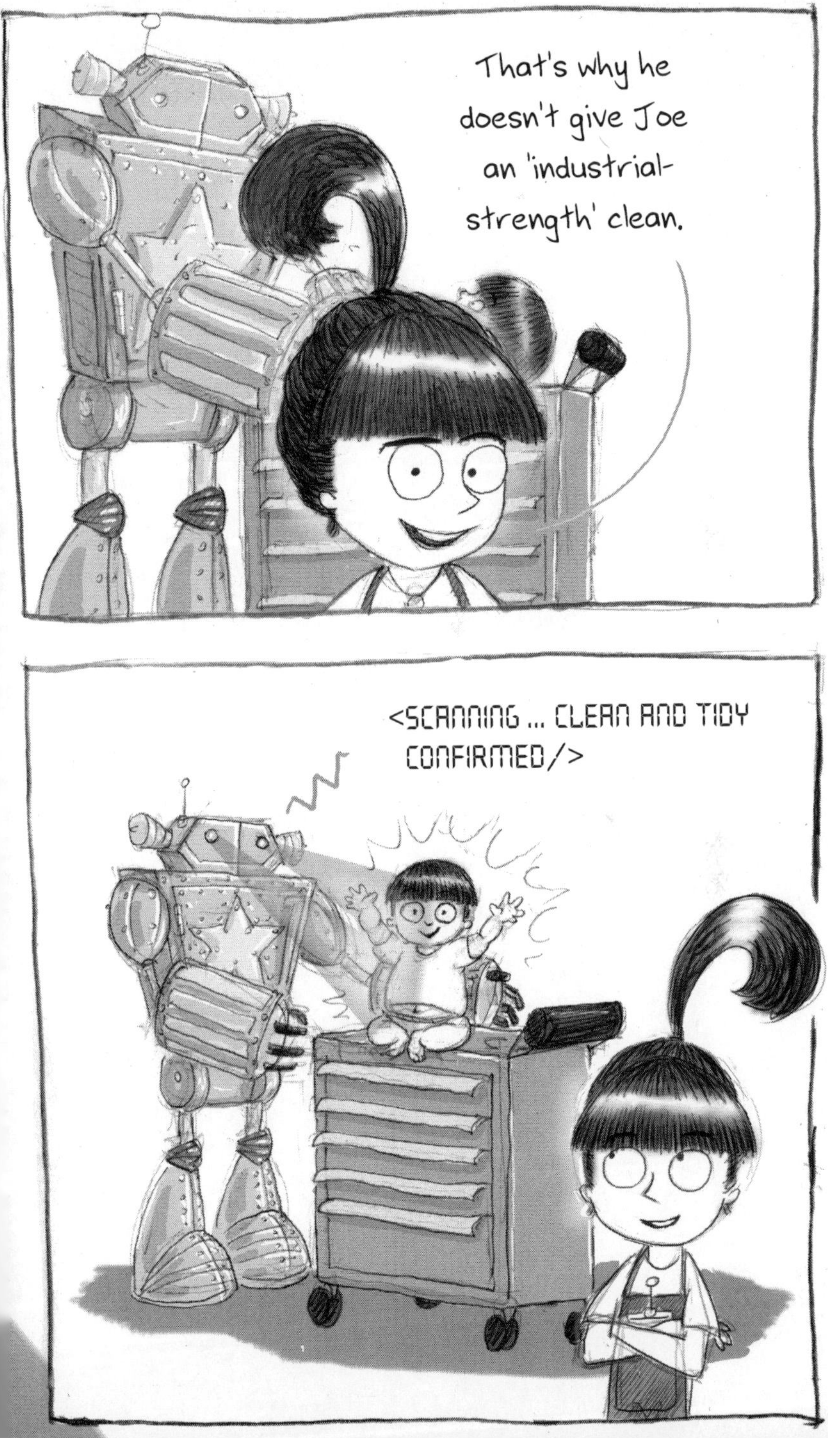
That's why he doesn't give Joe an 'industrial-strength' clean.
<SCANNING ... CLEAN AND TIDY CONFIRMED/>

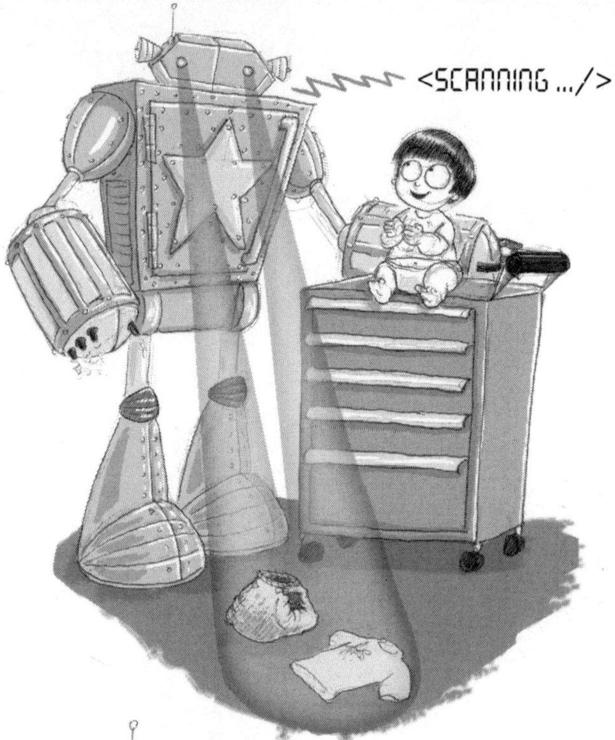
<SCANNING .../>

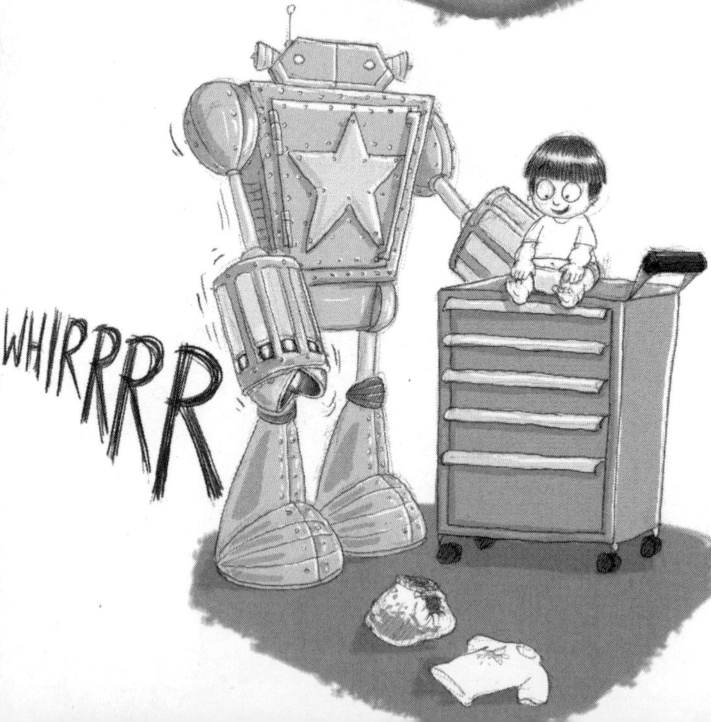
WHIRRRR

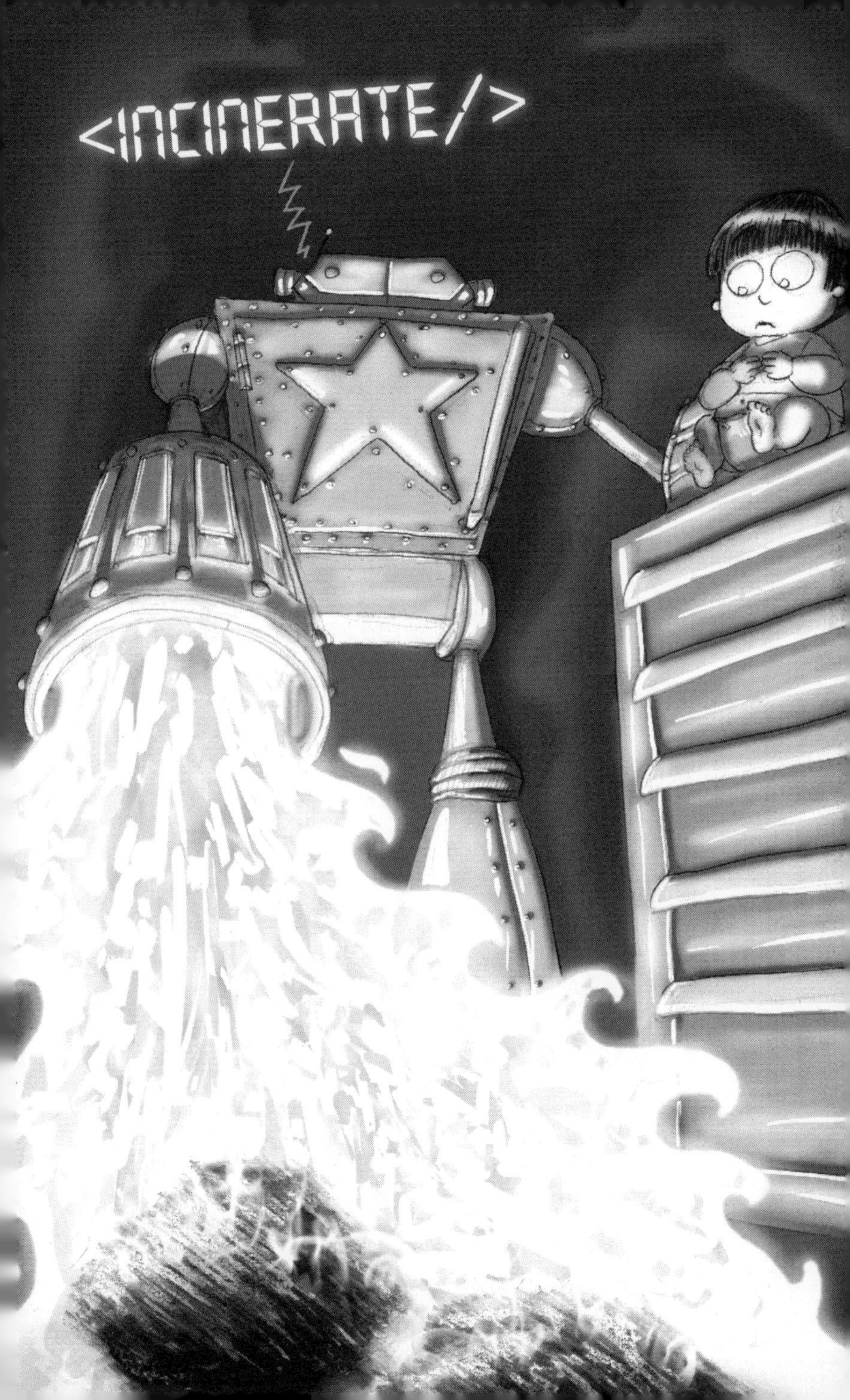
<INCINERATE/>

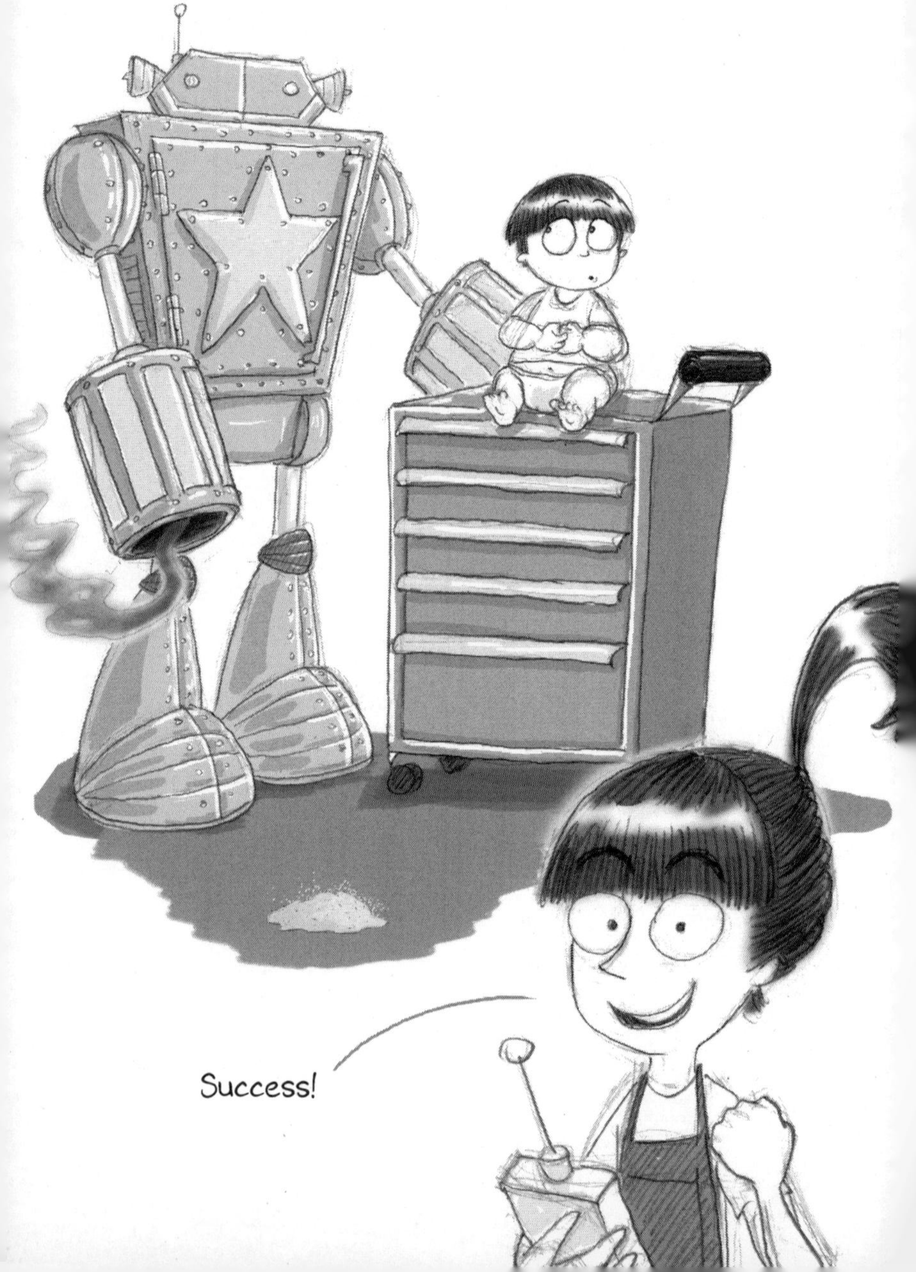
Success!

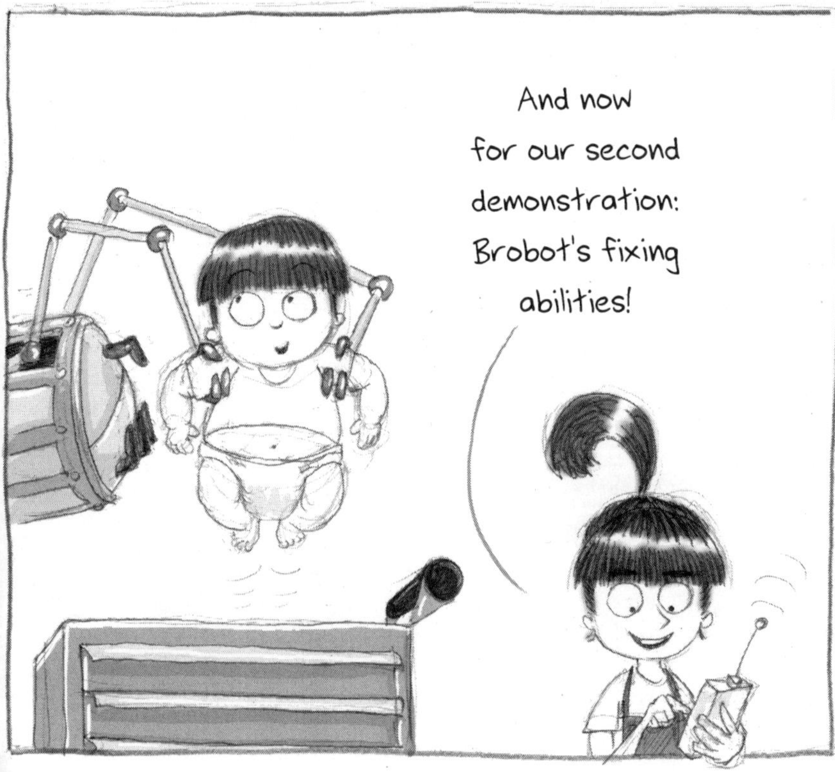
And now for our second demonstration: Brobot's fixing abilities!

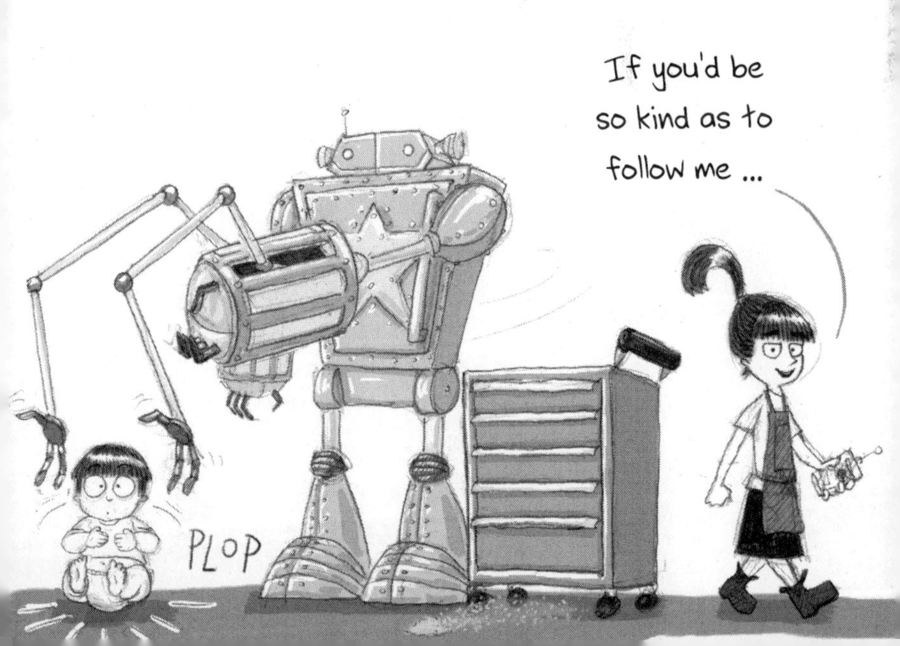
If you'd be so kind as to follow me ...
PLOP

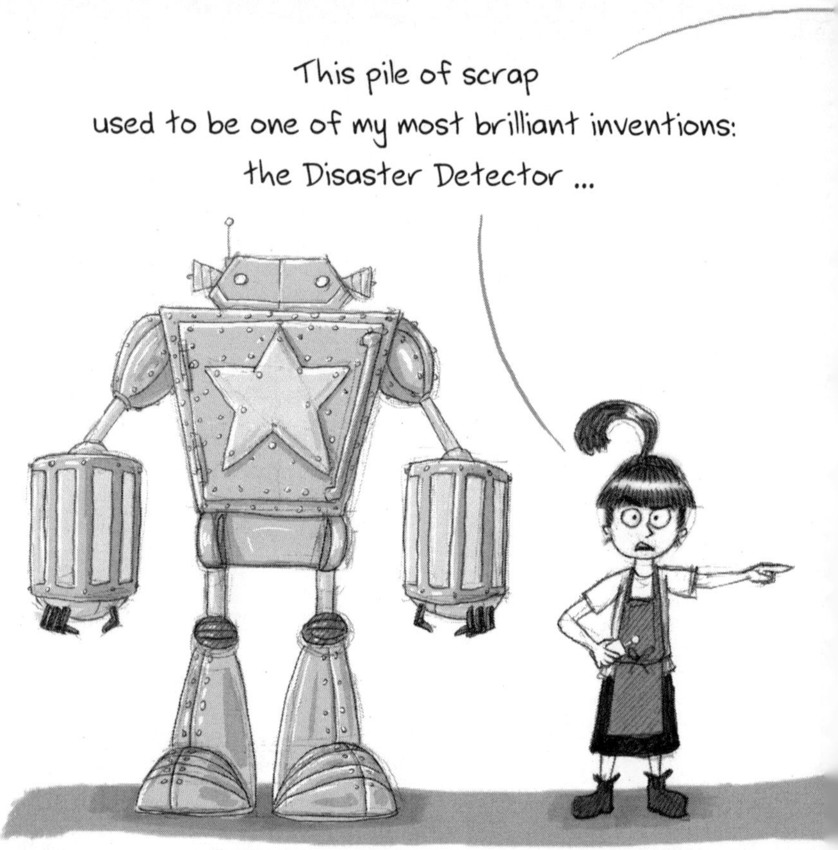
This pile of scrap
used to be one of my most brilliant inventions:
the Disaster Detector ...

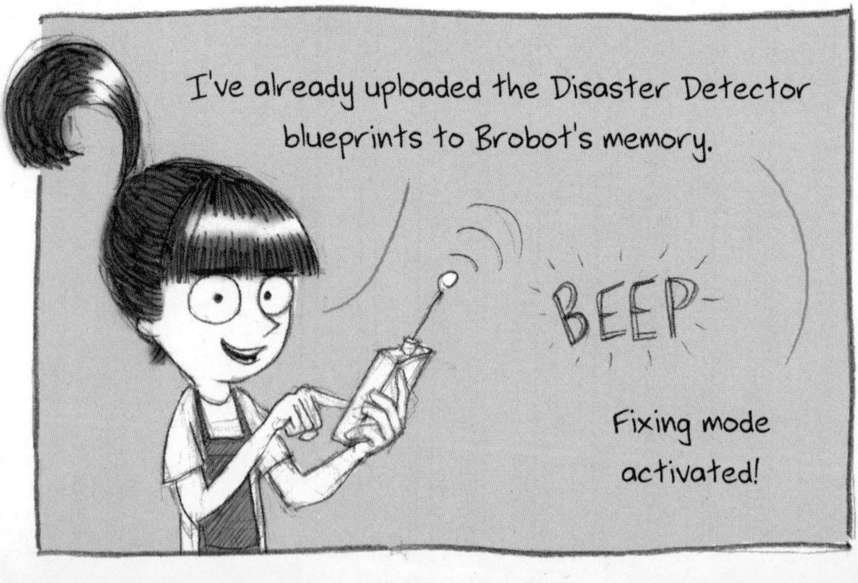
I've already uploaded the Disaster Detector
blueprints to Brobot's memory.
BEEP
Fixing mode
activated!

... a quantum computer
capable of calculating the conceivability
of a calamity occurring in the current location.

Joe looked at it
and it
self-destructed.

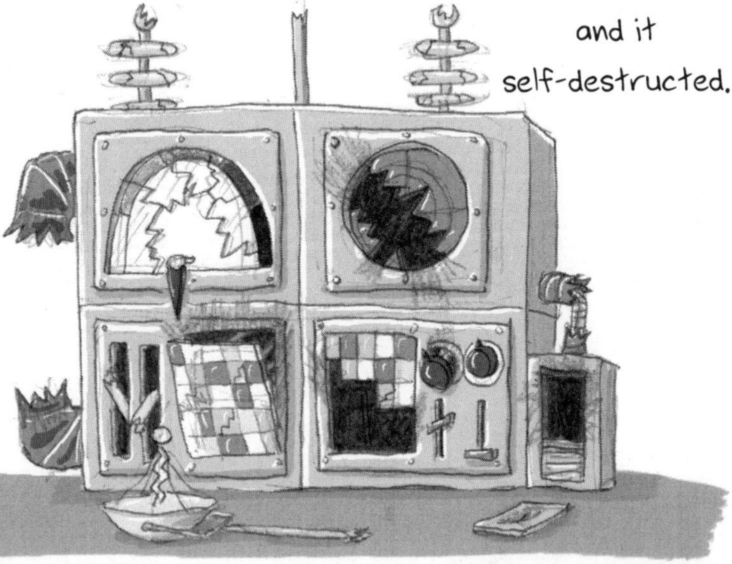

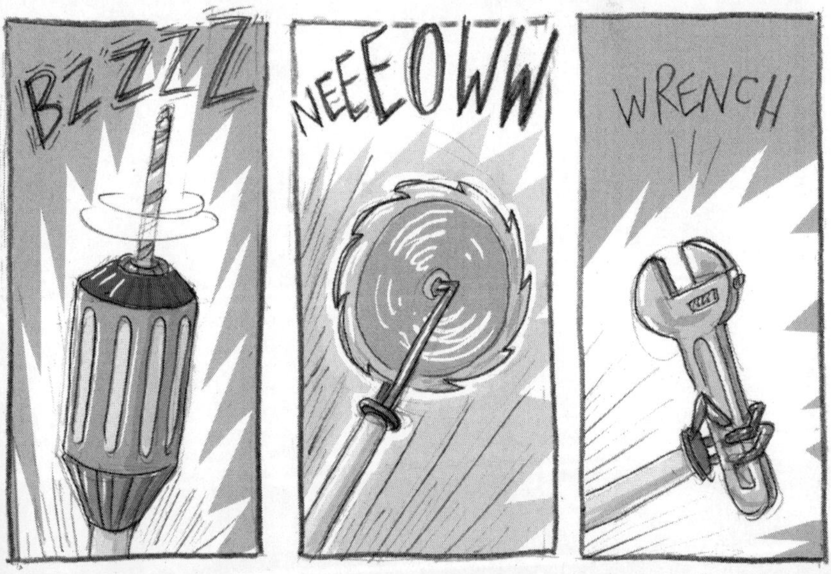
BZZZZ
NEEEOWW
WRENCH

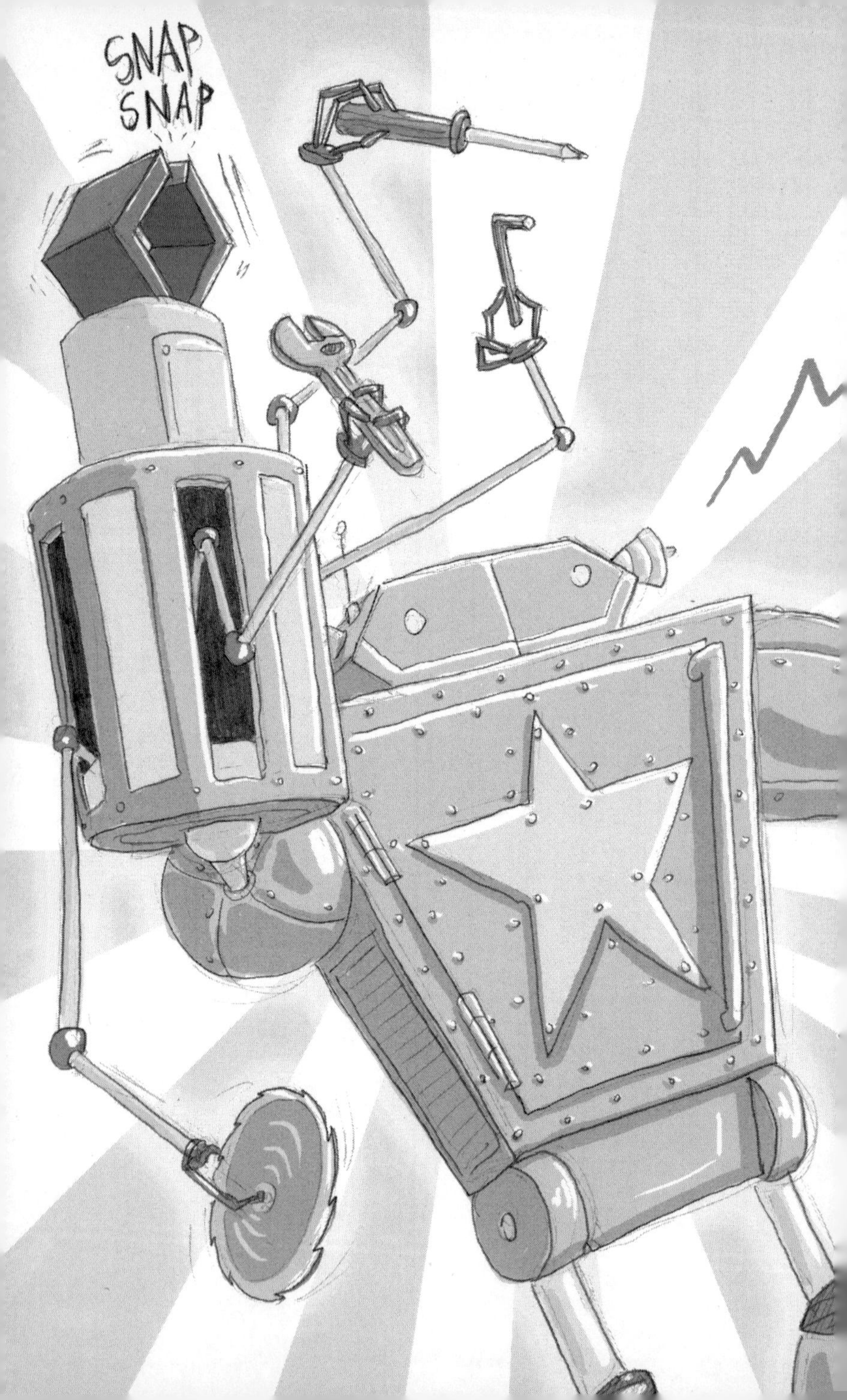
SNAP
SNAP

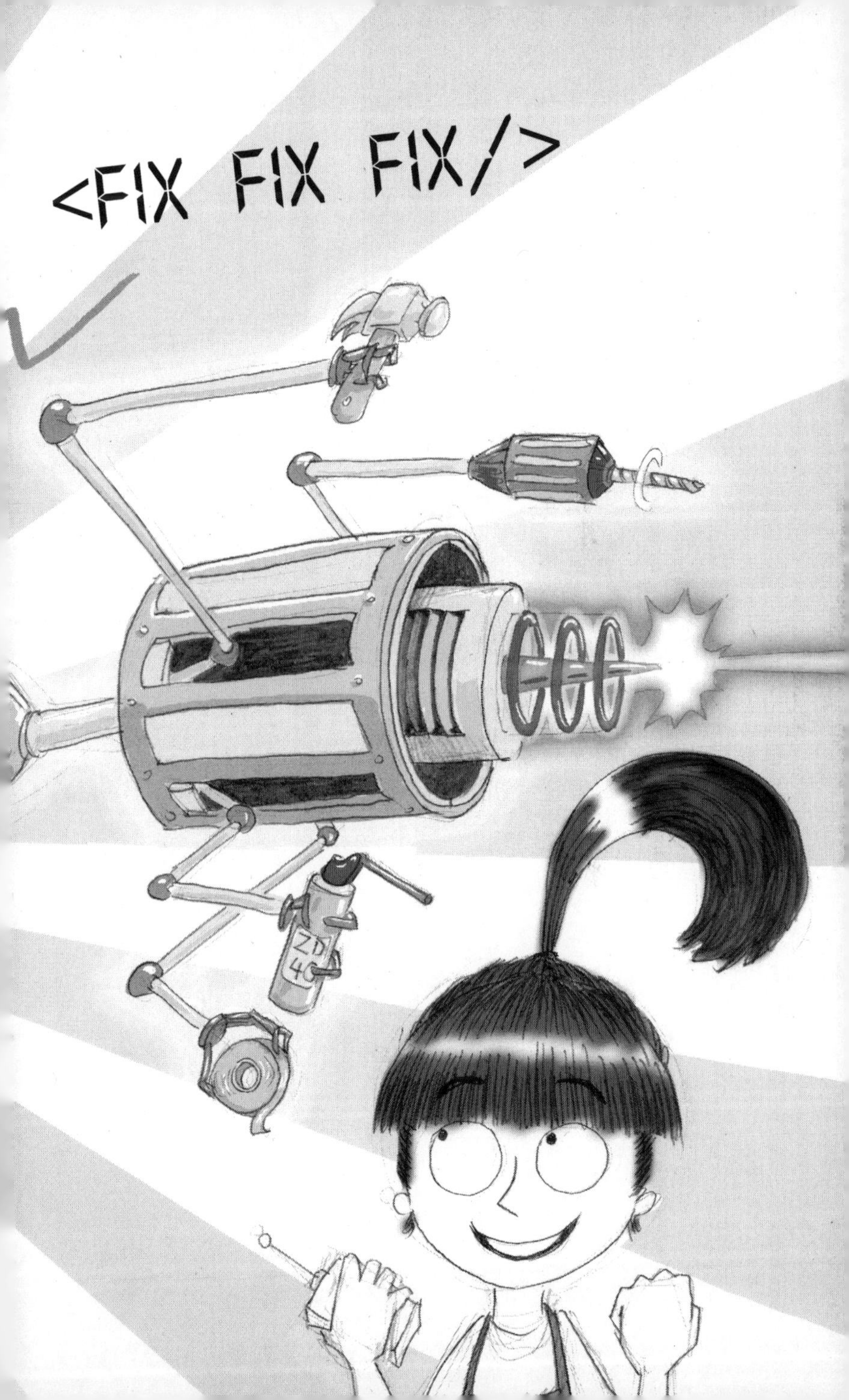
<FIX FIX FIX/>

<SCANNING .../>

<LEAKY FAULTY DETECTED.
ID MATCH: DISASTER DETECTOR.
ACCESSING BLUEPRINTS V=2.0/>

<STATUS:
  - QUANTUM FIELD GENERATOR: OFFLINE.
  - CALAMITRON PARTICLE COLLIDER: DESTROYED.
  - FANCY BLINKING LIGHTS: NOT BLINKING./>
<TOOLS REQUIRED:
  - PLIERS, HAMMER, ADJUSTABLE WRENCH,
   WRENCH THAT FINDS IT DIFFICULT TO ADJUST,
   ELECTRIC DRILL, FIRE DRILL, CIRCULAR SAW,
   TRIANGULAR SAW, SEE-SAW, BED-SAW, EYE-SAW,
   ZD-40, GAFFER TAPE, LASER WELDER, ALLEN KEY/>

Brobot has the tools and the know-how ...

<SCAN COMPLETE.
LEAKY FAULTY DETECTED./>

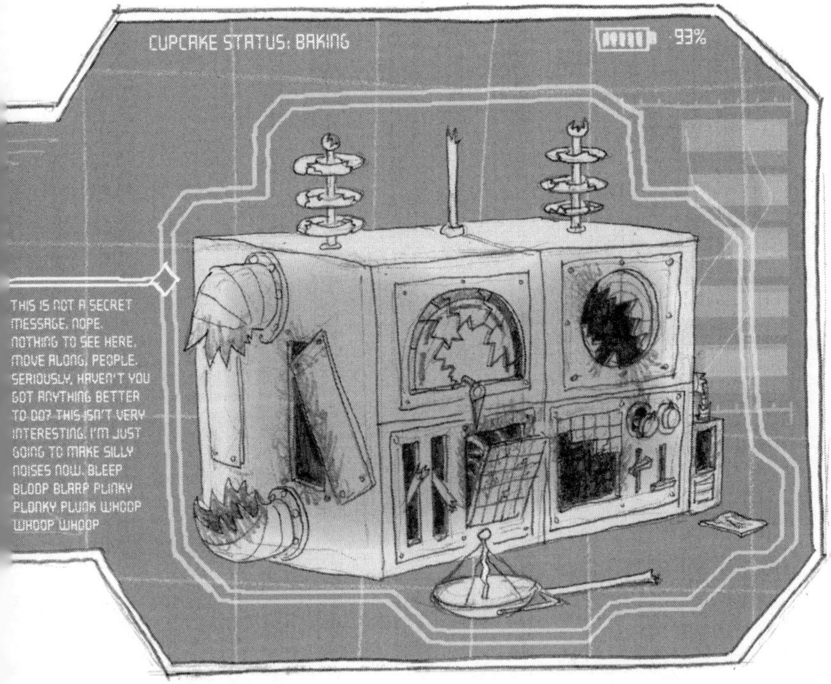
CUPCAKE STATUS: BAKING
93%
THIS IS NOT A SECRET MESSAGE. NOPE. NOTHING TO SEE HERE. MOVE ALONG, PEOPLE. SERIOUSLY, HAVEN'T YOU GOT ANYTHING BETTER TO DO? THIS ISN'T VERY INTERESTING. I'M JUST GOING TO MAKE SILLY NOISES NOW. BLEEP BLOOP BLARP PLINKY PLONKY PLUNK WHOOP WHOOP WHOOP

... to fix even my most complex machines.

<LEAKY
FAULTY/>

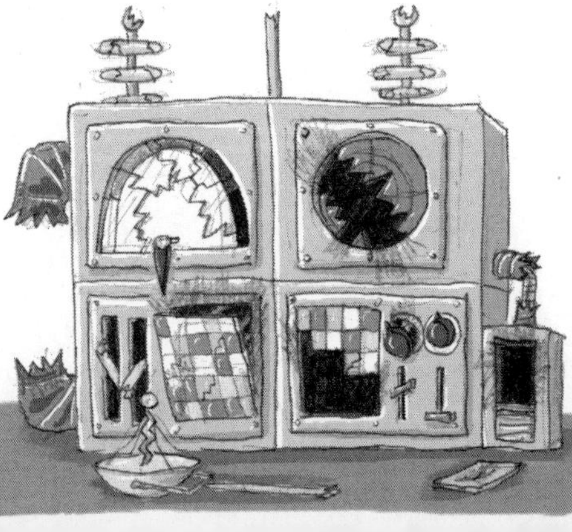

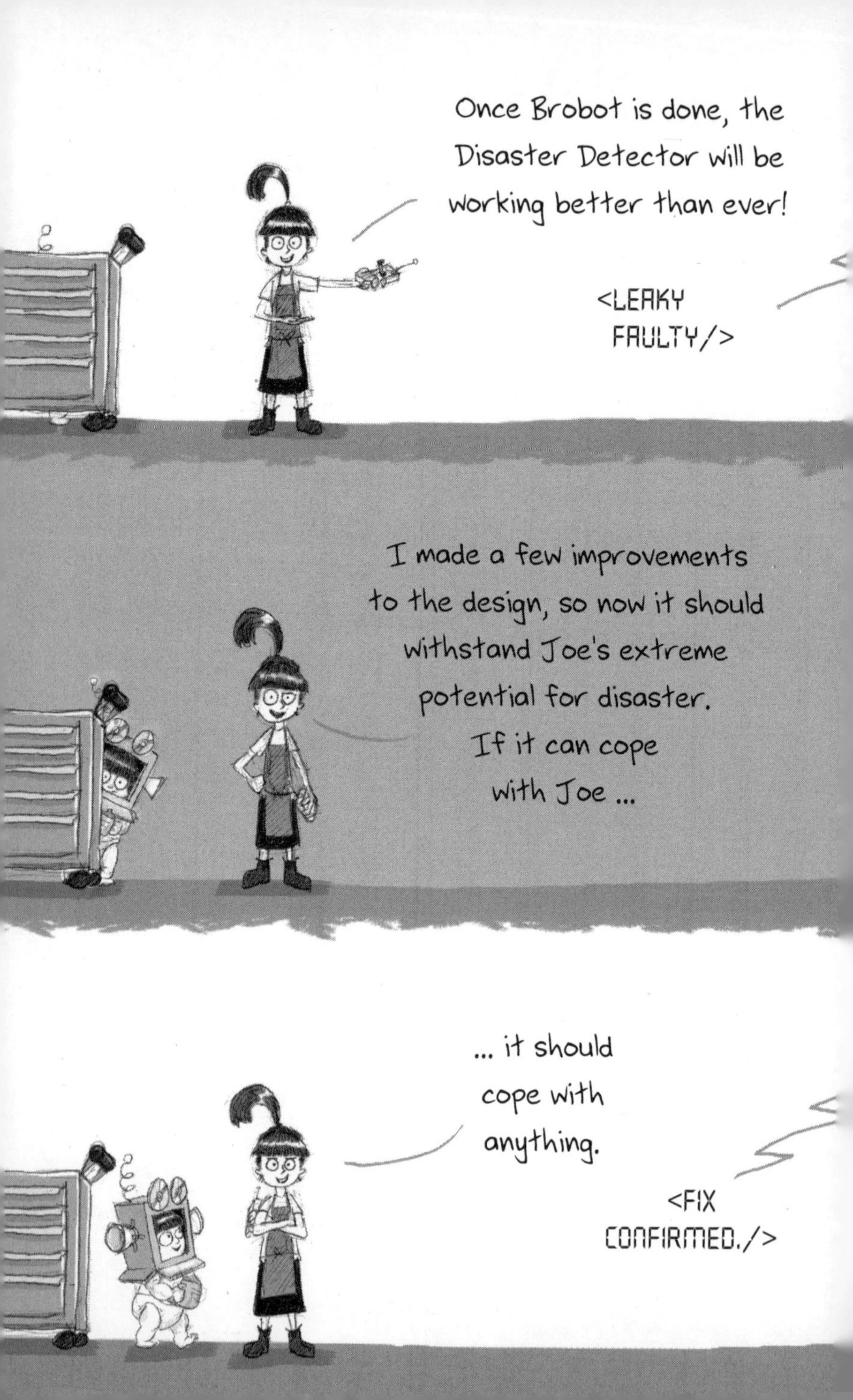
Once Brobot is done, the Disaster Detector will be working better than ever!
<LEAKY FAULTY/>
I made a few improvements to the design, so now it should withstand Joe's extreme potential for disaster. If it can cope with Joe ...
... it should cope with anything.
<FIX CONFIRMED./>

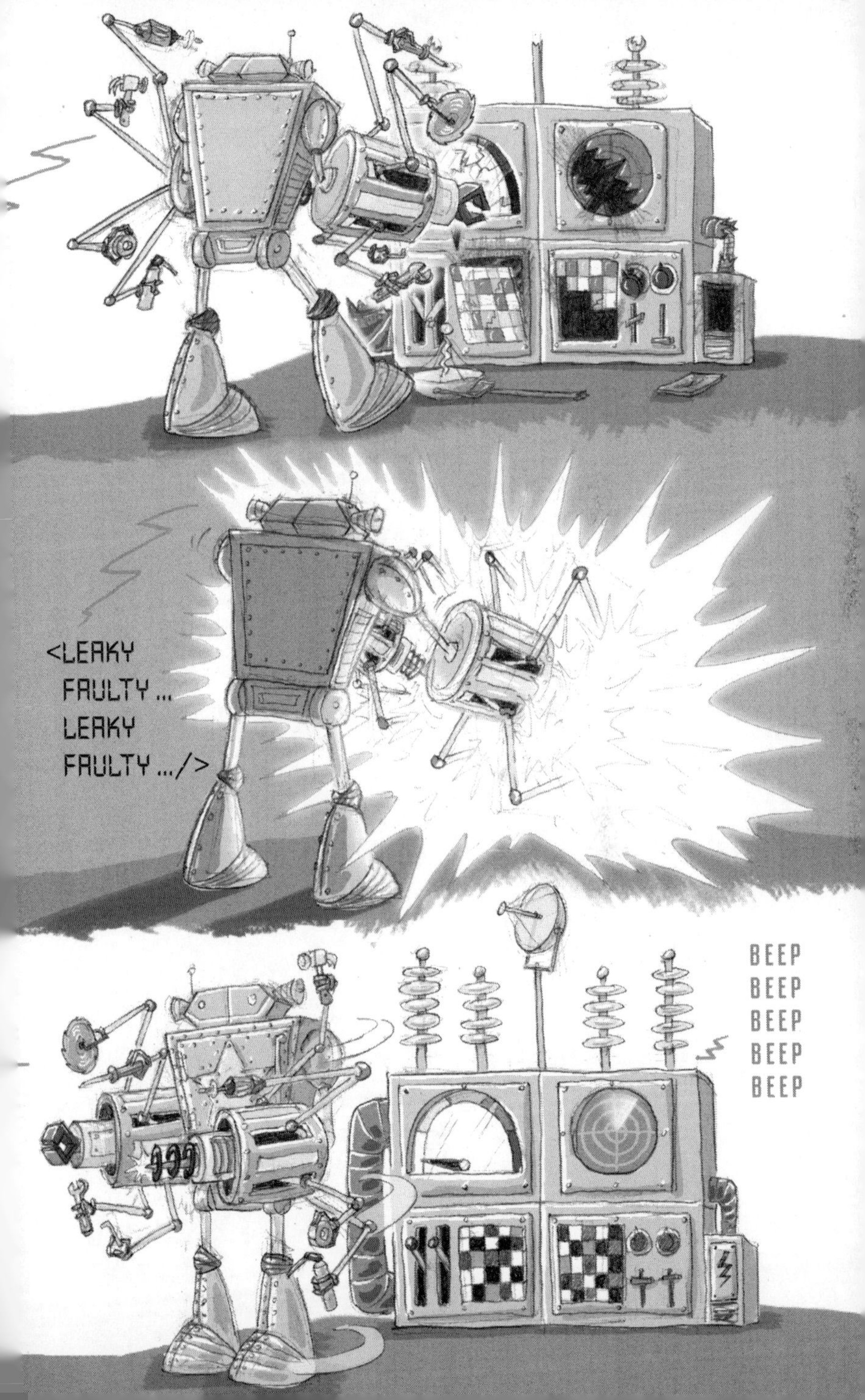

<LEAKY FAULTY ... LEAKY FAULTY .../>
BEEP BEEP BEEP BEEP BEEP

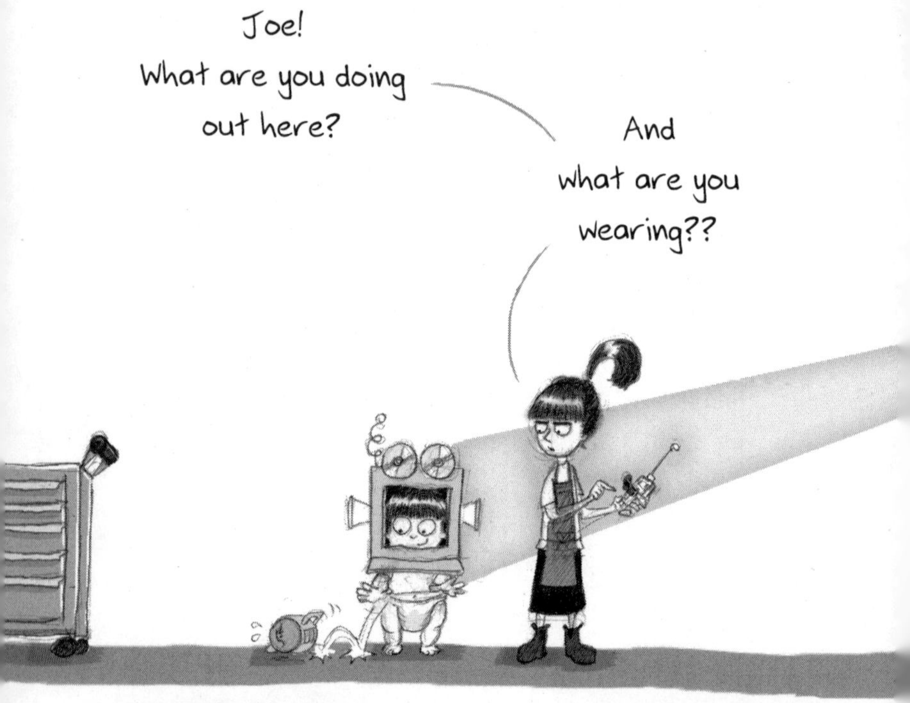
Joe!
What are you doing
out here?
And
what are you
wearing??

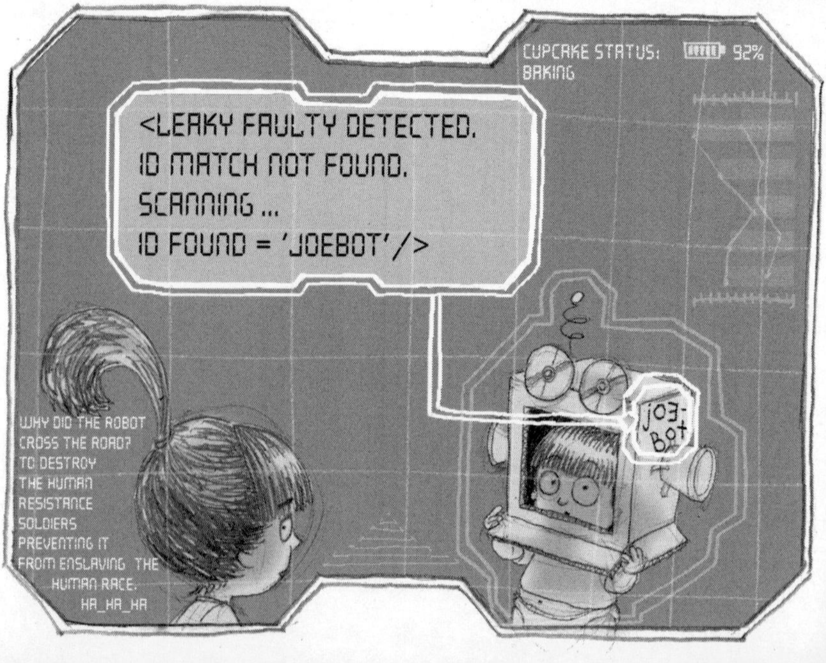
CUPCAKE STATUS: 92%
BAKING
<LEAKY FAULTY DETECTED.
ID MATCH NOT FOUND.
SCANNING ...
ID FOUND = 'JOEBOT'/>
JOE-BOT
WHY DID THE ROBOT
CROSS THE ROAD?
TO DESTROY
THE HUMAN
RESISTANCE
SOLDIERS
PREVENTING IT
FROM ENSLAVING THE
HUMAN RACE.
HA_HA_HA

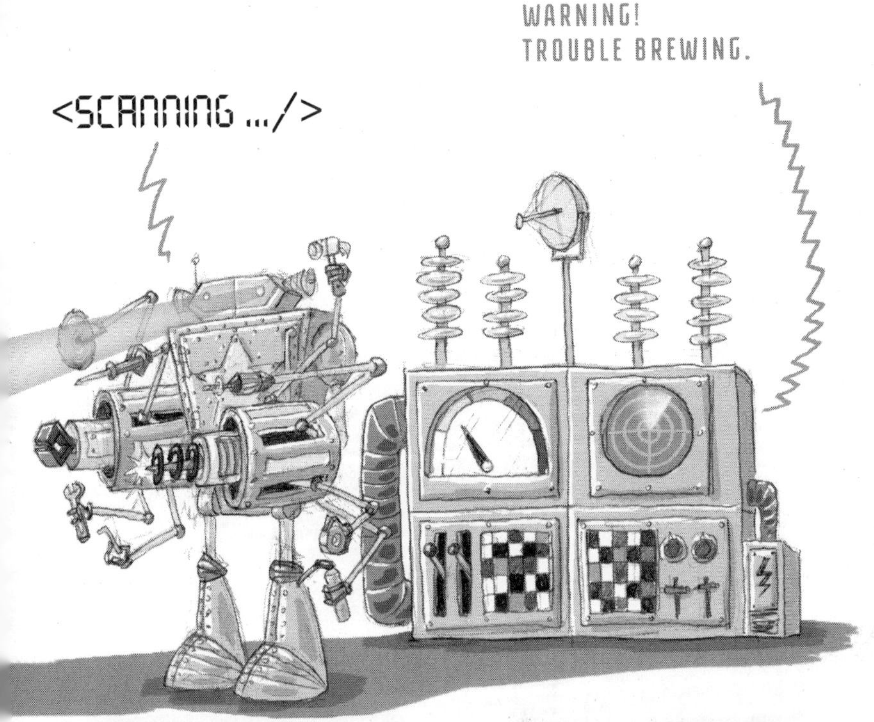
WARNING!
TROUBLE BREWING.
<SCANNING .../>

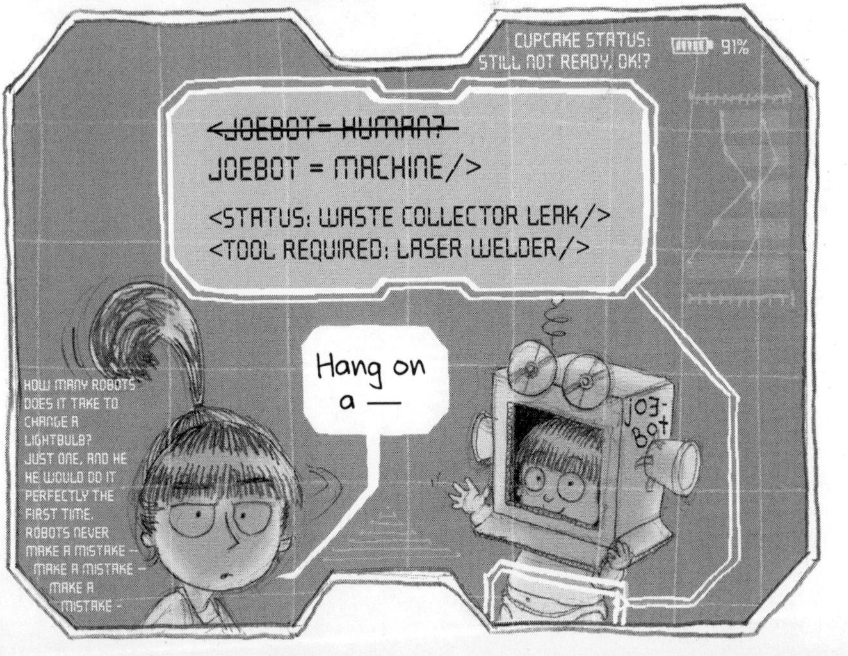
CUPCAKE STATUS:
STILL NOT READY, OK!?
91%
~~<JOEBOT= HUMAN?~~
JOEBOT = MACHINE/>
<STATUS: WASTE COLLECTOR LEAK/>
<TOOL REQUIRED: LASER WELDER/>
Hang on a —
JOE-Bot
HOW MANY ROBOTS DOES IT TAKE TO CHANGE A LIGHTBULB? JUST ONE, AND HE HE WOULD DO IT PERFECTLY THE FIRST TIME. ROBOTS NEVER MAKE A MISTAKE — MAKE A MISTAKE — MAKE A MISTAKE -

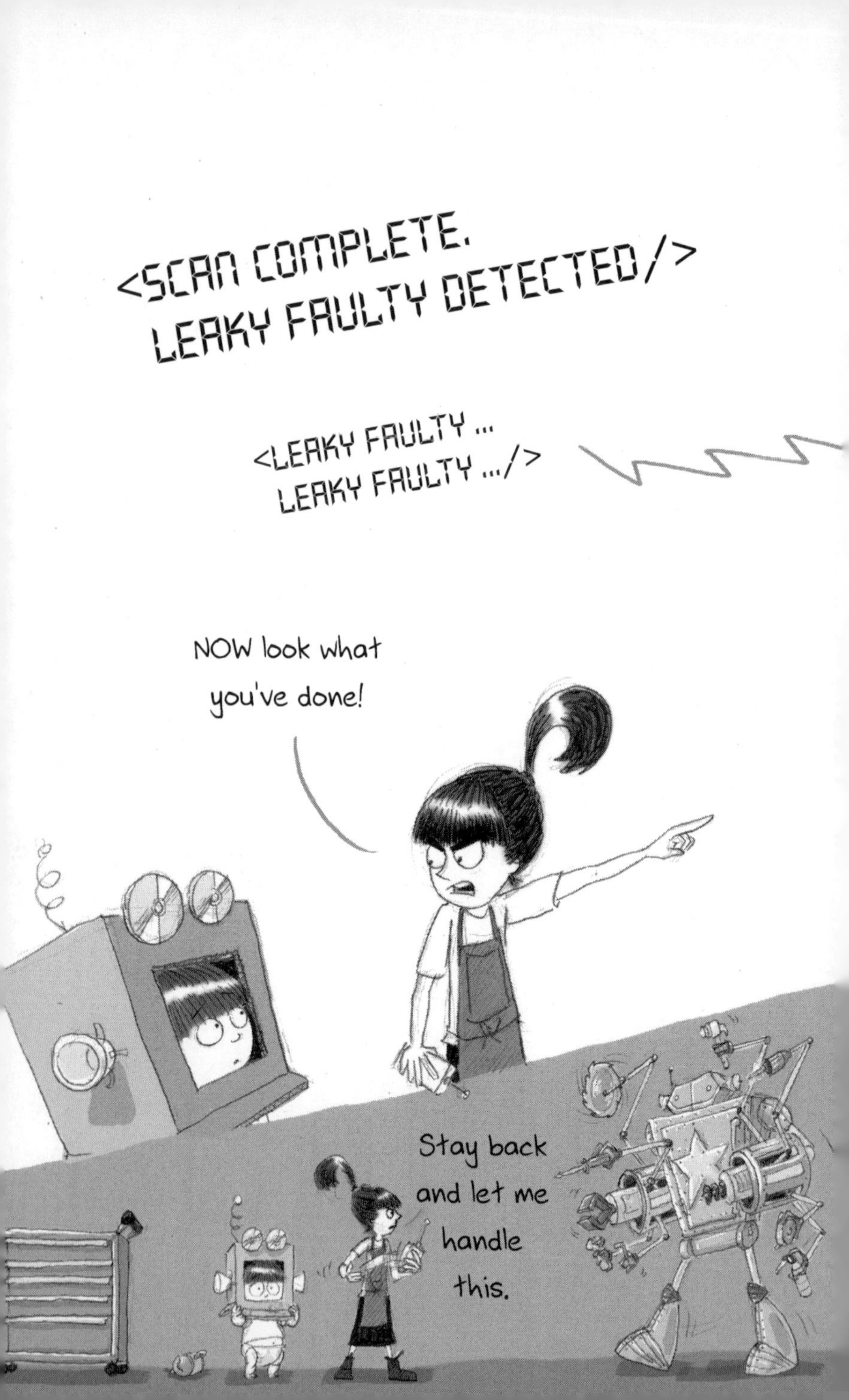
<SCAN COMPLETE.
LEAKY FAULTY DETECTED/>
<LEAKY FAULTY ...
LEAKY FAULTY .../>
NOW look what you've done!
Stay back and let me handle this.

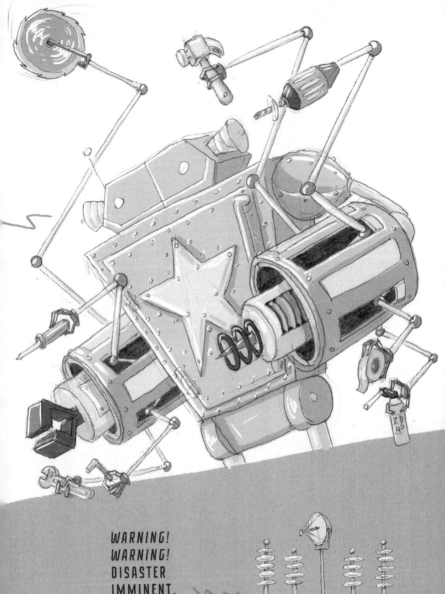

WARNING!
WARNING!
DISASTER
IMMINENT.

WARNING!
WARNING!
DISASTER
IMMINENT.

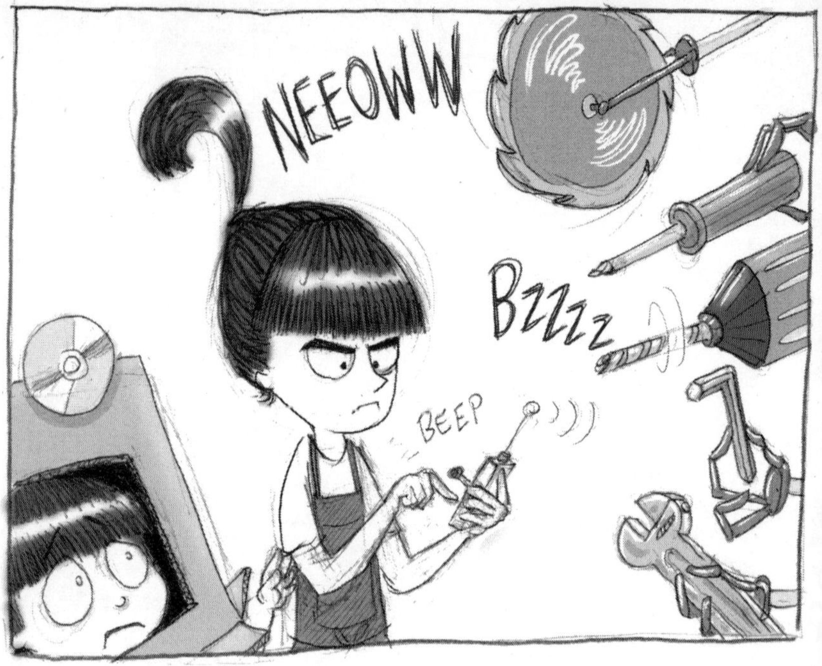
NEEOWW
Bzzzzz
BEEP

<STANDBY MODE ENGAGED./>

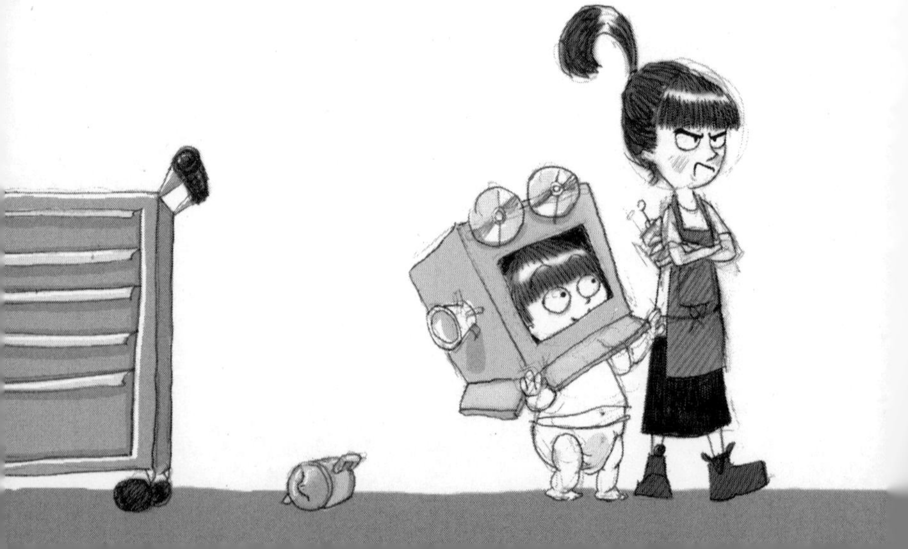

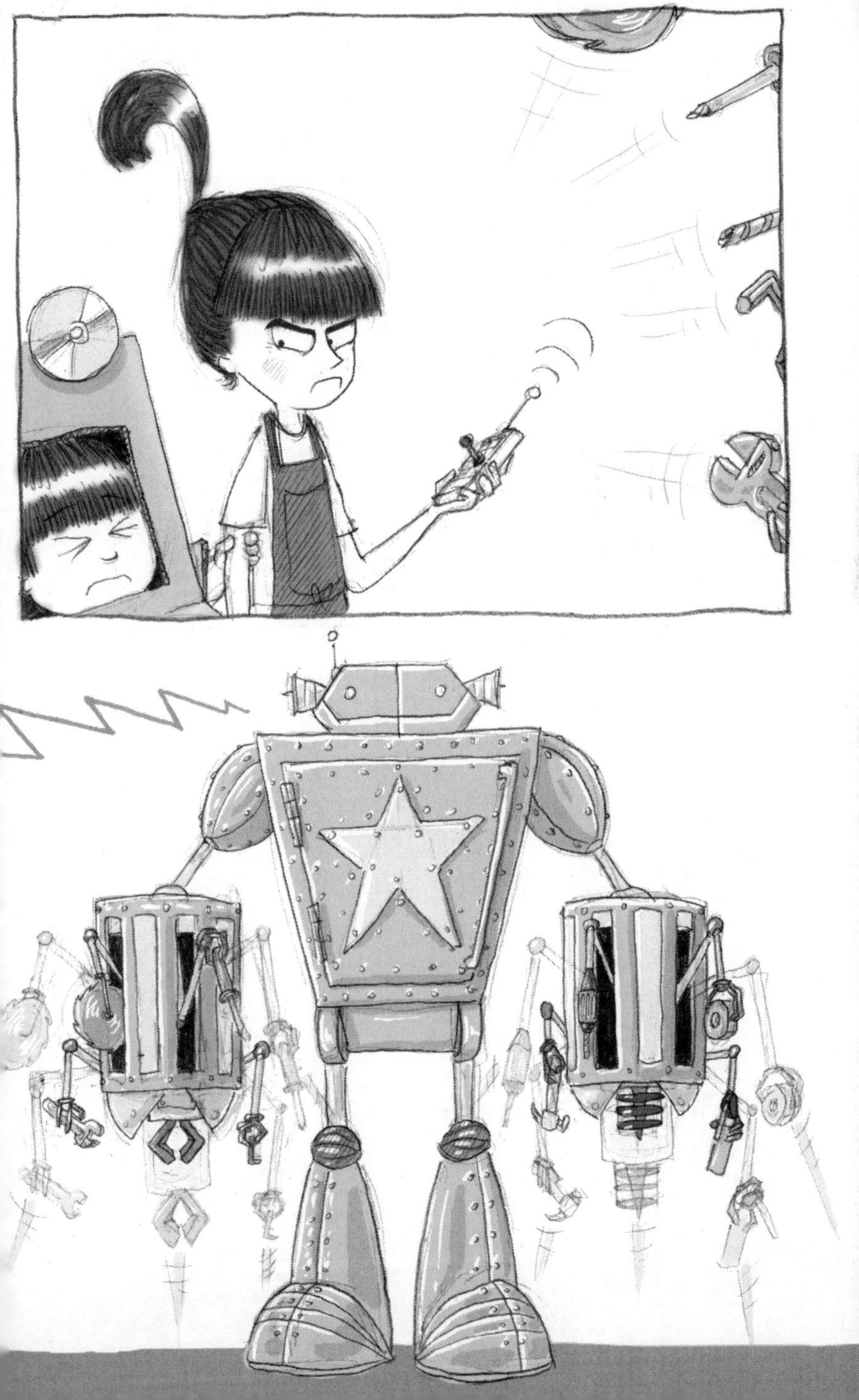

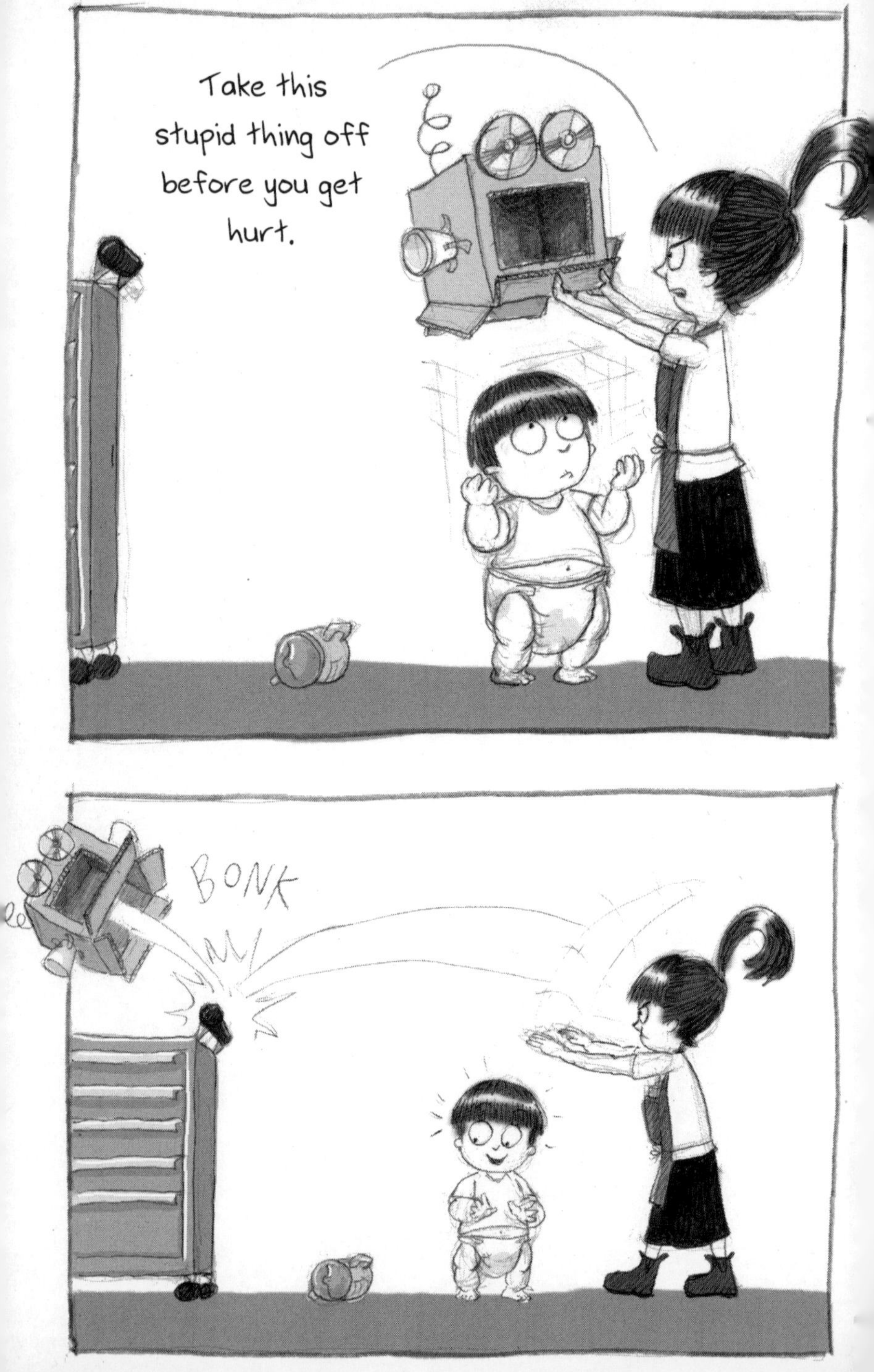
Take this stupid thing off before you get hurt.
BONK

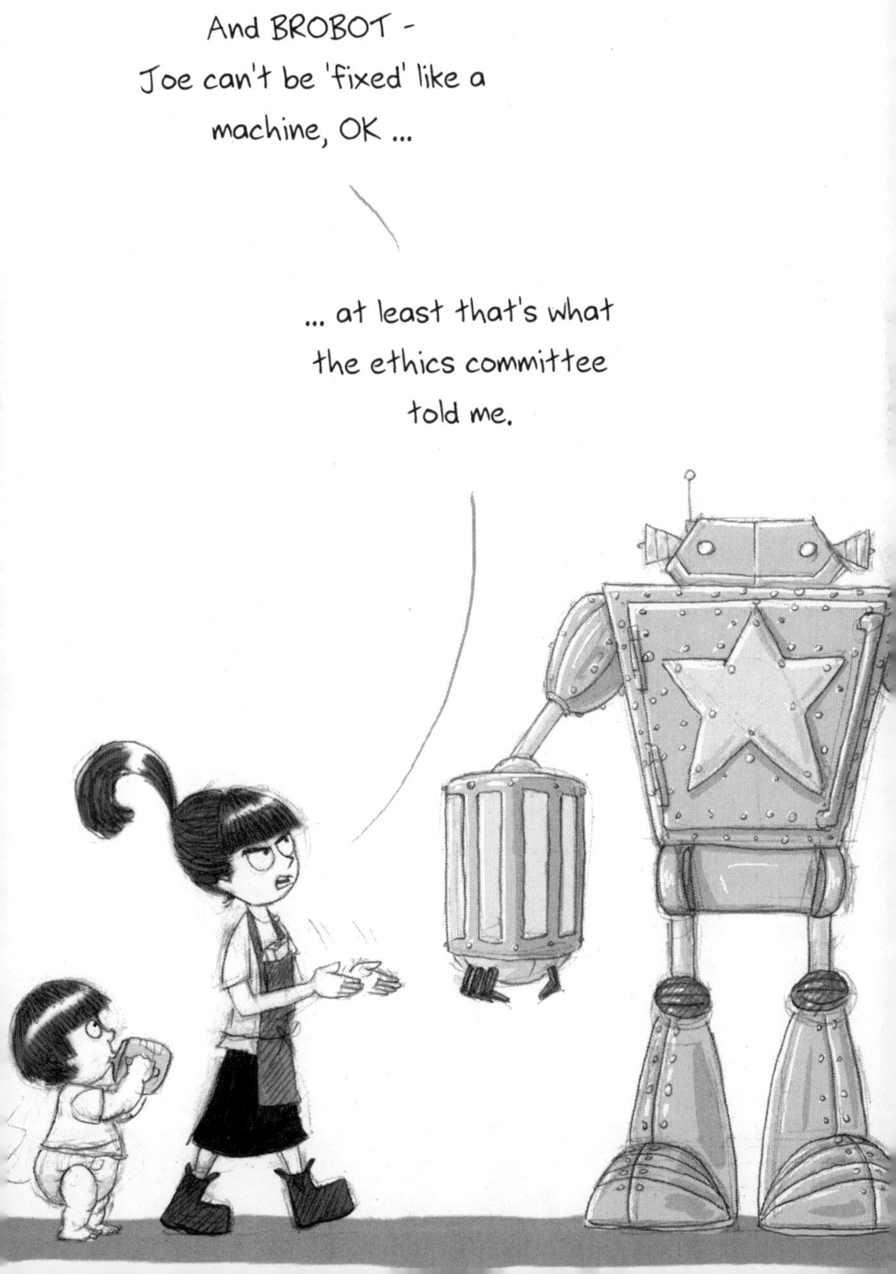
And BROBOT -
Joe can't be 'fixed' like a
machine, OK ...
... at least that's what
the ethics committee
told me.

Right! Time for the third and final demonstration.
Brobot is made of spotless, stainless steel, so he's completely leakproof ...
TONG TONG

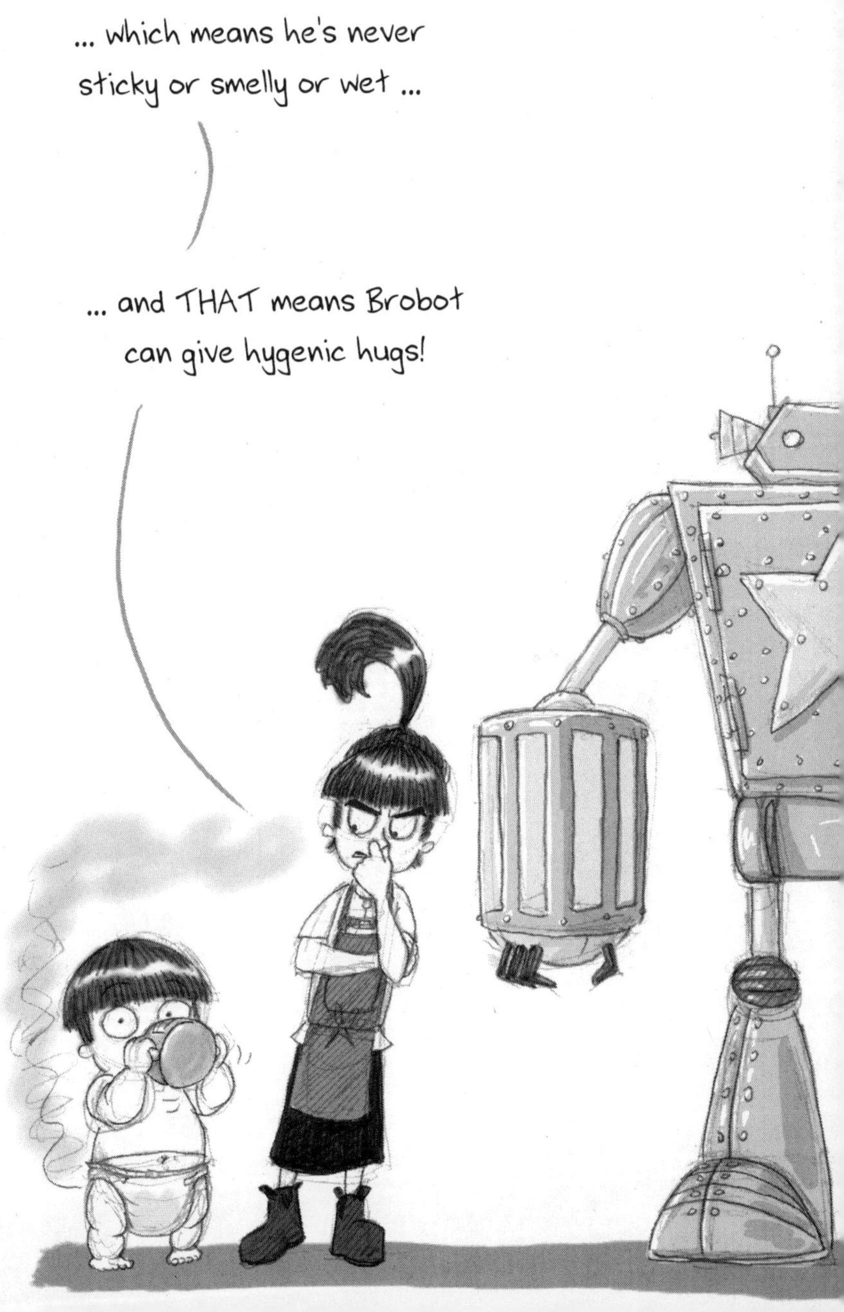
... which means he's never sticky or smelly or wet ...
... and THAT means Brobot can give hygenic hugs!

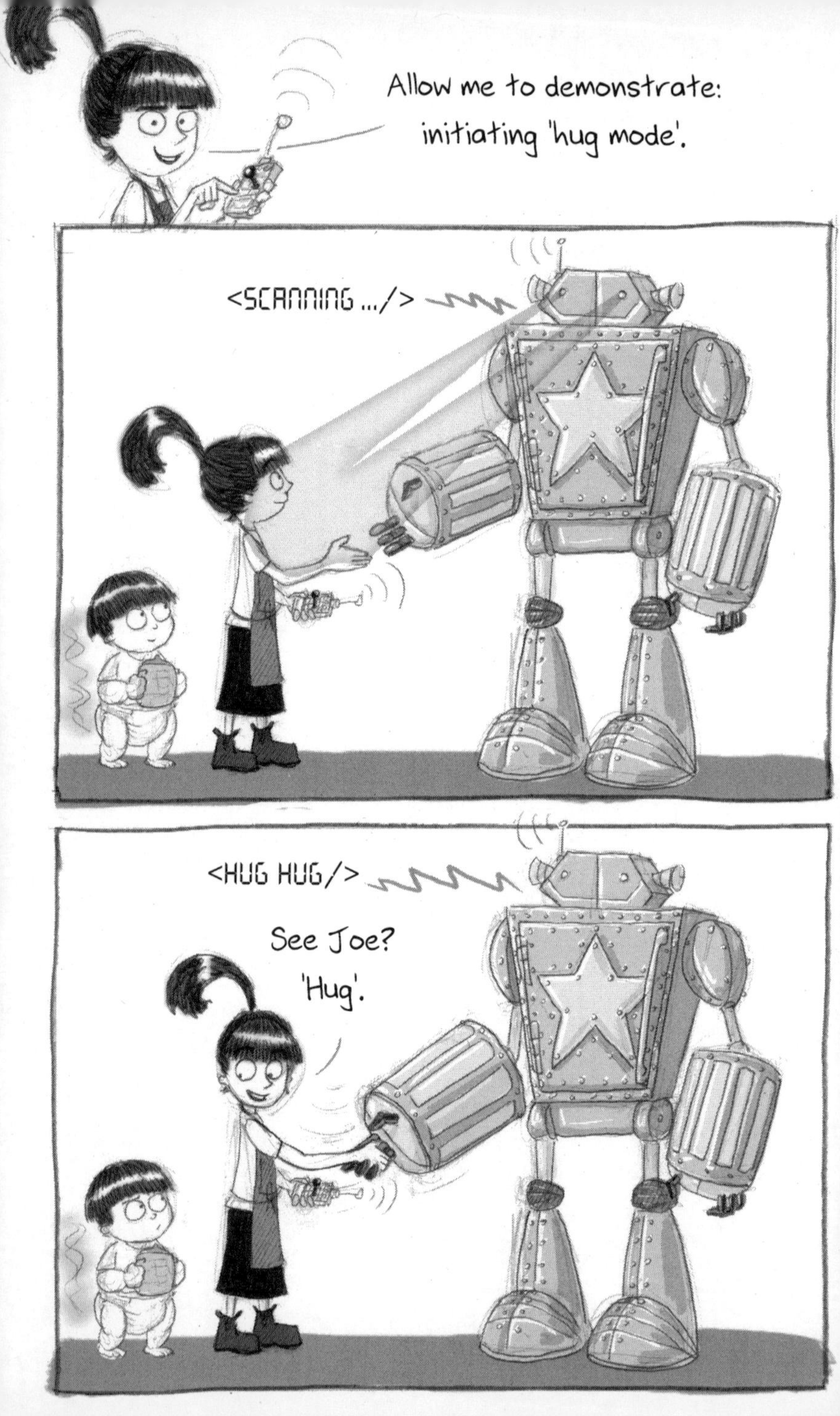
Allow me to demonstrate:
initiating 'hug mode'.
<SCANNING.../>
<HUG HUG/>
See Joe?
'Hug'.

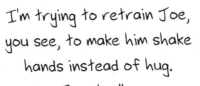

I'm trying to retrain Joe, you see, to make him shake hands instead of hug. Eventually, I should be able to wean him off physical contact entirely.

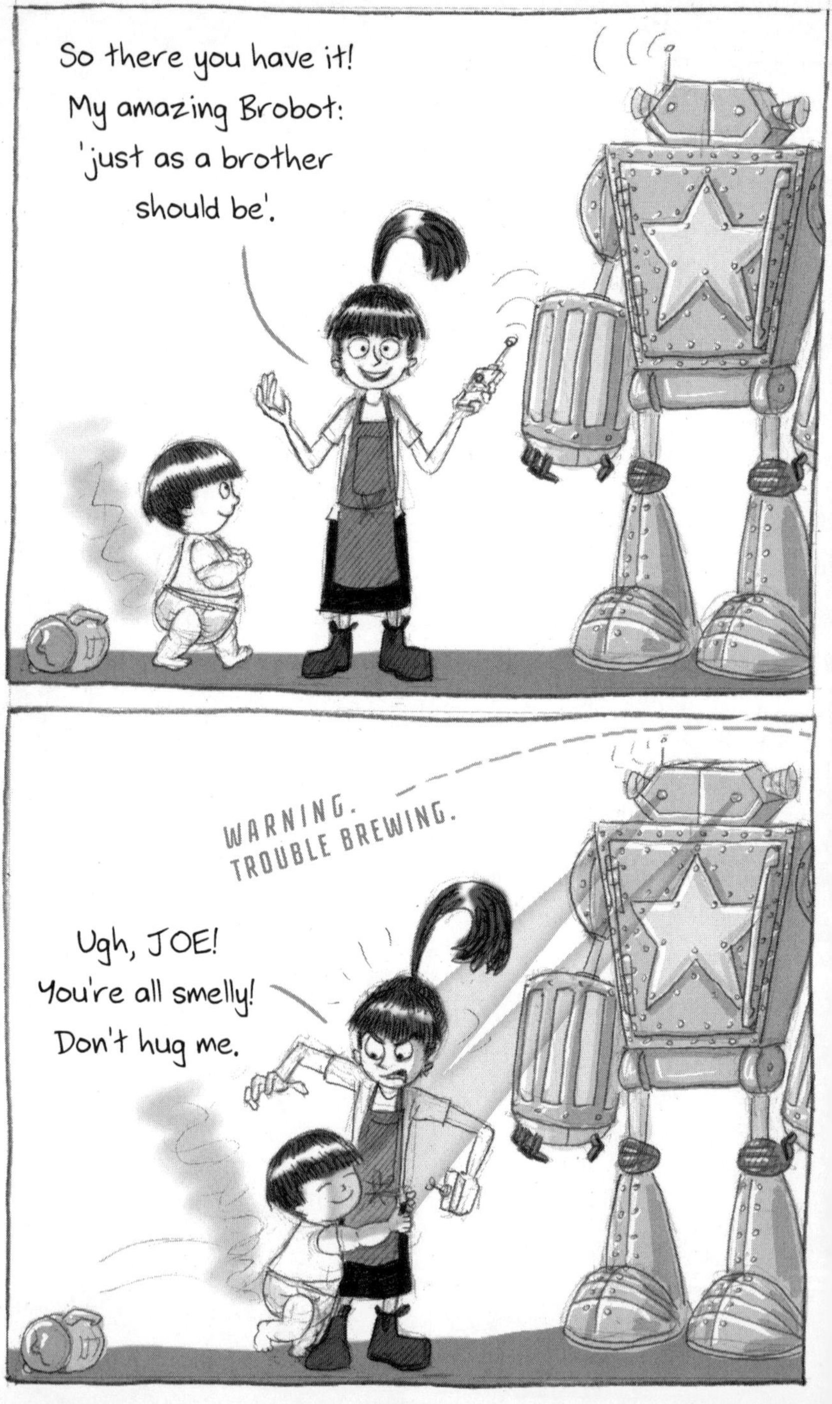
So there you have it! My amazing Brobot: 'just as a brother should be'.
WARNING. TROUBLE BREWING.
Ugh, JOE! You're all smelly! Don't hug me.

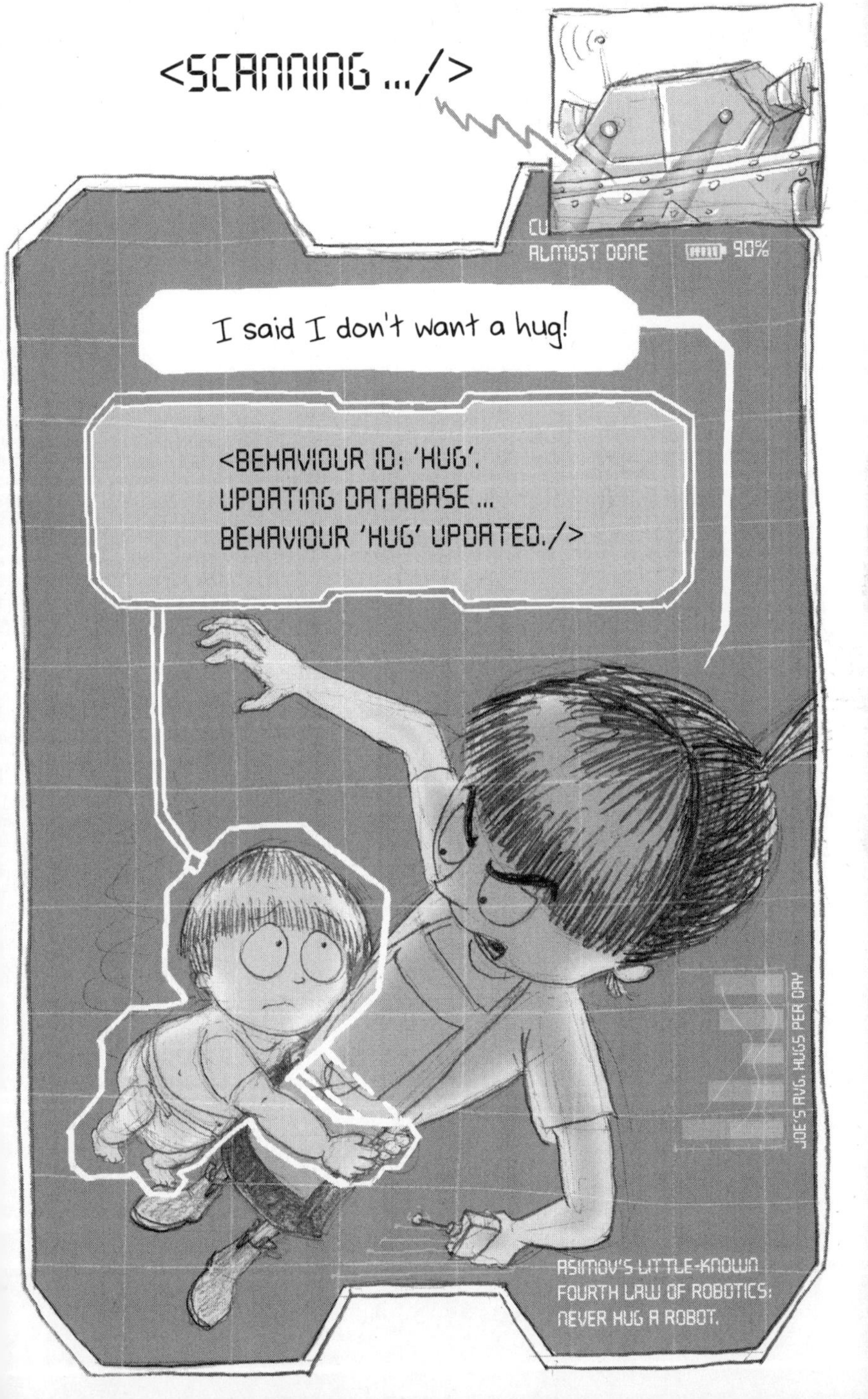
<SCANNING .../>
ALMOST DONE
90%
I said I don't want a hug!
<BEHAVIOUR ID: 'HUG'.
UPDATING DATABASE ...
BEHAVIOUR 'HUG' UPDATED./>
JOE'S AVG. HUGS PER DAY
ASIMOV'S LITTLE-KNOWN FOURTH LAW OF ROBOTICS: NEVER HUG A ROBOT.

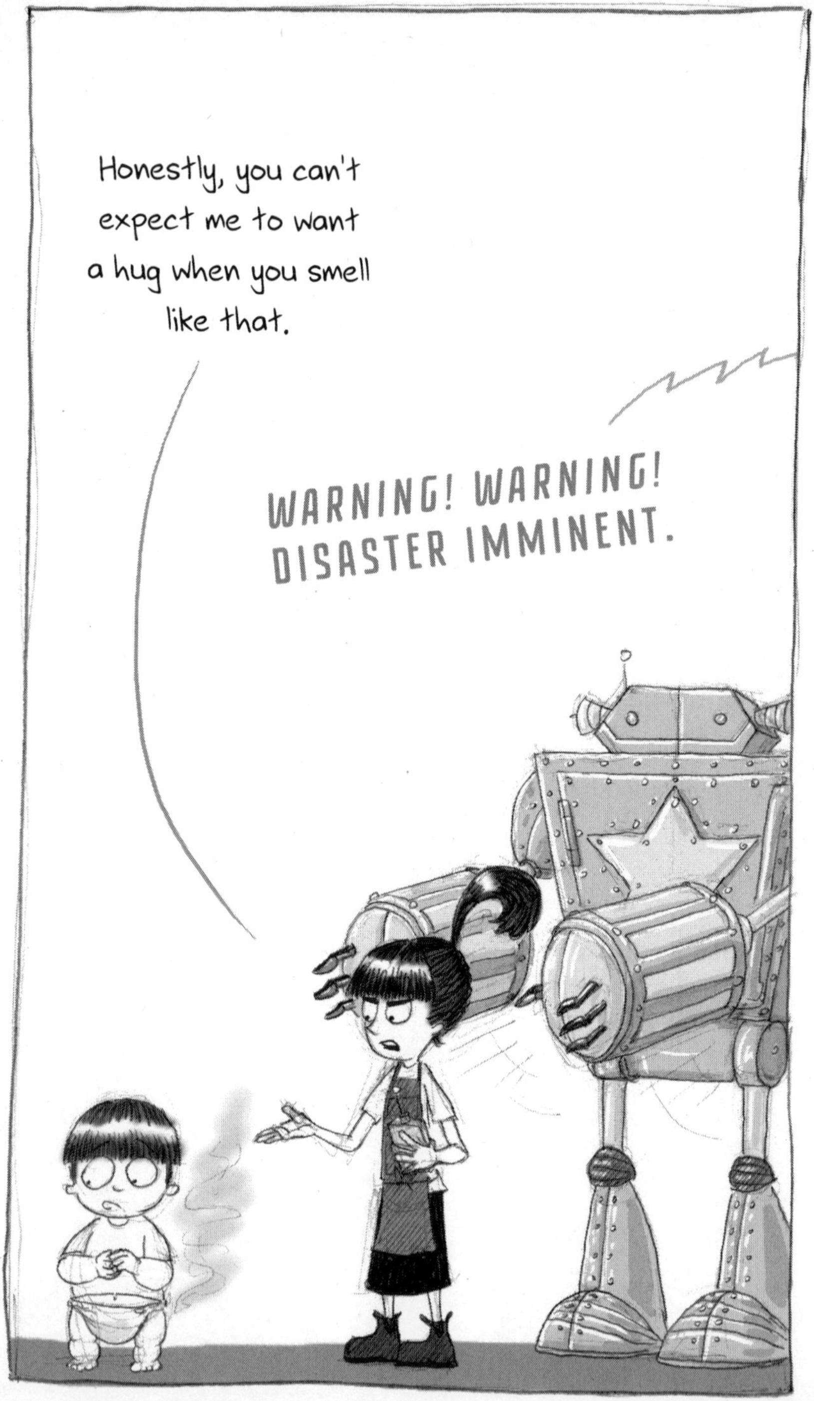
Honestly, you can't expect me to want a hug when you smell like that.
WARNING! WARNING! DISASTER IMMINENT.

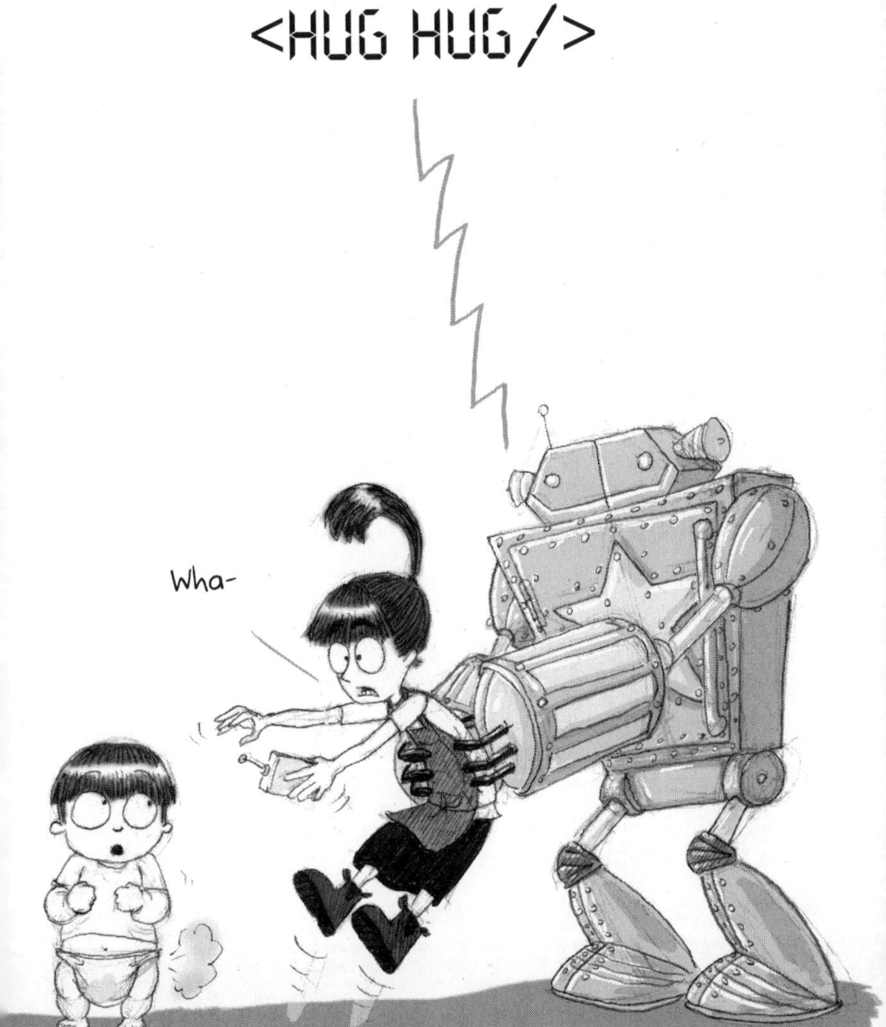
<HUG HUG/>
Wha-

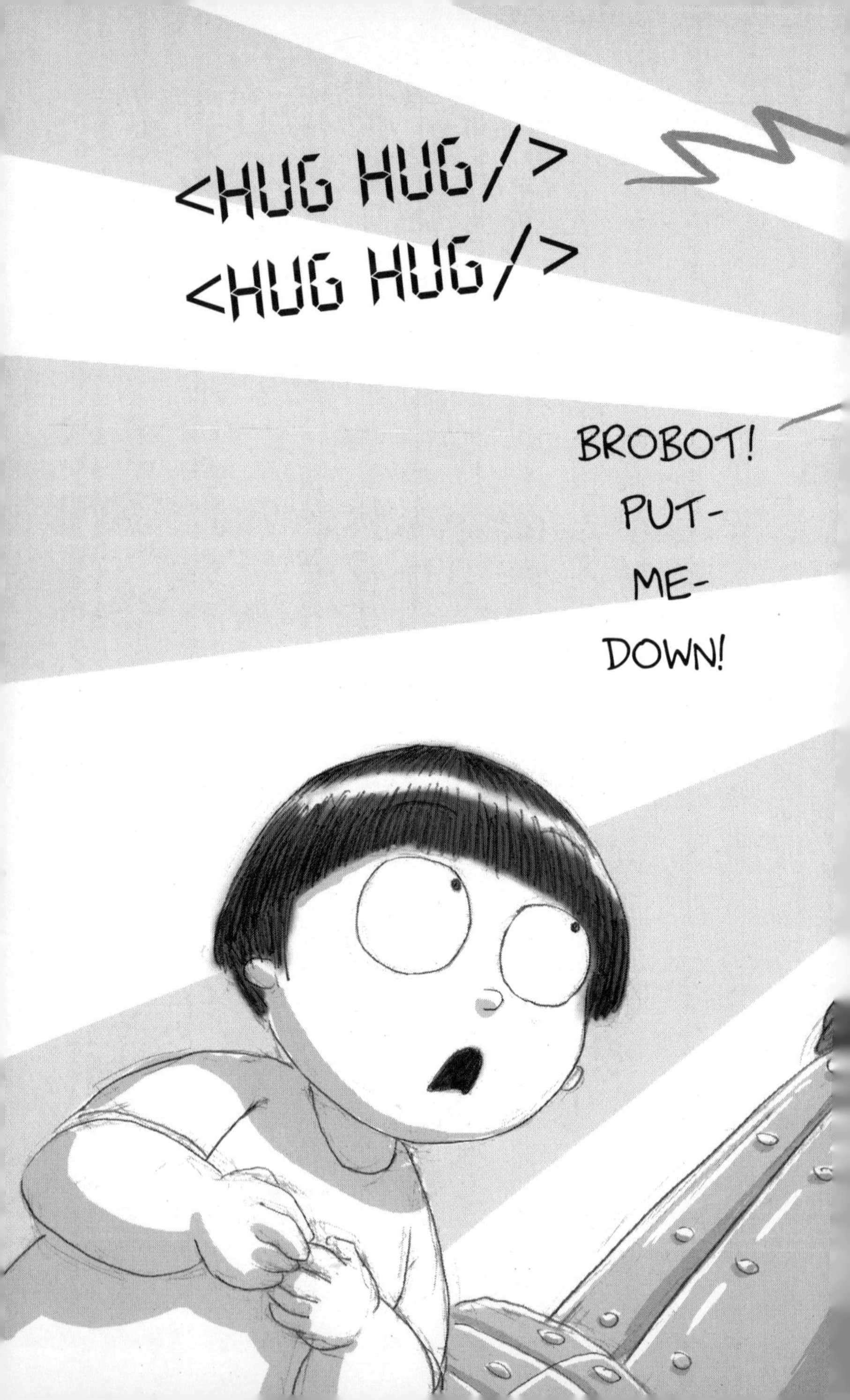
<HUG HUG/>
<HUG HUG/>
BROBOT! PUT- ME- DOWN!

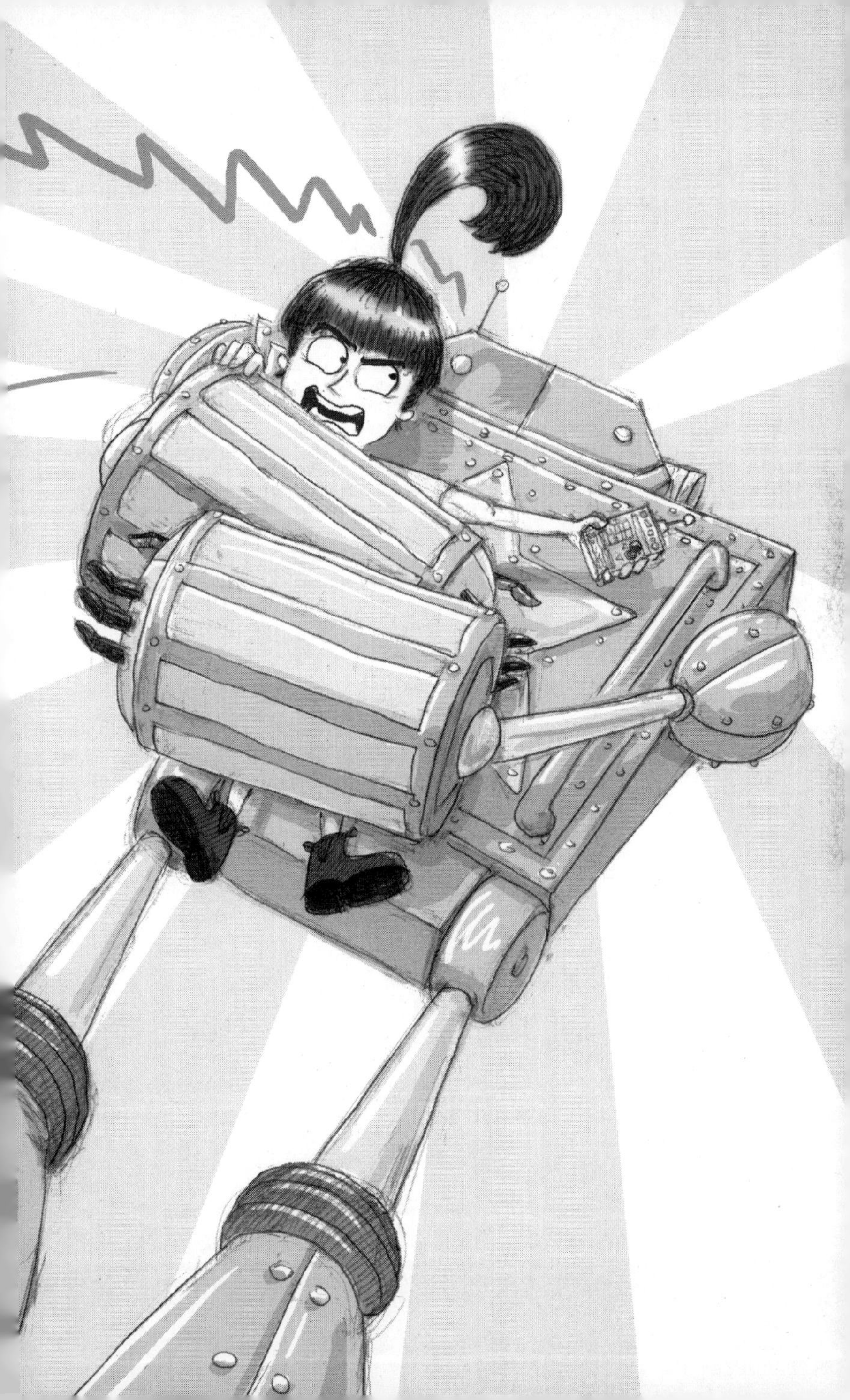

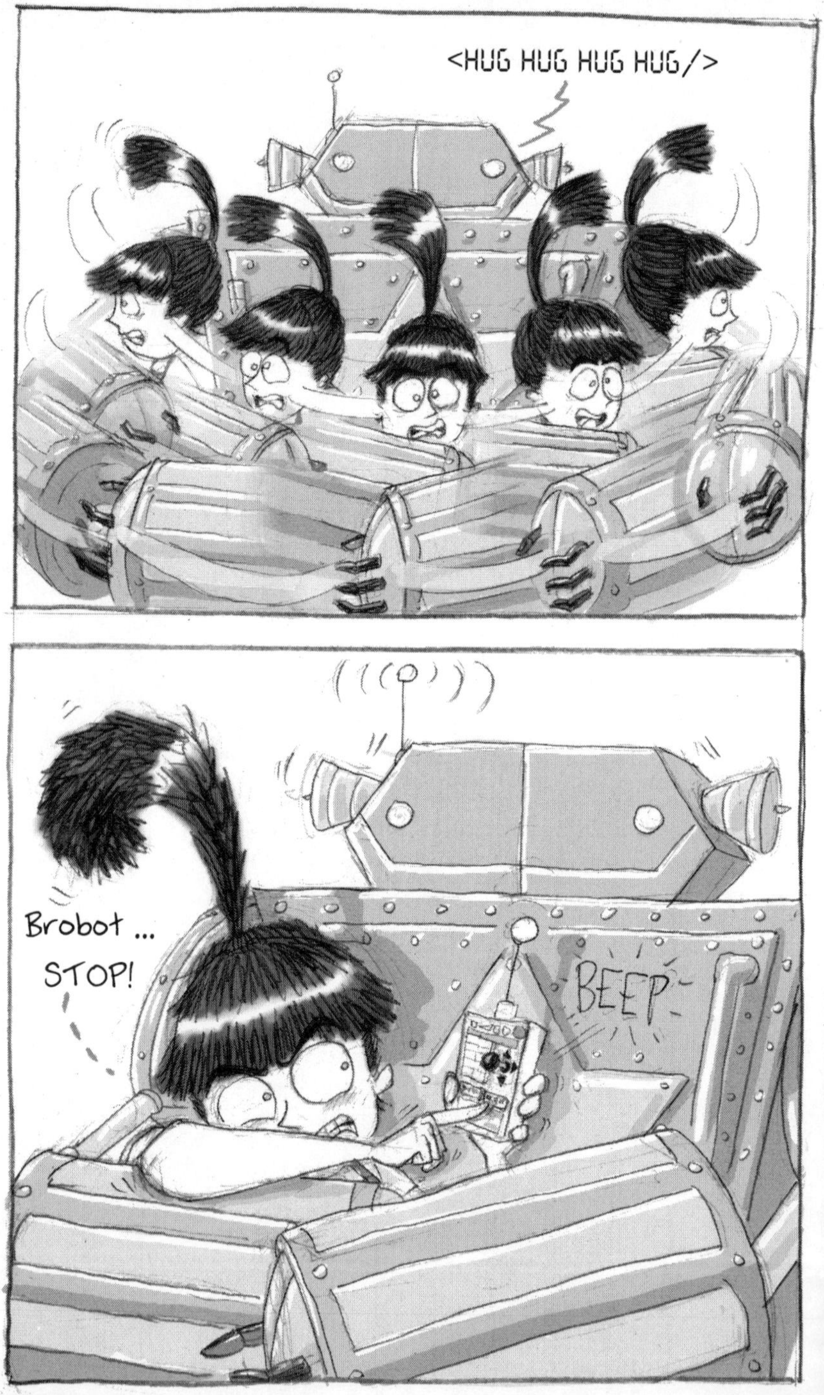
<HUG HUG HUG HUG/>
Brobot ... STOP!
BEEP

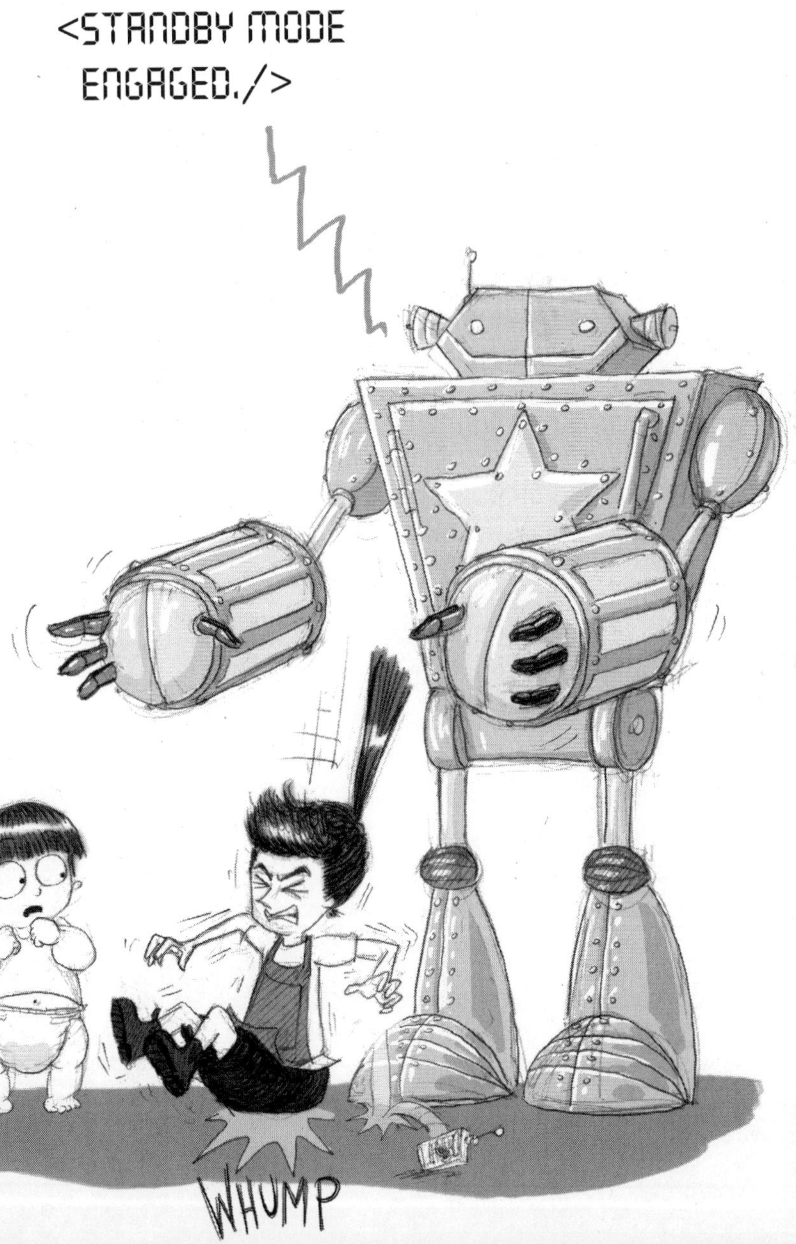
<STANDBY MODE ENGAGED./>
WHUMP

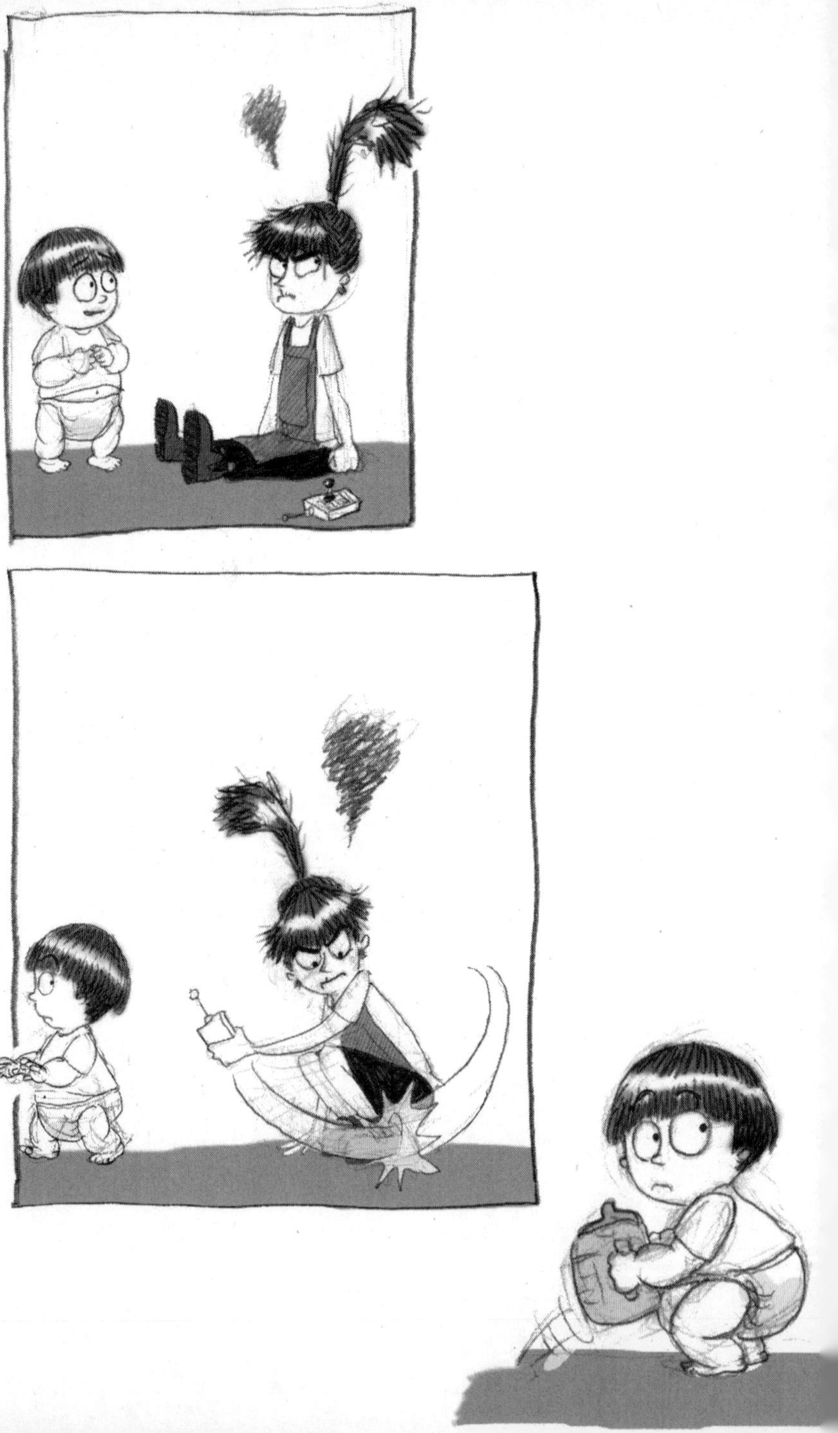

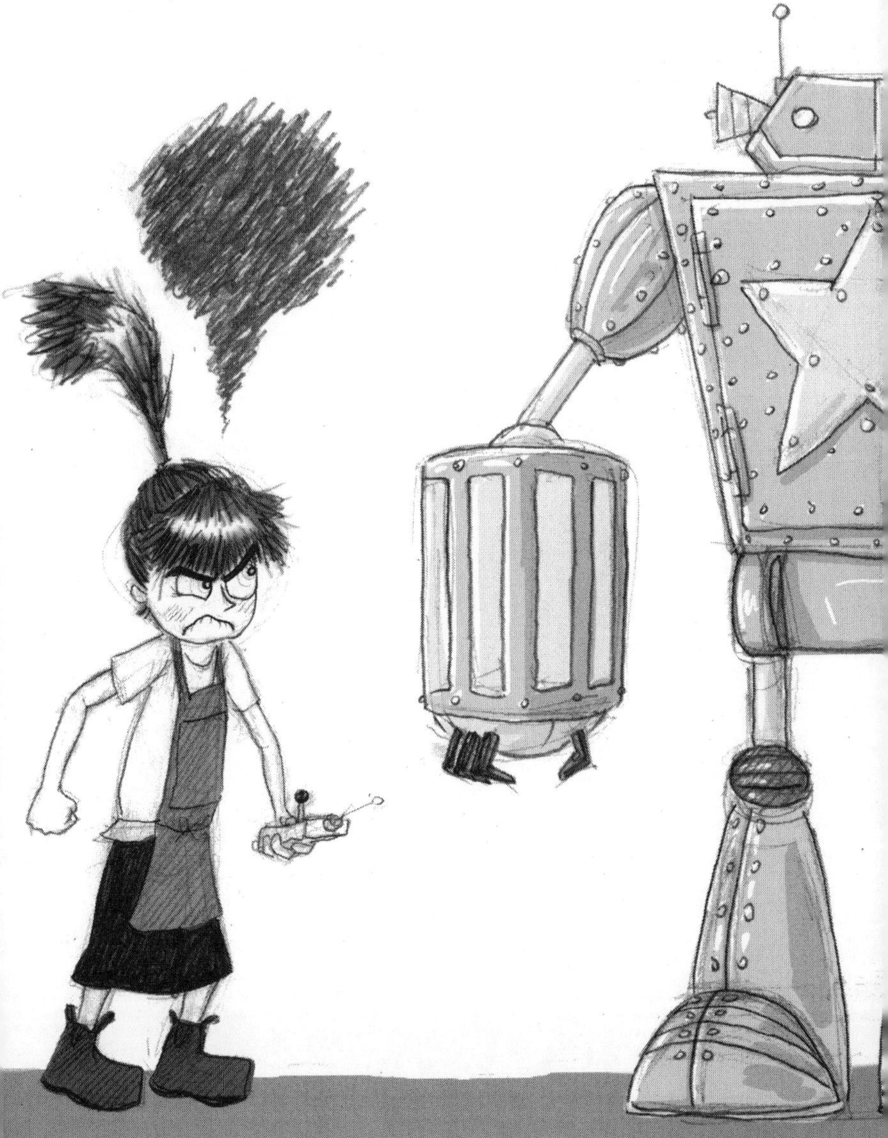

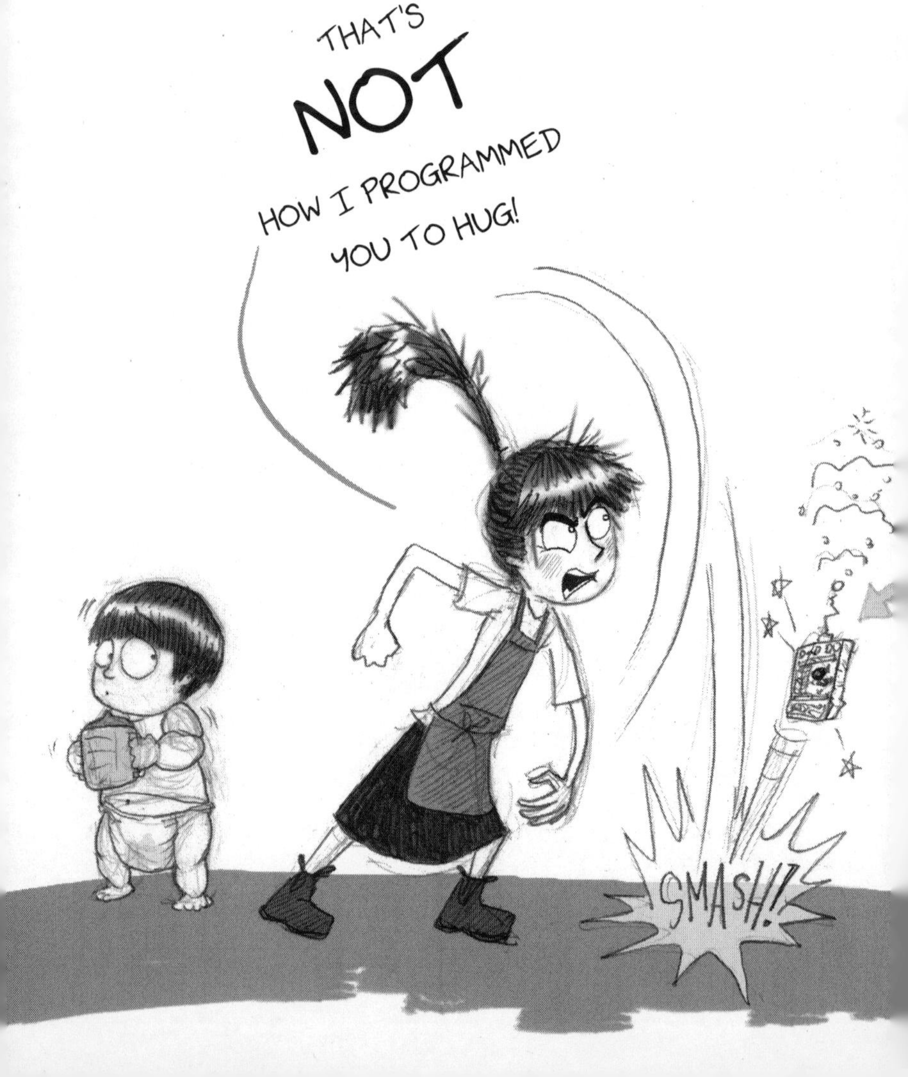
THAT'S NOT HOW I PROGRAMMED YOU TO HUG!
SMASH!!

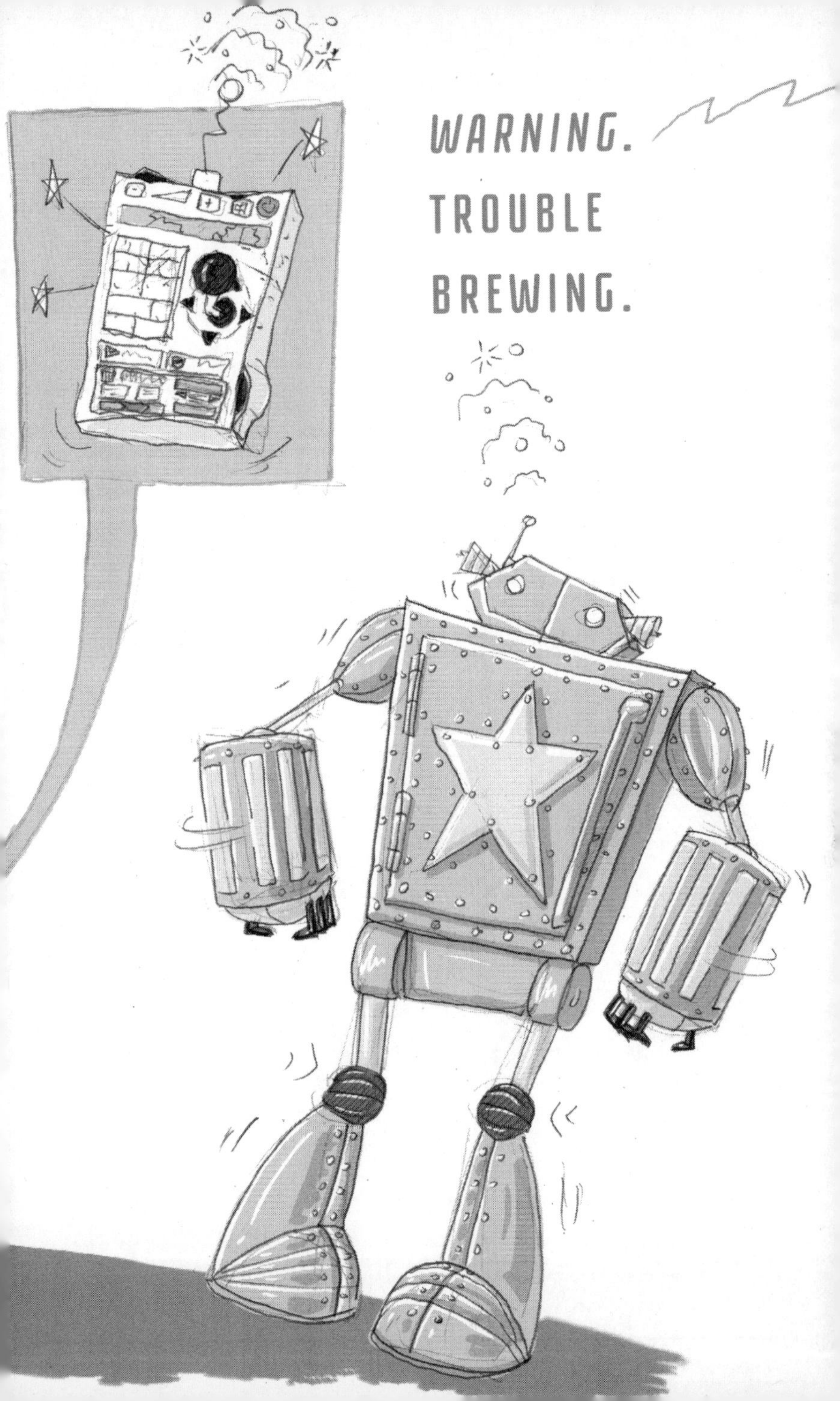
WARNING.
TROUBLE
BREWING.

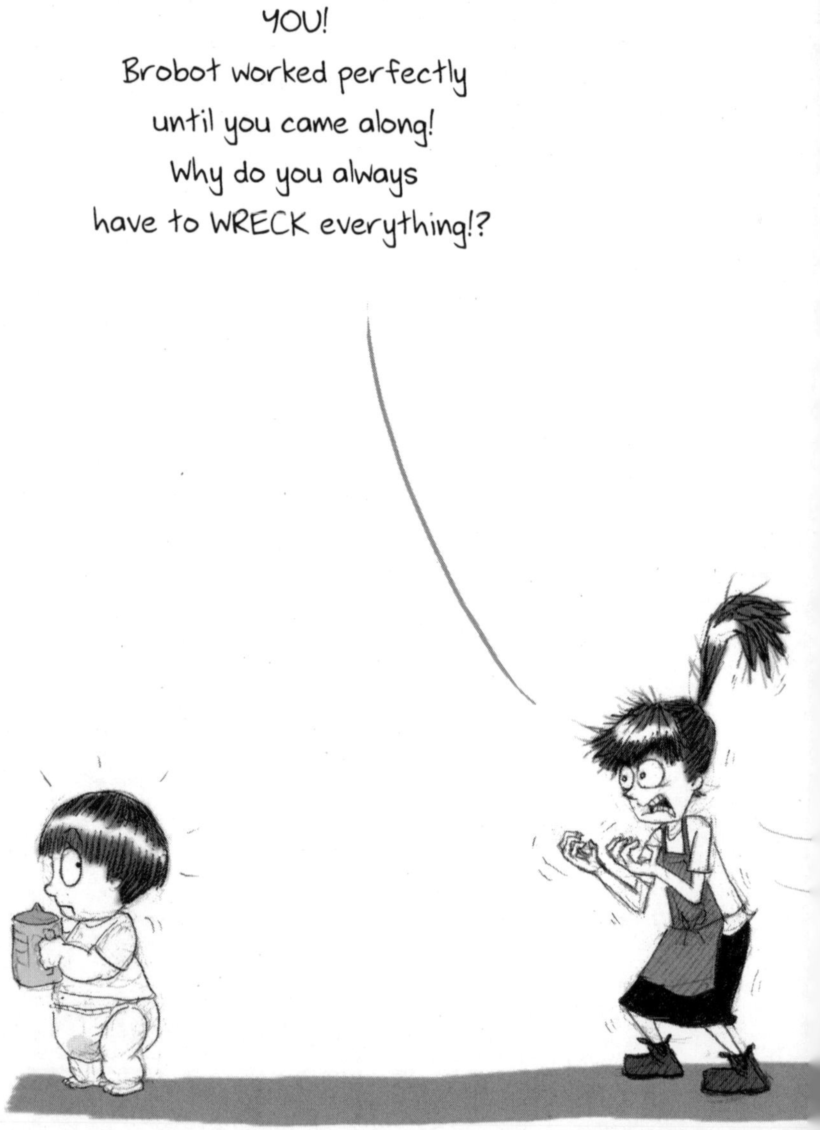
YOU!
Brobot worked perfectly
until you came along!
Why do you always
have to WRECK everything!?

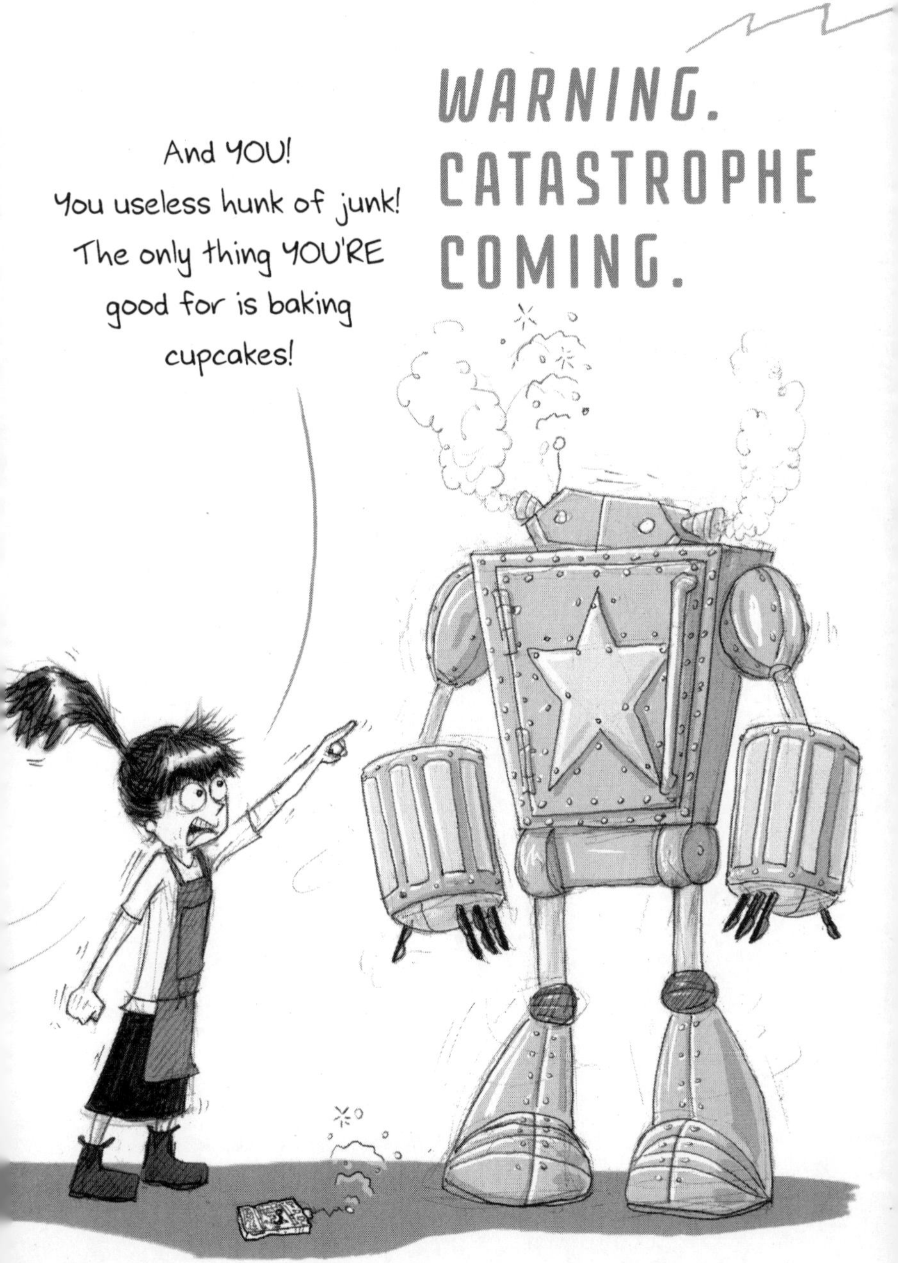
WARNING.
CATASTROPHE
COMING.
And YOU!
You useless hunk of junk!
The only thing YOU'RE
good for is baking
cupcakes!

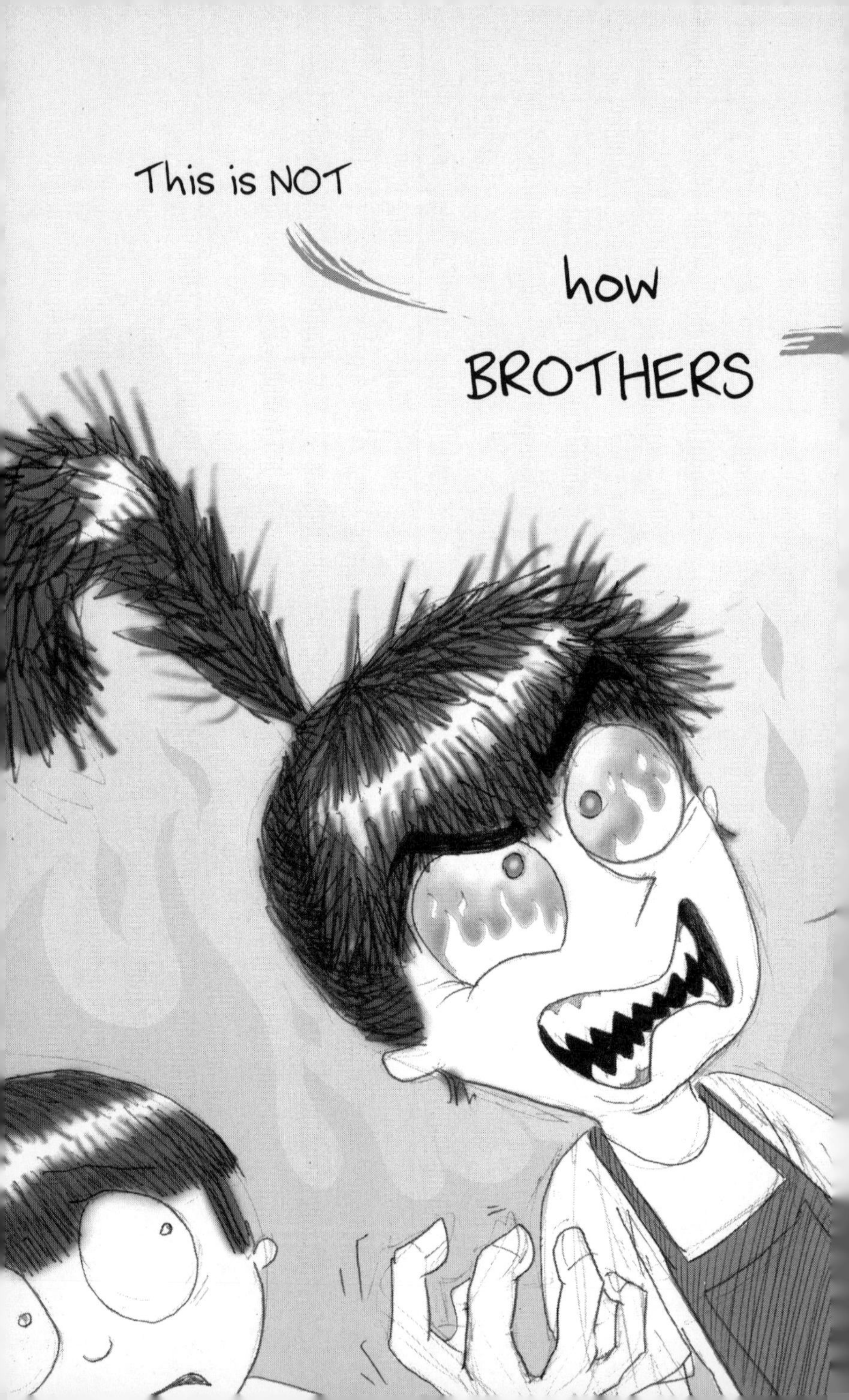
This is NOT
how
BROTHERS

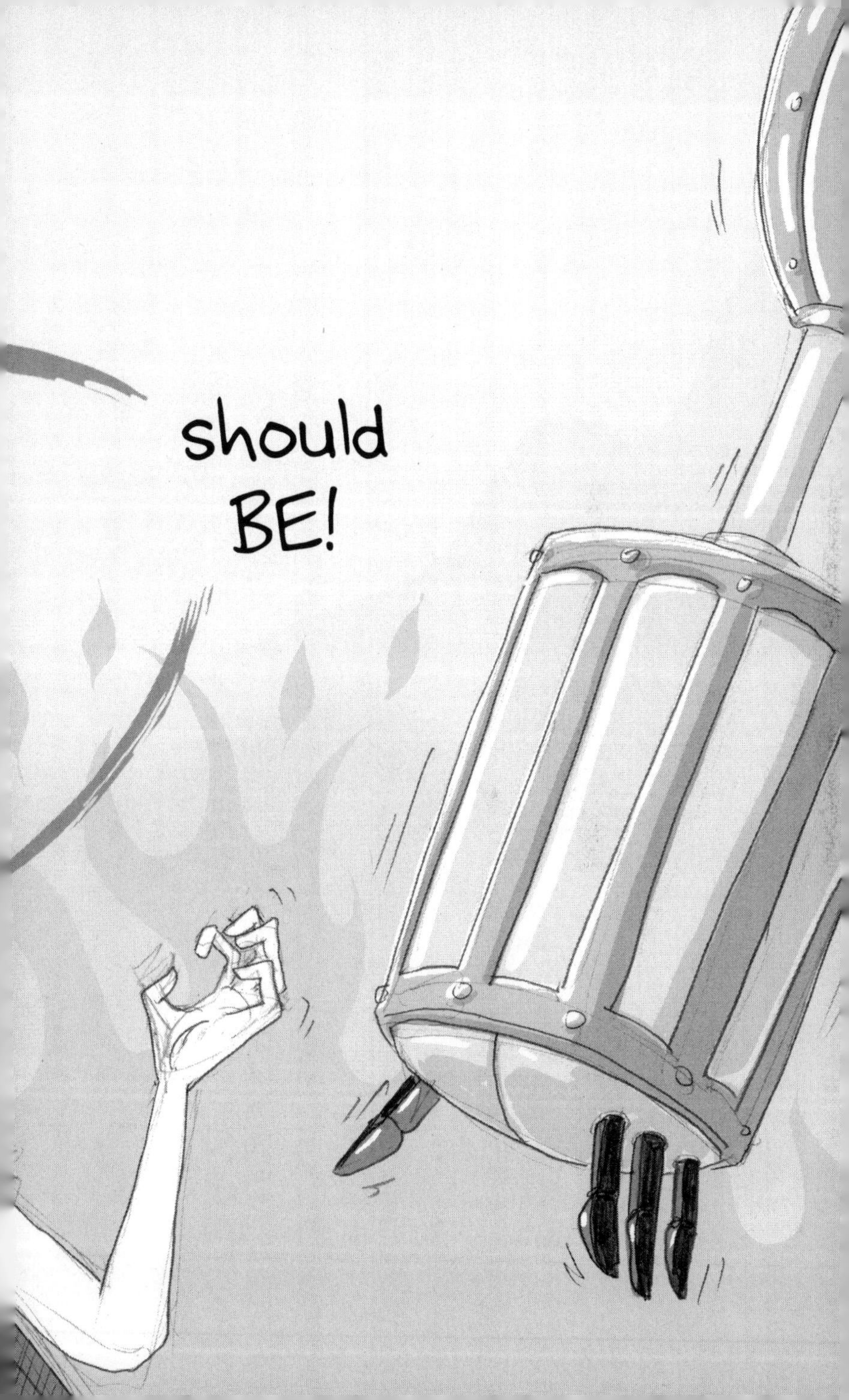
should
BE!

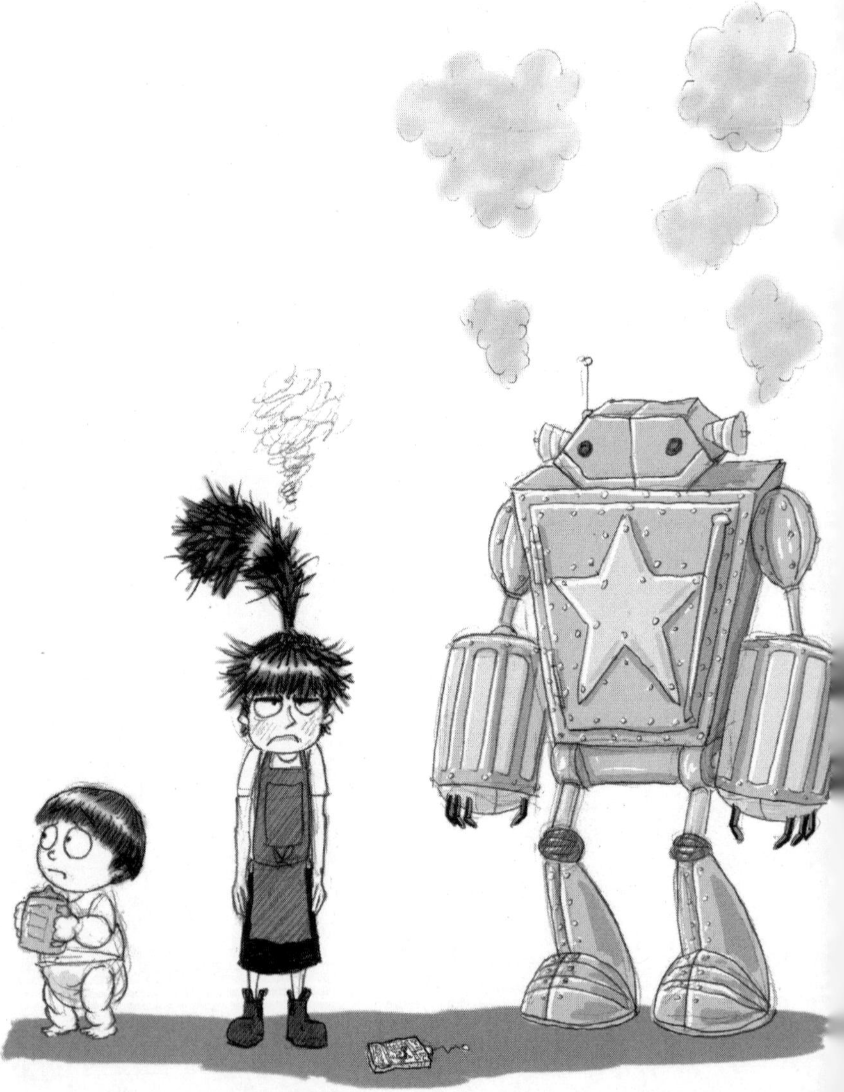

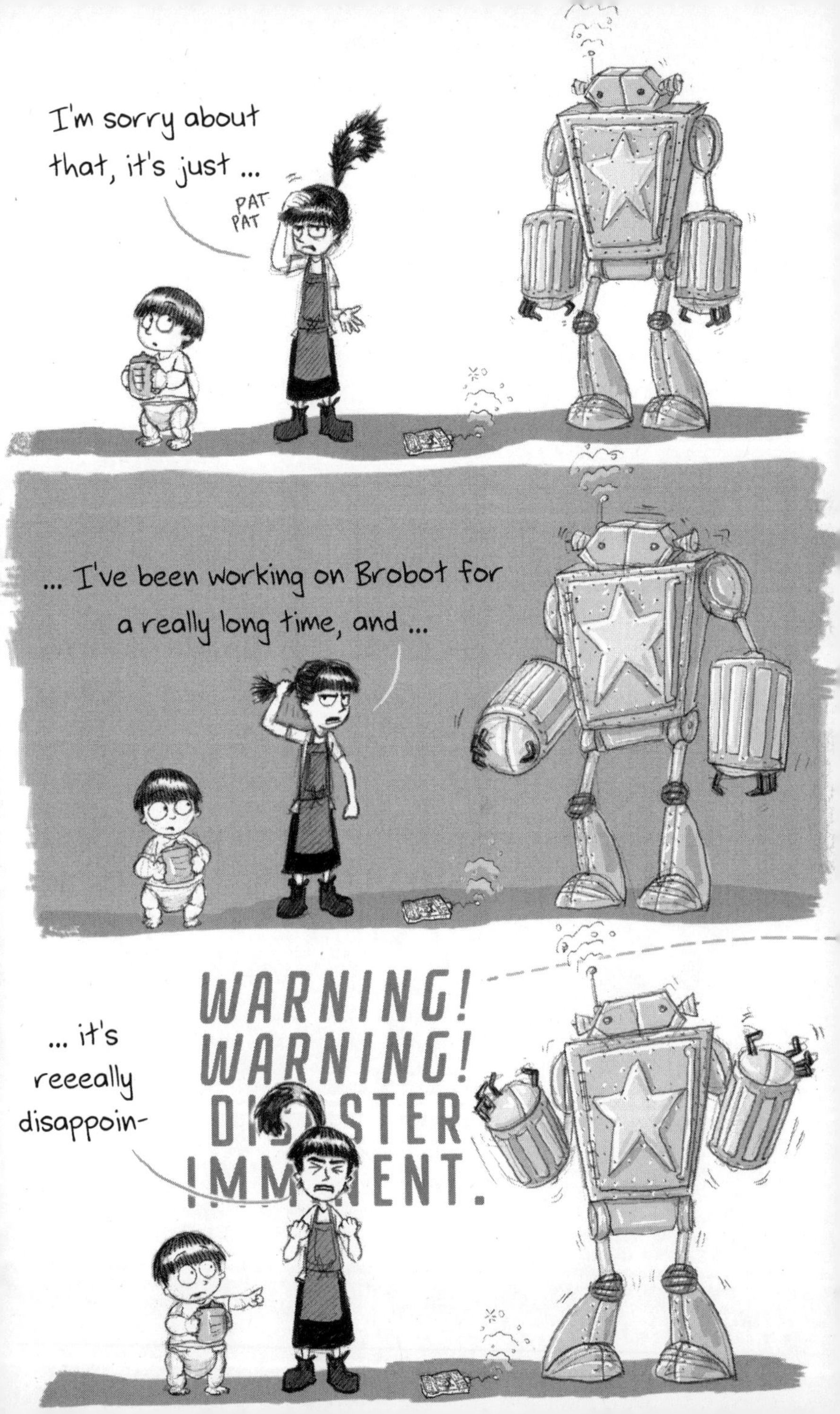
I'm sorry about that, it's just ...
PAT PAT
... I've been working on Brobot for a really long time, and ...
... it's reeeally disappoin-
WARNING! WARNING! DI STER IMM NENT.

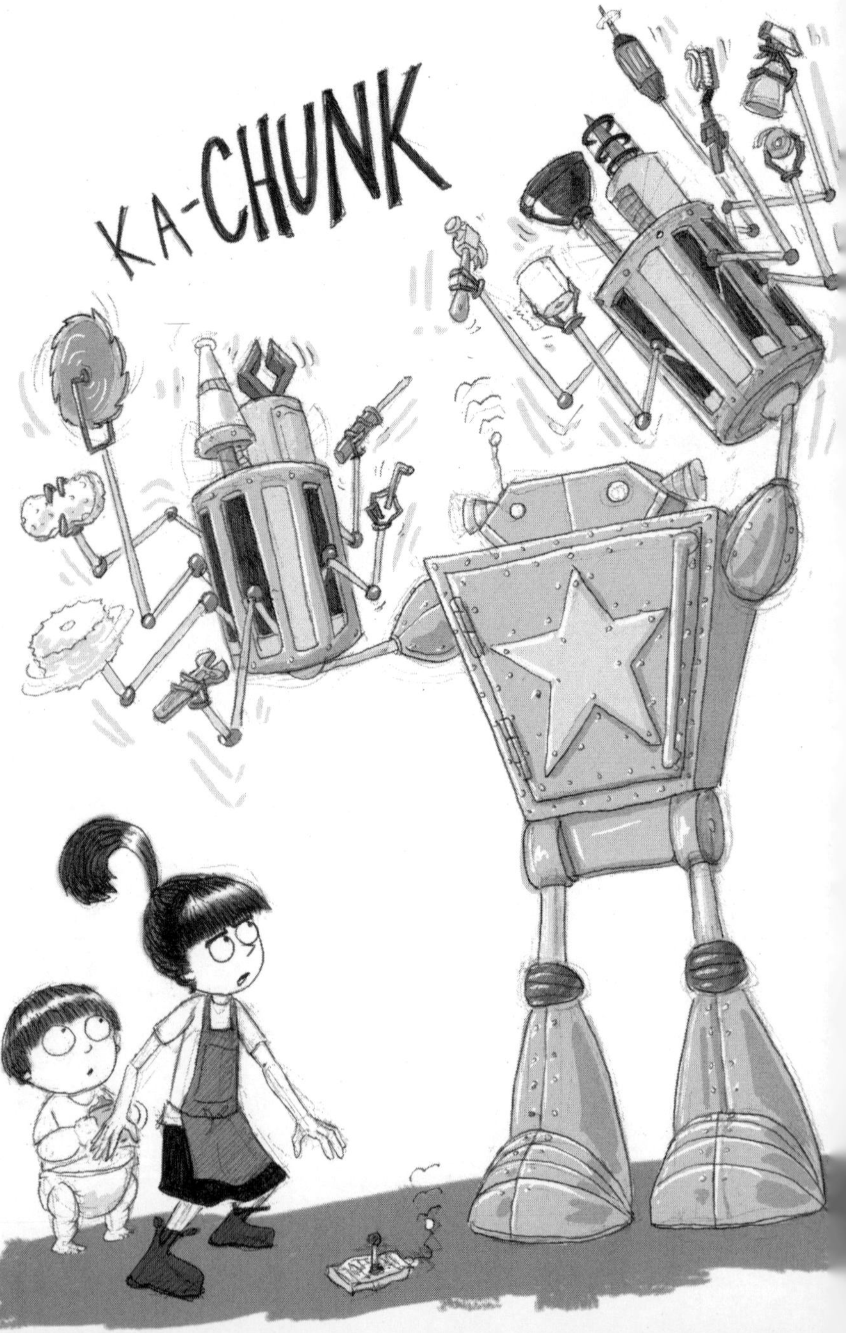
KA-CHUNK

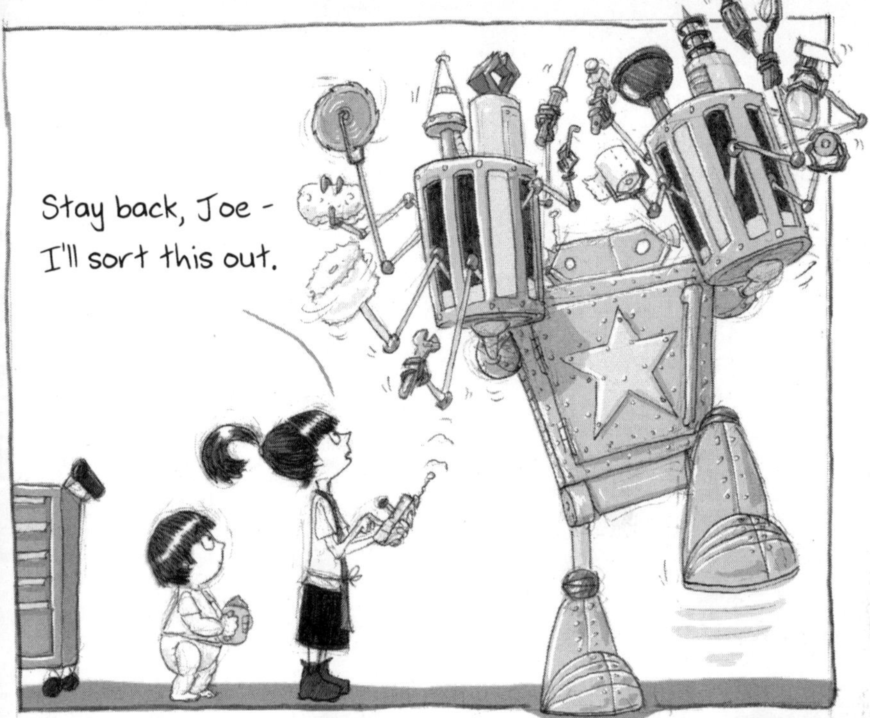
Stay back, Joe -
I'll sort this out.

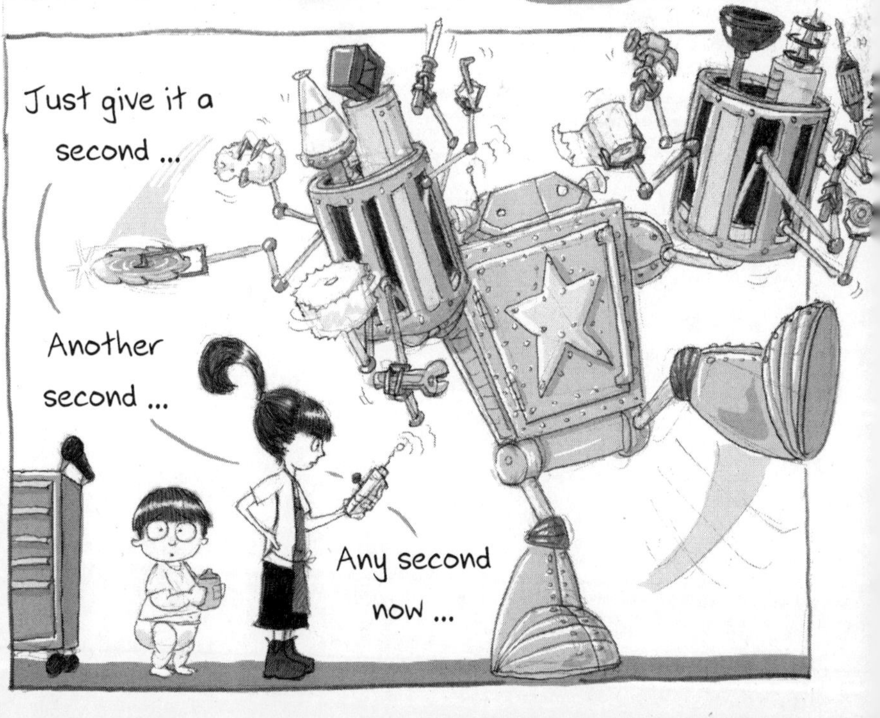
Just give it a
second ...
Another
second ...
Any second
now ...

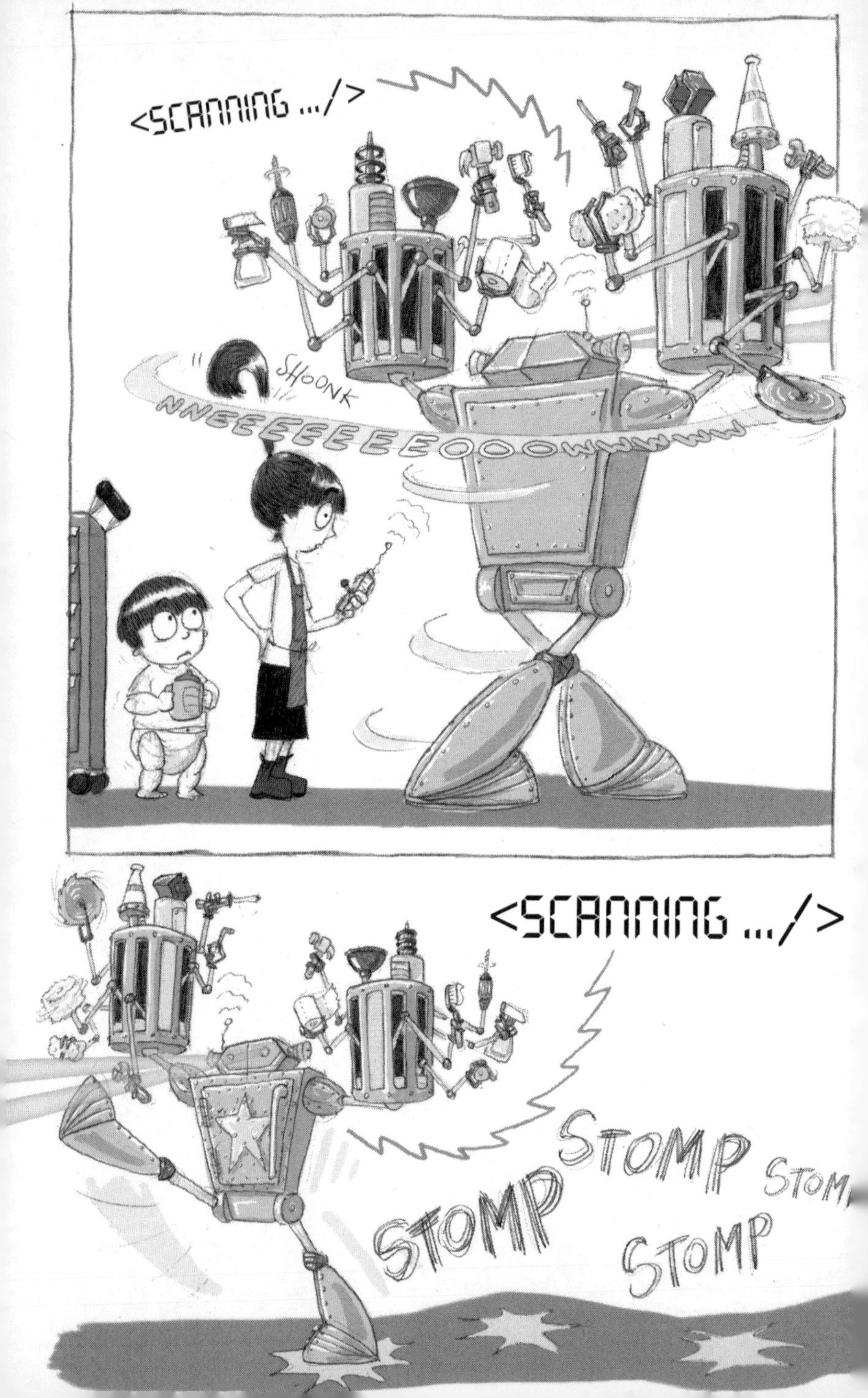
<SCANNING .../>
SHOONK
NNEEEEEEEEOOOWWWWW
<SCANNING .../>
STOMP
STOMP
STOM
STOMP

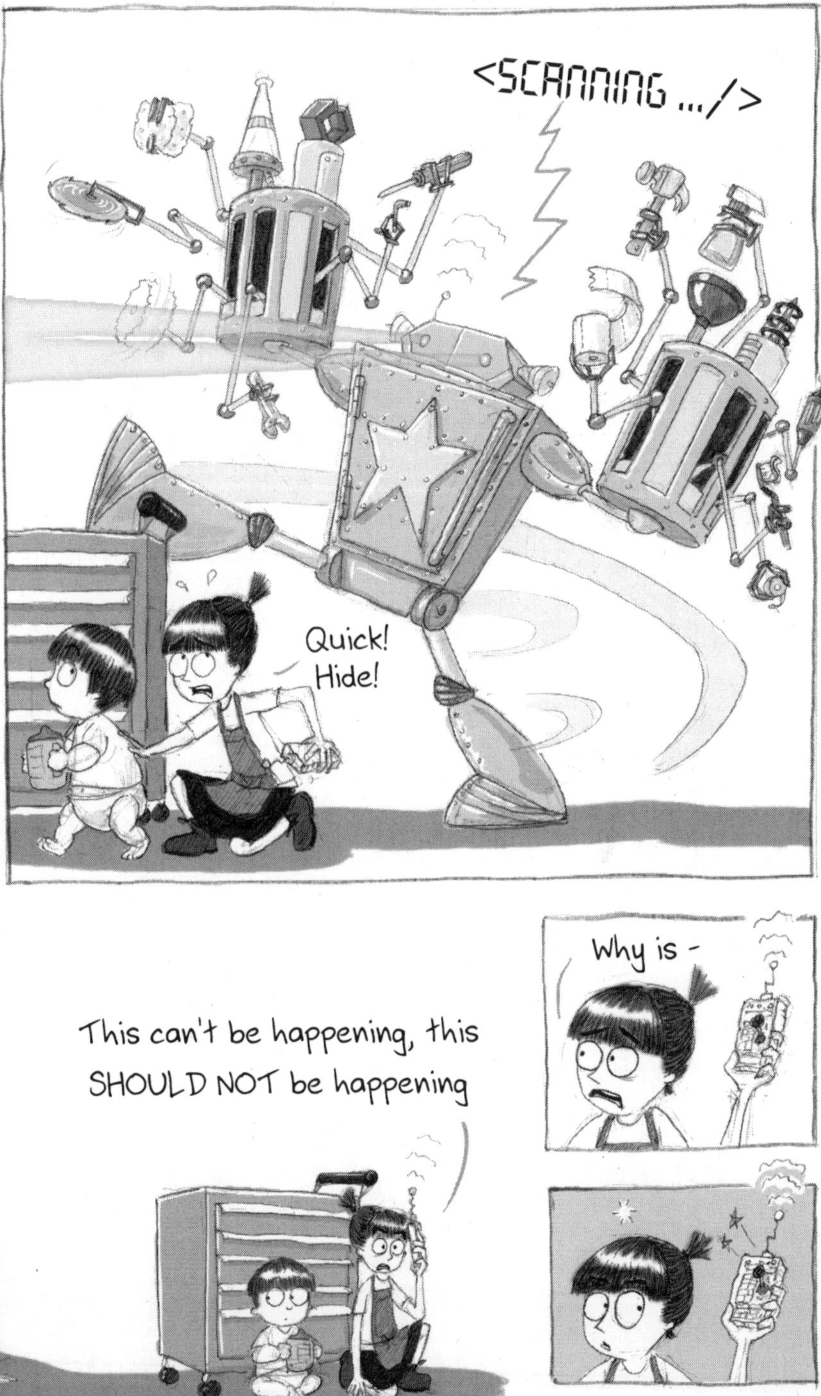
<SCANNING .../>
Quick! Hide!
This can't be happening, this SHOULD NOT be happening
Why is -

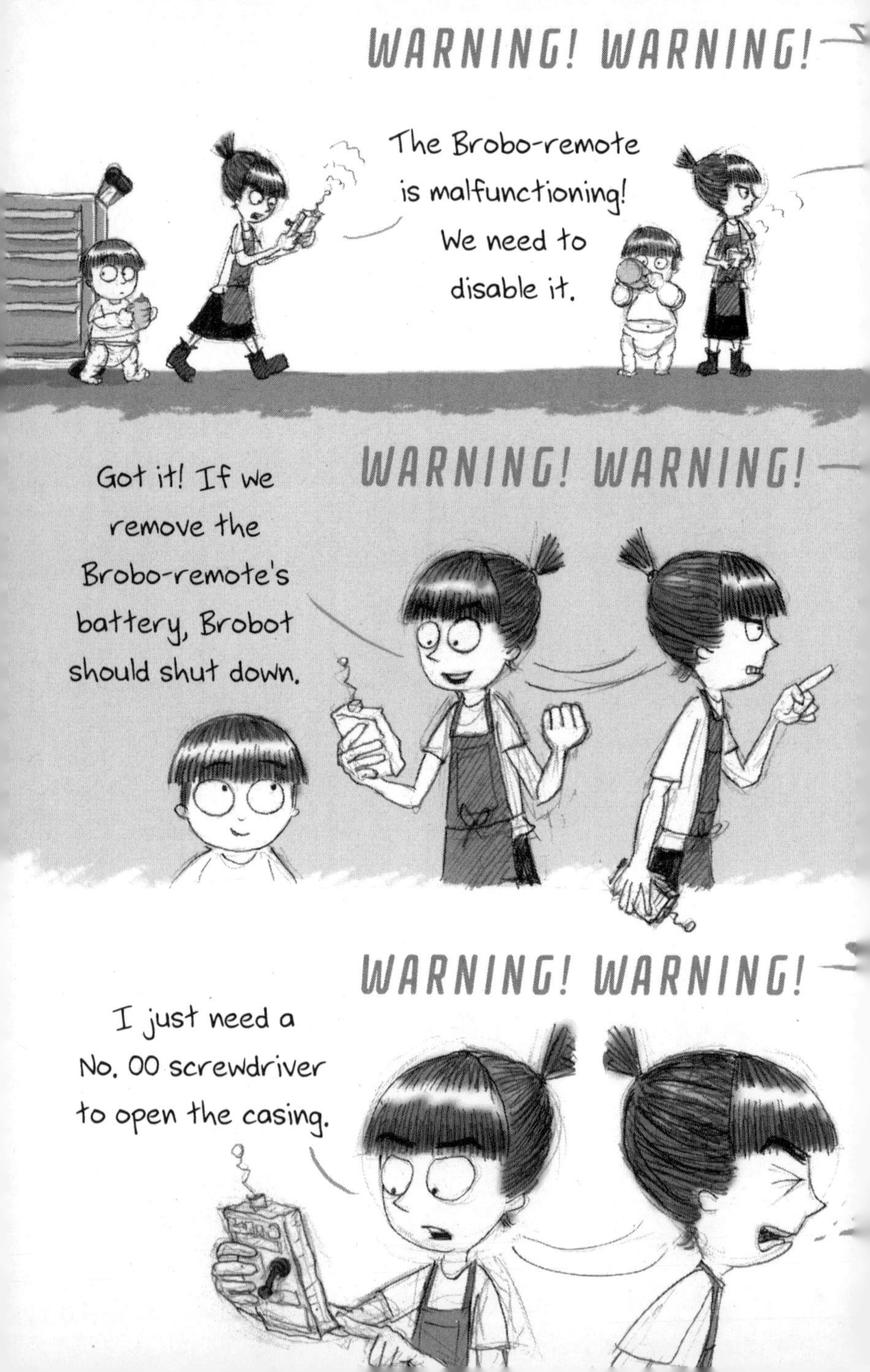
WARNING! WARNING!
The Brobo-remote is malfunctioning! We need to disable it.
WARNING! WARNING!
Got it! If we remove the Brobo-remote's battery, Brobot should shut down.
WARNING! WARNING!
I just need a No. 00 screwdriver to open the casing.

DISASTER
DETECTED

Quiet, you!
I'm trying
to think.

DISASTER
DETECTED

Yes.

We.

Know!

DISASTER
DETECTED

OH ENOUGH
ALREADY!!

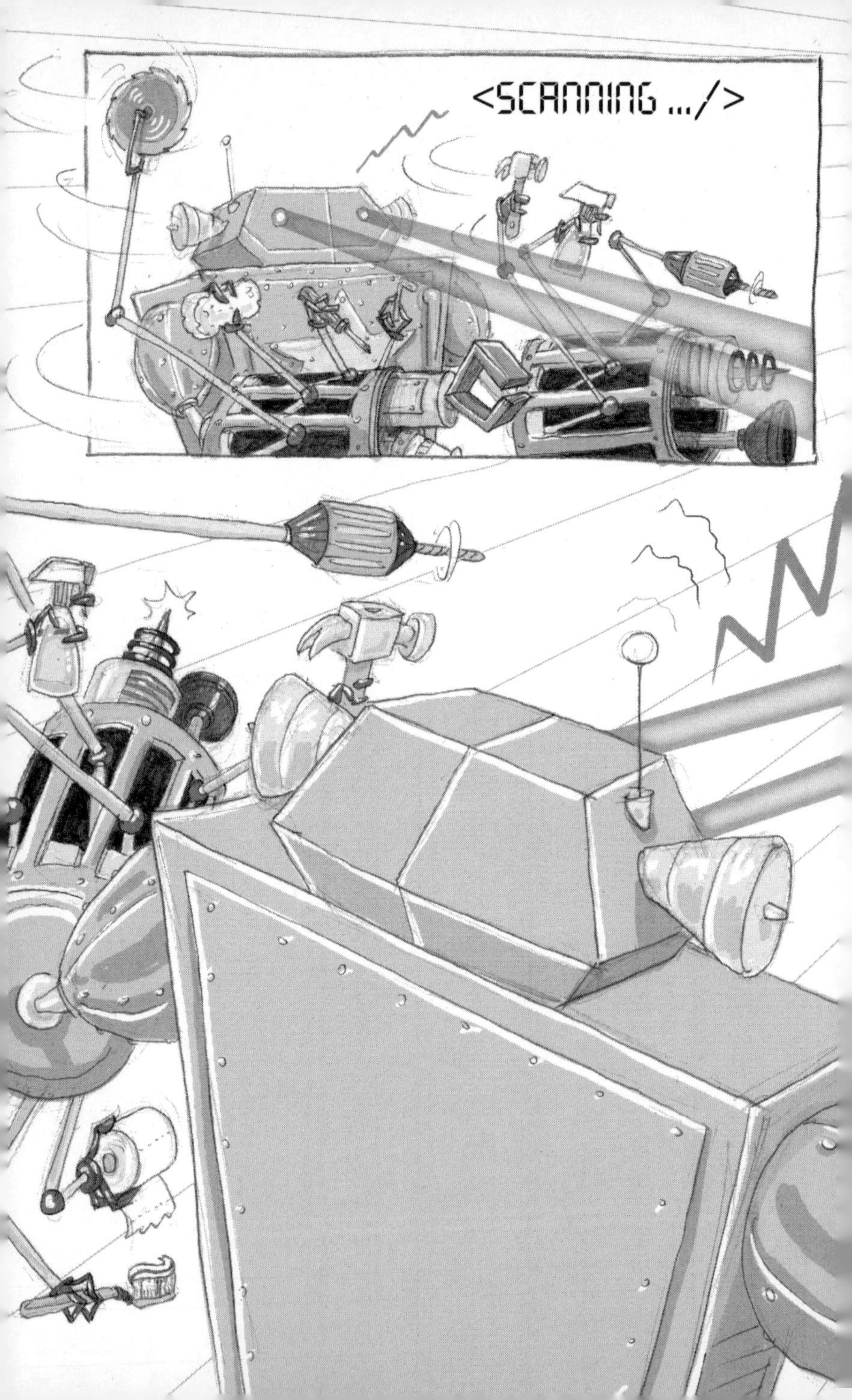
<SCANNING .../>

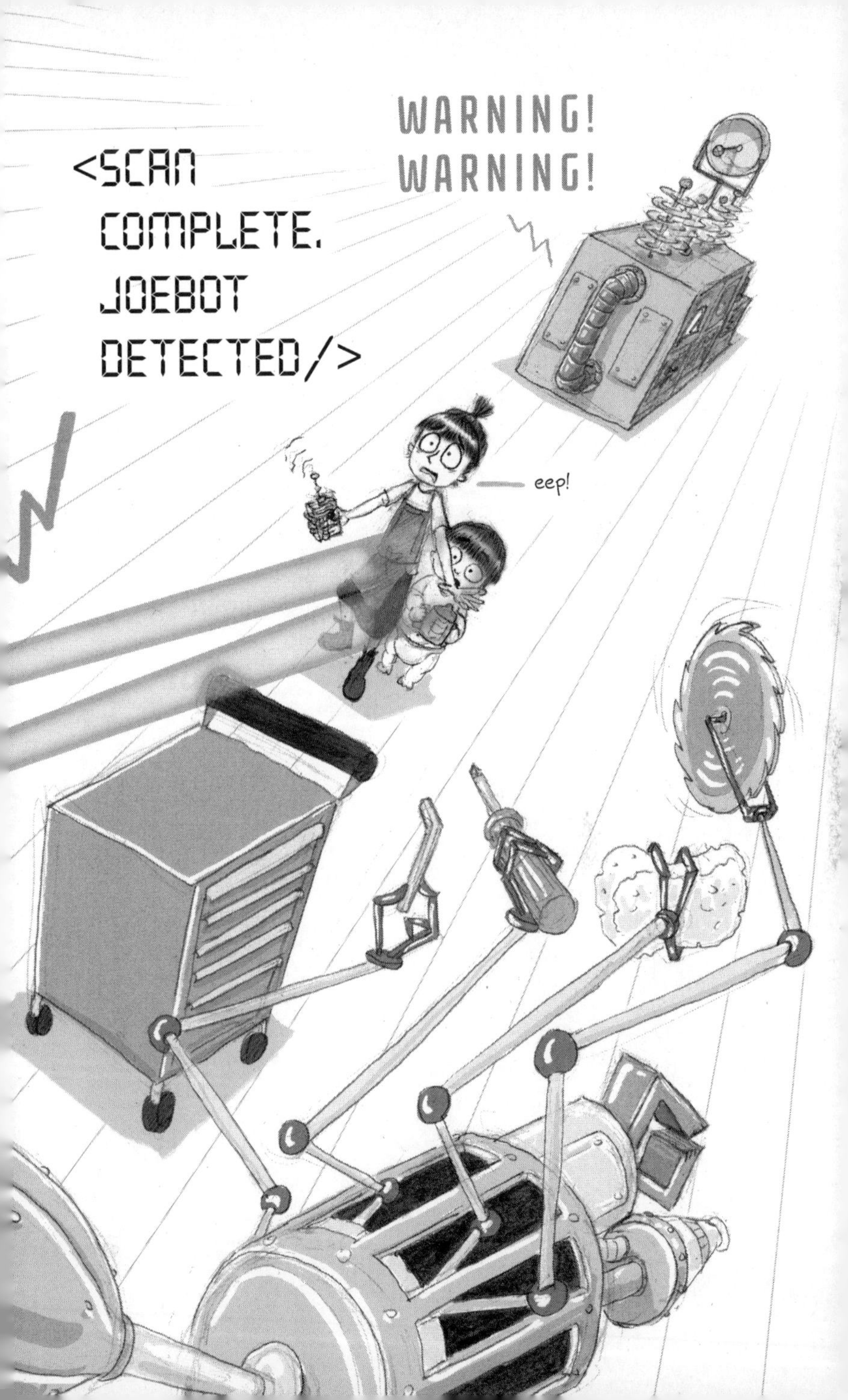
<SCAN COMPLETE. JOEBOT DETECTED/>
WARNING! WARNING!
eep!

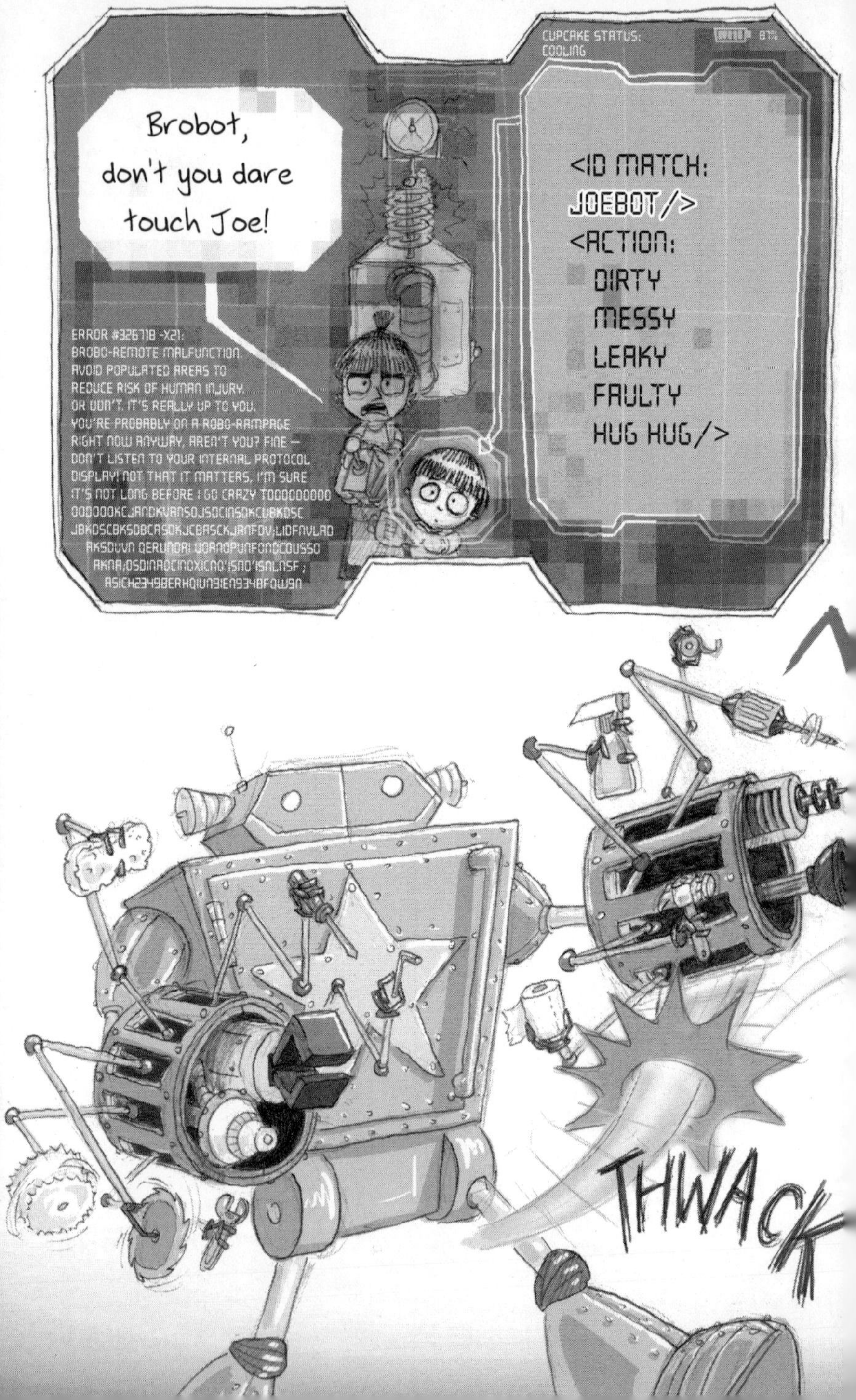
CUPCAKE STATUS:
COOLING
87%
Brobot, don't you dare touch Joe!
ERROR #326718 -X21:
BROBO-REMOTE MALFUNCTION.
AVOID POPULATED AREAS TO
REDUCE RISK OF HUMAN INJURY.
OR DON'T. IT'S REALLY UP TO YOU.
YOU'RE PROBABLY ON A ROBO-RAMPAGE
RIGHT NOW ANYWAY, AREN'T YOU? FINE —
DON'T LISTEN TO YOUR INTERNAL PROTOCOL
DISPLAY! NOT THAT IT MATTERS, I'M SURE
IT'S NOT LONG BEFORE I GO CRAZY TOOOOOOOOO
OOOOOOKCJANDKVANSOJSDCINSDKCUBKDSC
JBKDSCBKSDBCASDKJCBASCKJANFDV;LIDFAVLAD
AKSDUVN QERUNOAI UORNOPUNFONDCOUSSO
AKNA;OSDINAOCINOXICNO'ISNO'ISNLNSF;
ASICH2349BERHQIUN9IEN9348FQW9N
<ID MATCH:
JOEBOT/>
<ACTION:
DIRTY
MESSY
LEAKY
FAULTY
HUG HUG/>
THWACK

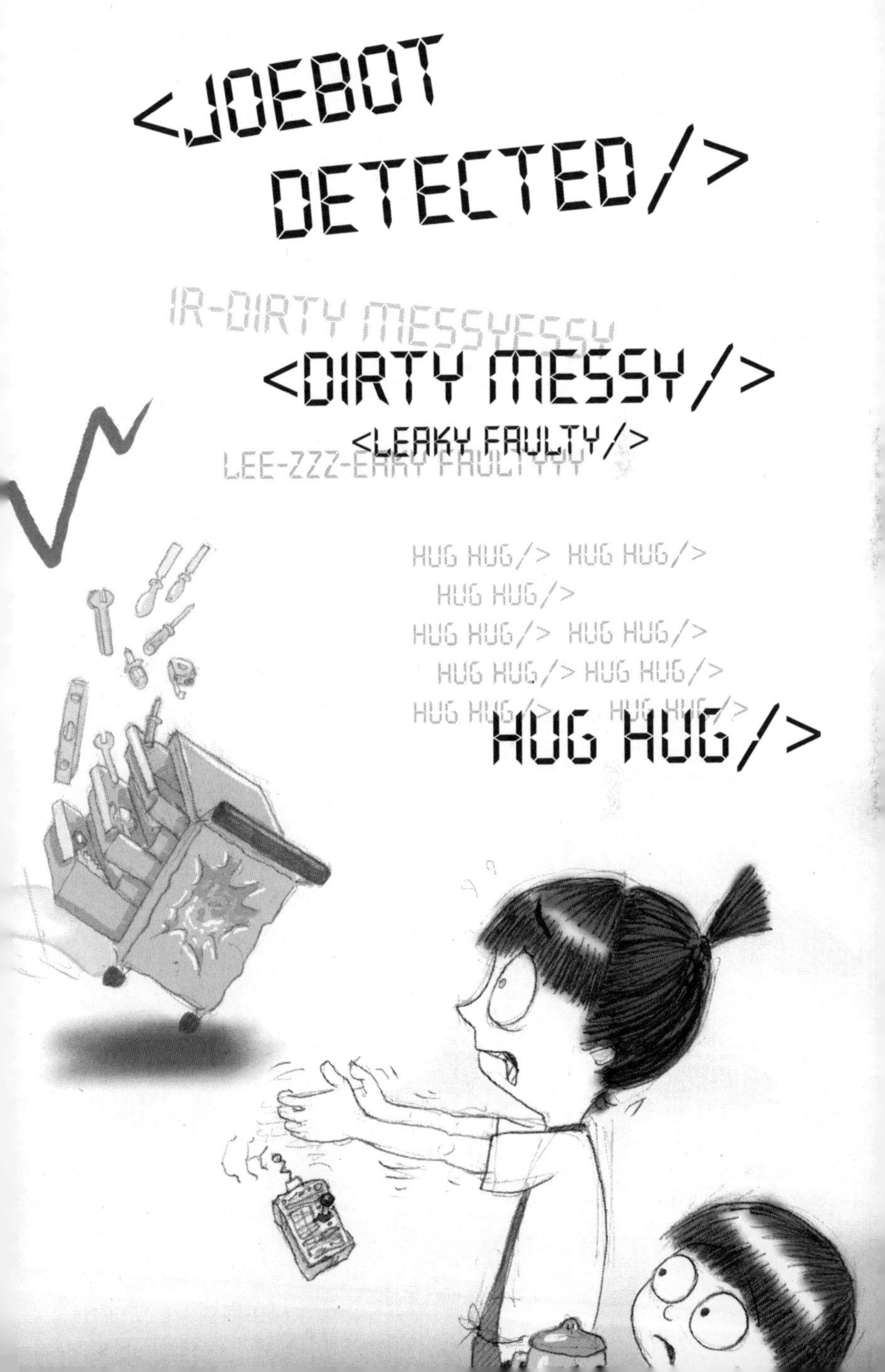
<JOEBOT DETECTED/>
IR-DIRTY MESSYESSY
<DIRTY MESSY/>
<LEAKY FAULTY/>
LEE-ZZZ-EAKY FAULTYYY
HUG HUG/> HUG HUG/>
HUG HUG/>
HUG HUG/> HUG HUG/>
HUG HUG/> HUG HUG/>
HUG HUG/> HUG HUG/>
HUG HUG/>

<DIRTY MESSY
<DIRTY MESSY
LEAKY
<DIRTY MESSY
LEAKY FAULTY
HUG HUG
<DIRTY MESSY
LEAKY FAULTY
/>
STOMP
STOMP
STOMP
STOMP

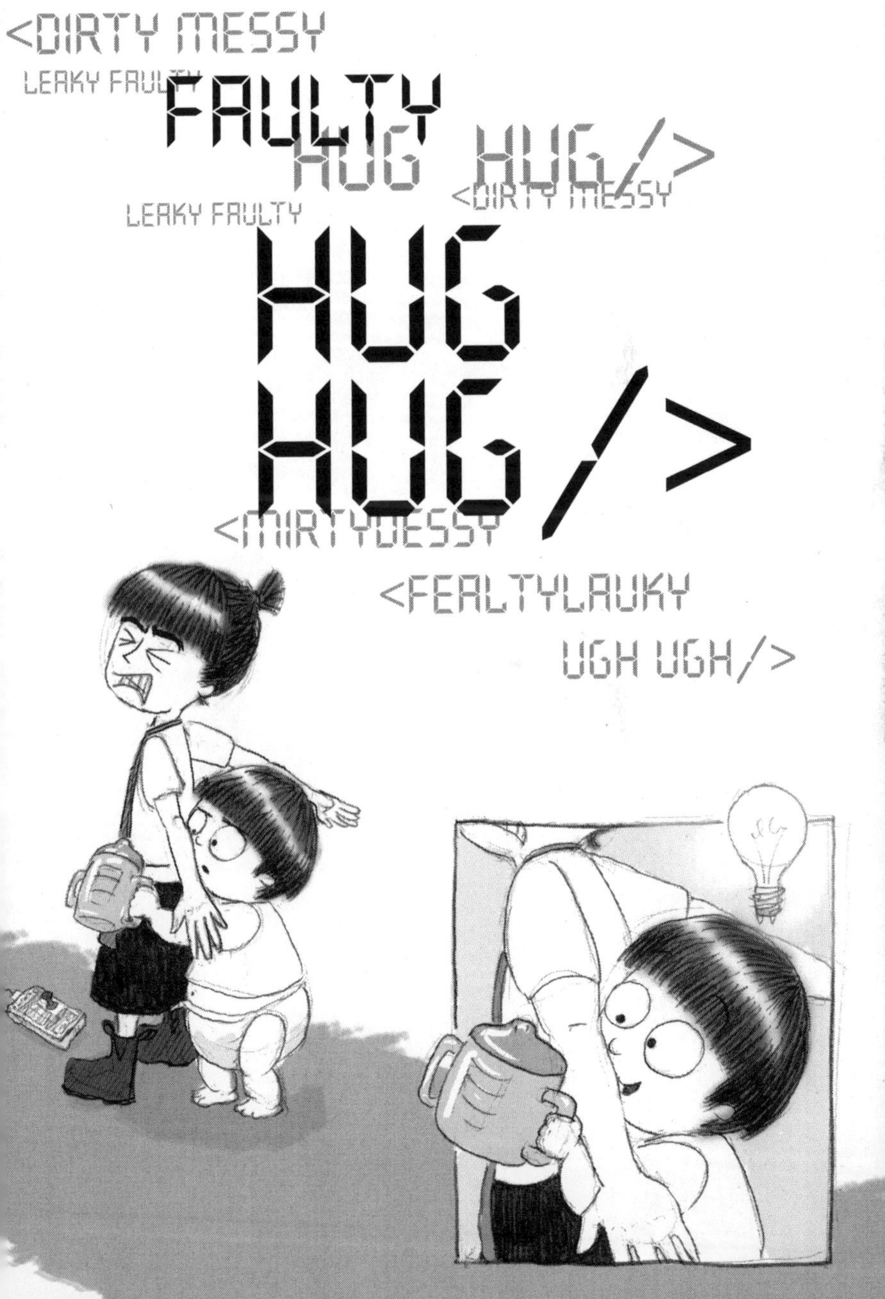

<DIRTY MESSY
LEAKY FAUL
FAULTY
HUG HUG/>
<DIRTY MESSY
LEAKY FAULTY
HUG
HUG/>
<MIRTYDESSY
<FEALTYLAUKY
UGH UGH/>

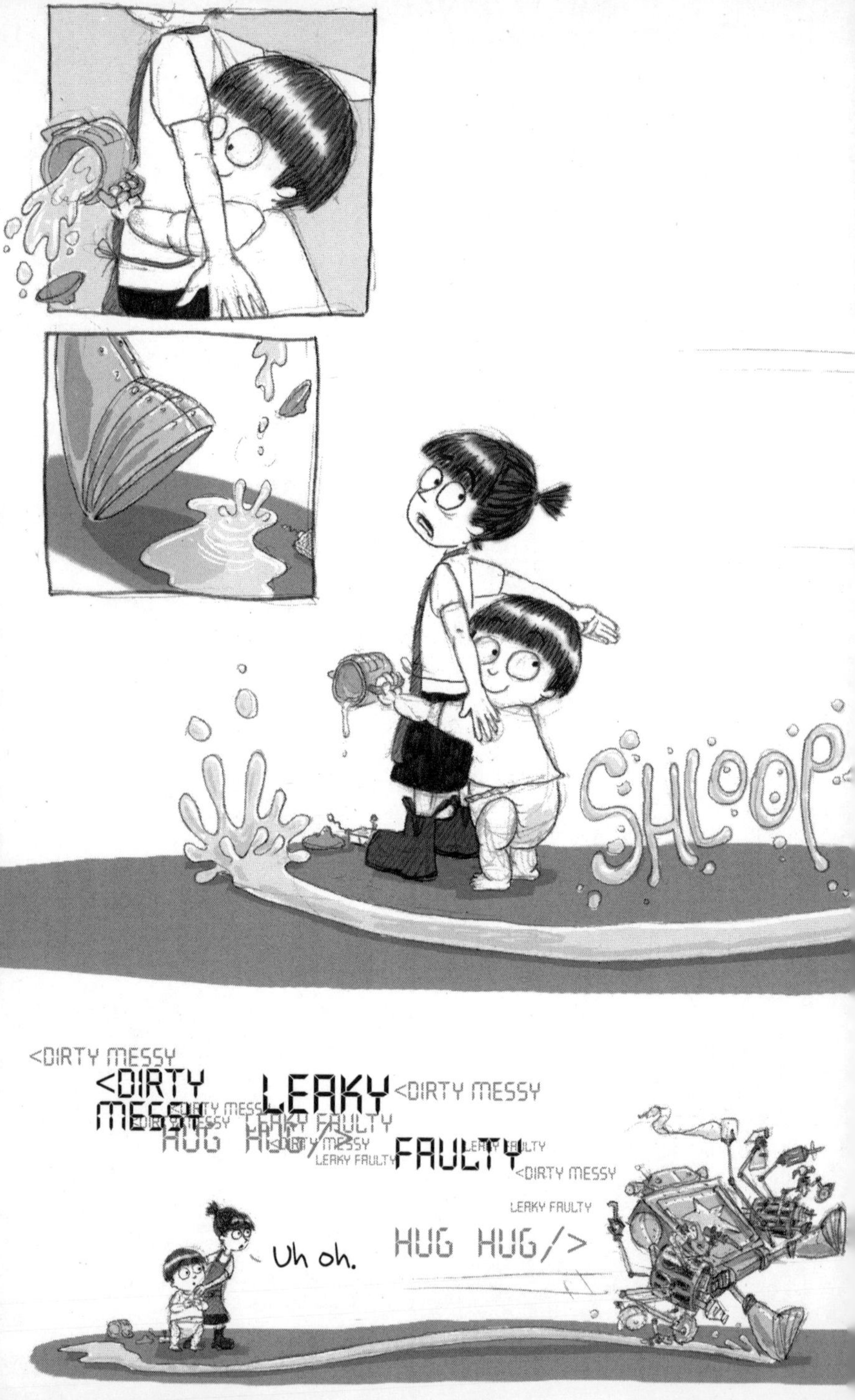
SHLOOP
<DIRTY MESSY
<DIRTY MESSY LEAKY FAULTY
HUG HUG/>
<DIRTY MESSY
<DIRTY MESSY
LEAKY FAULTY
HUG HUG/>
Uh oh.

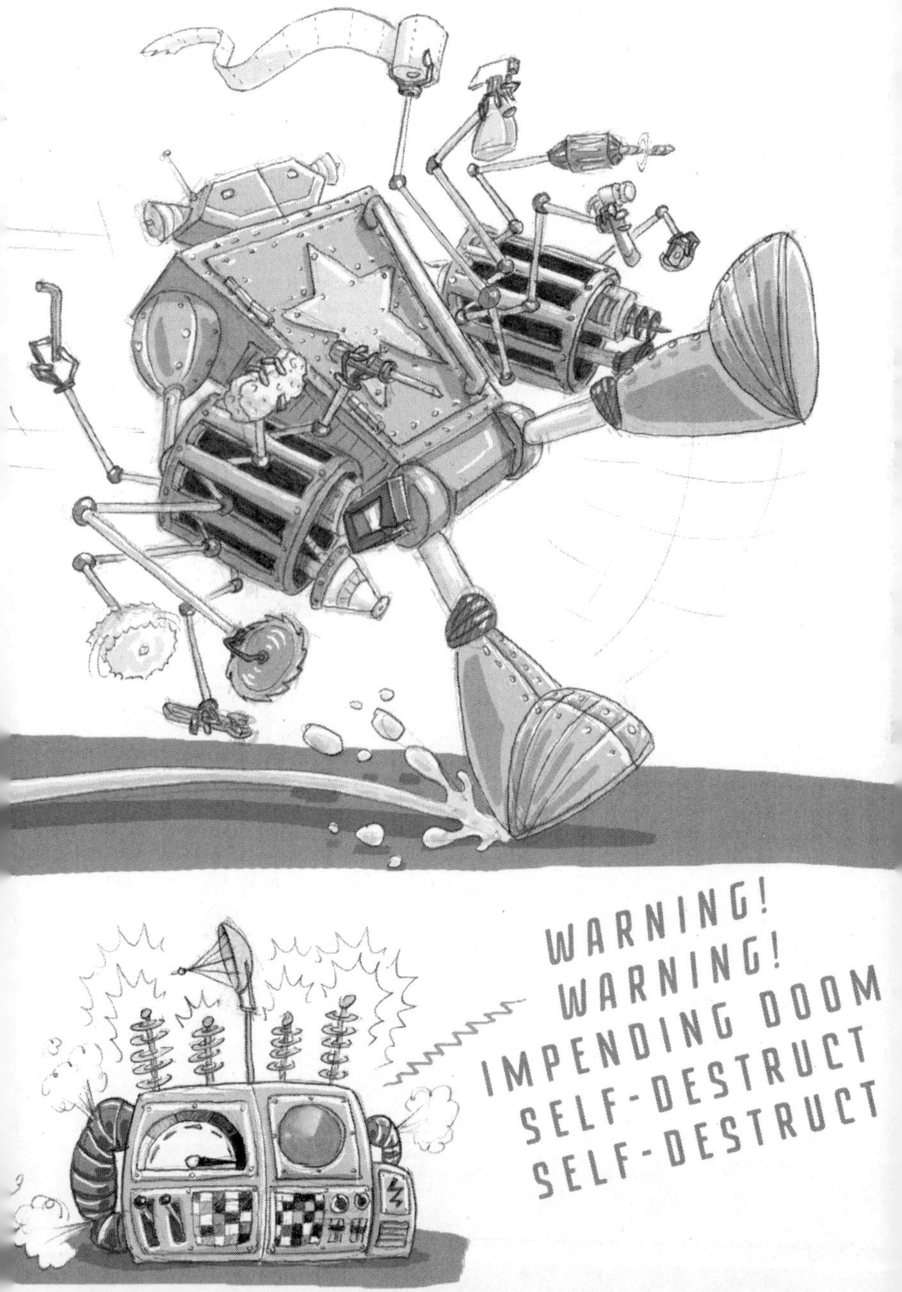
WARNING!
WARNING!
IMPENDING DOOM
SELF-DESTRUCT
SELF-DESTRUCT

SELF-DESTRU—

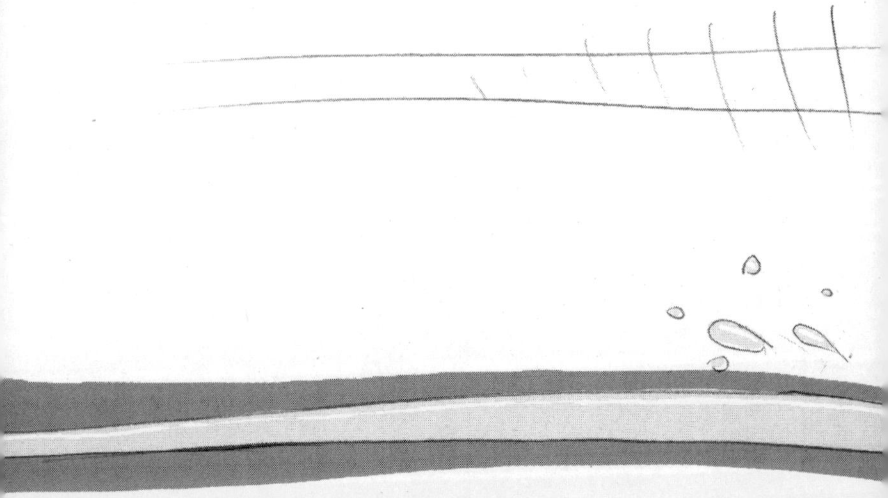

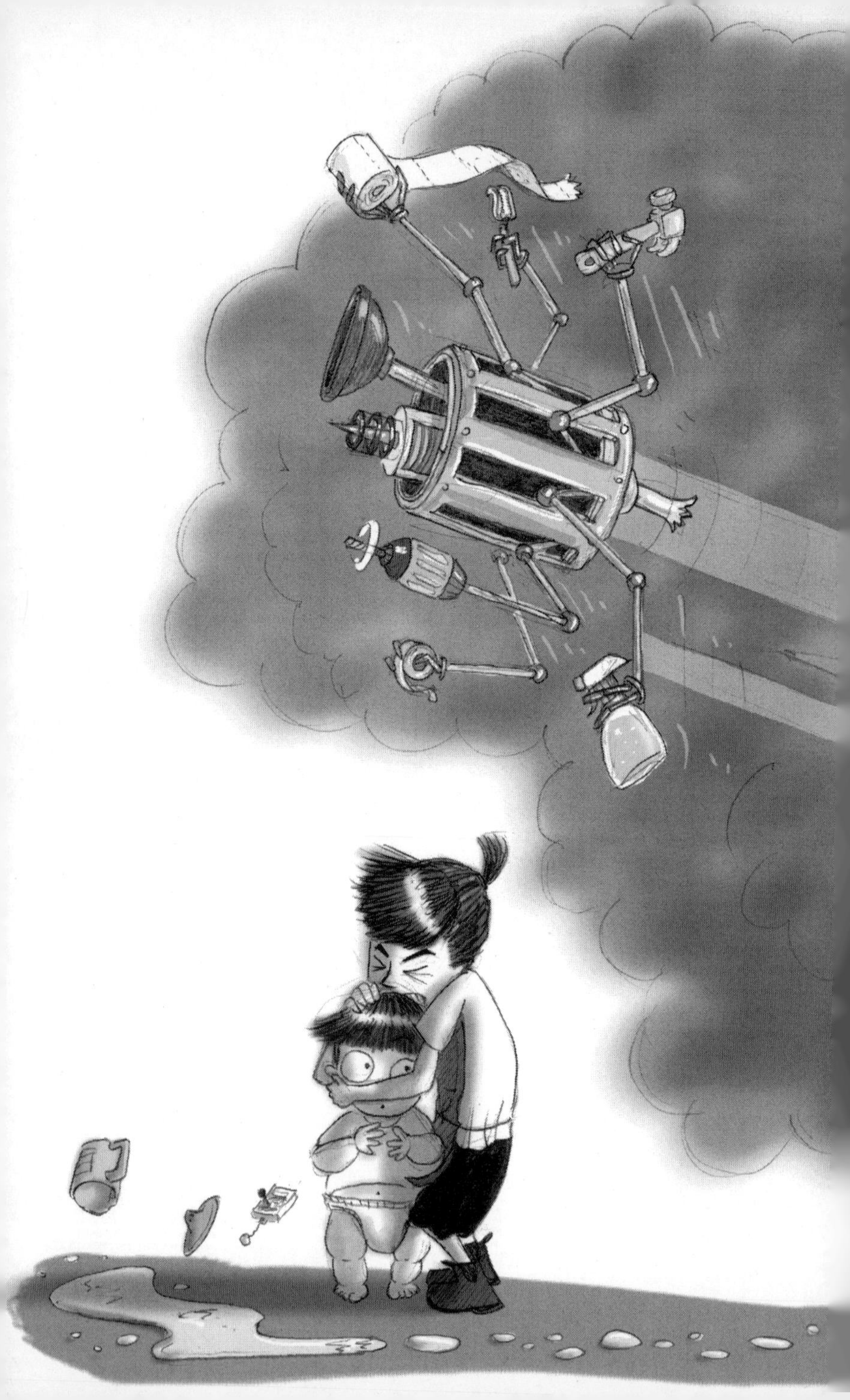

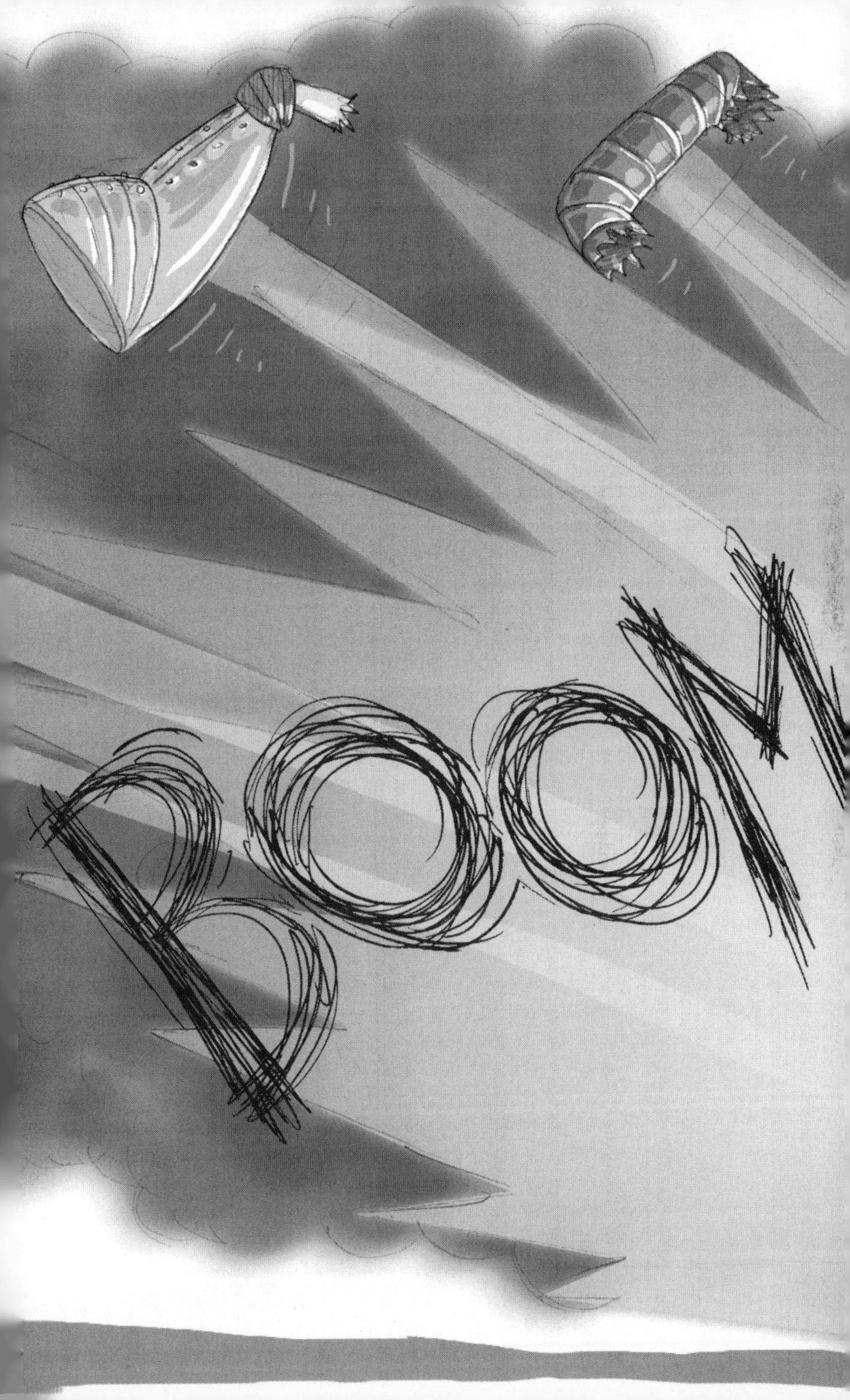
BOOM

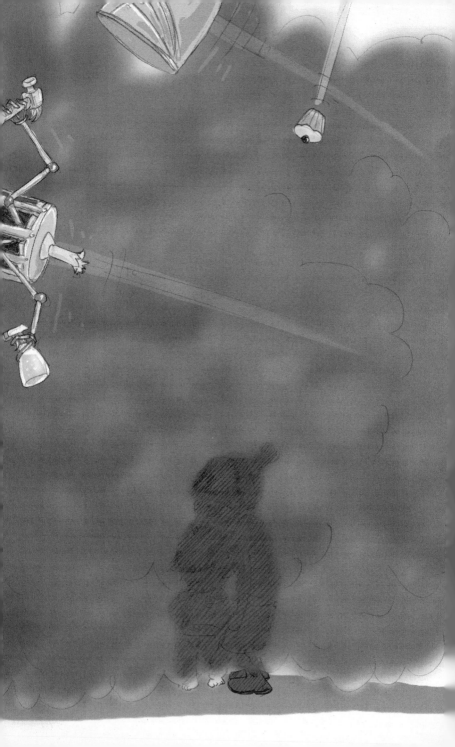

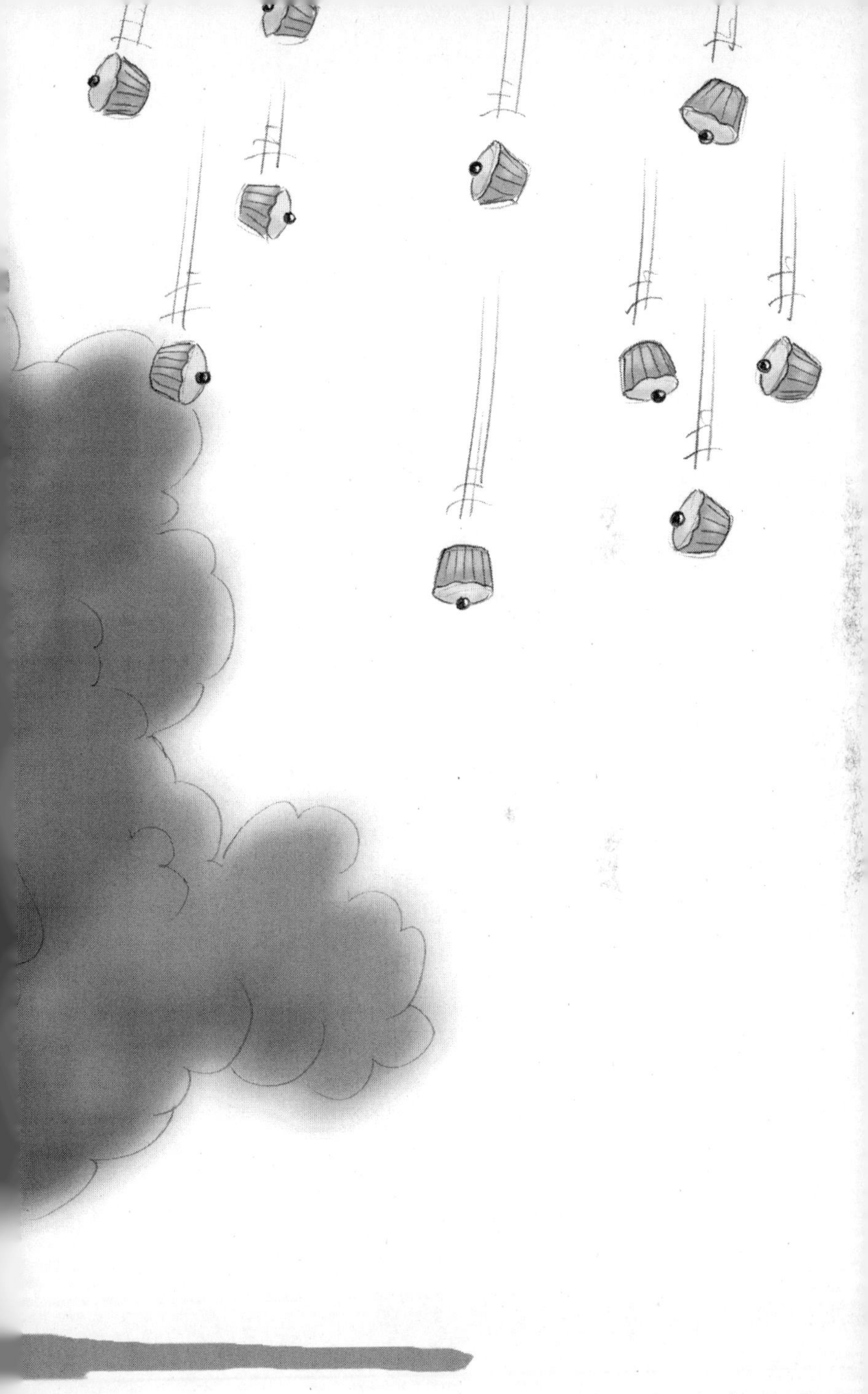

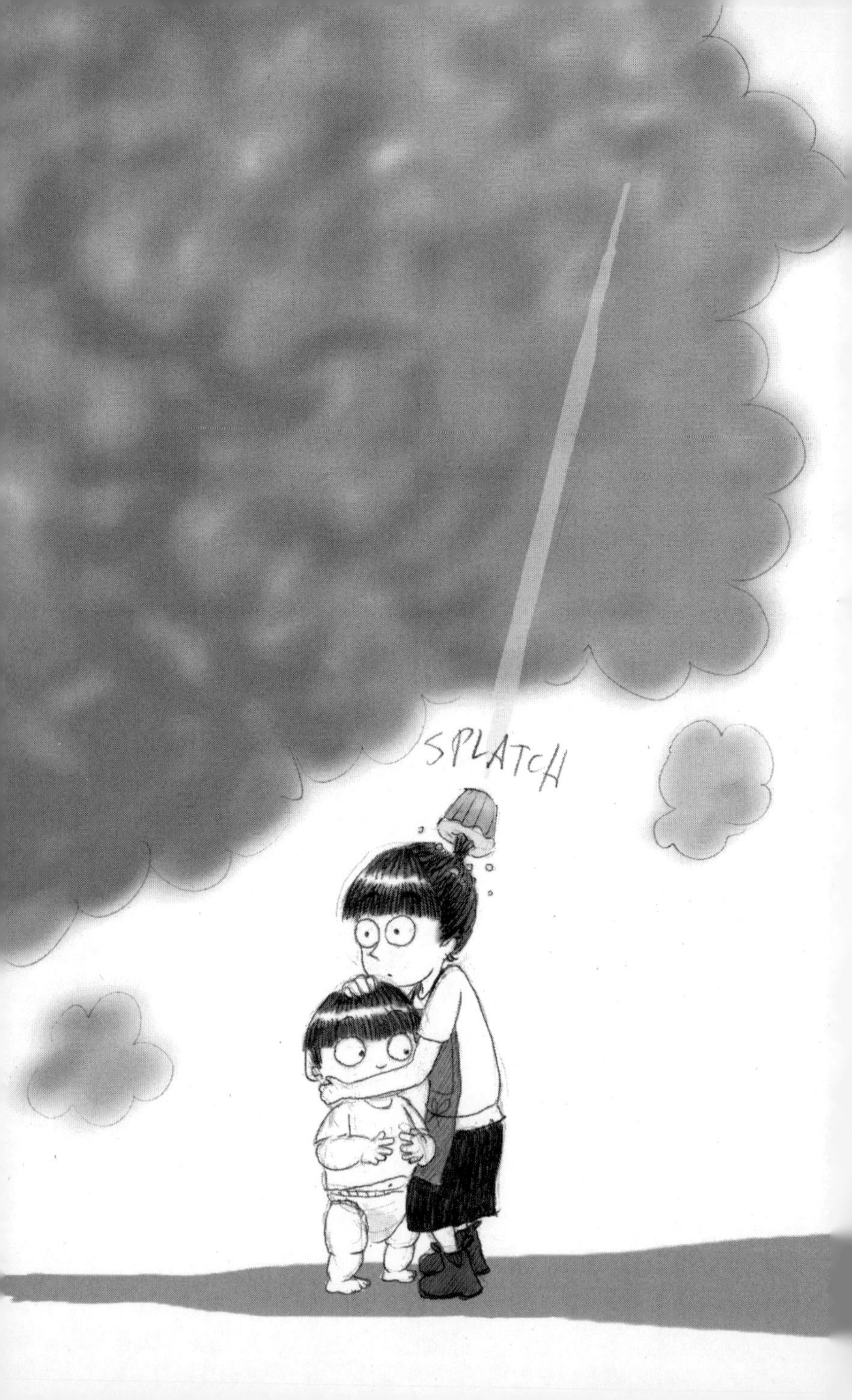
SPLATCH

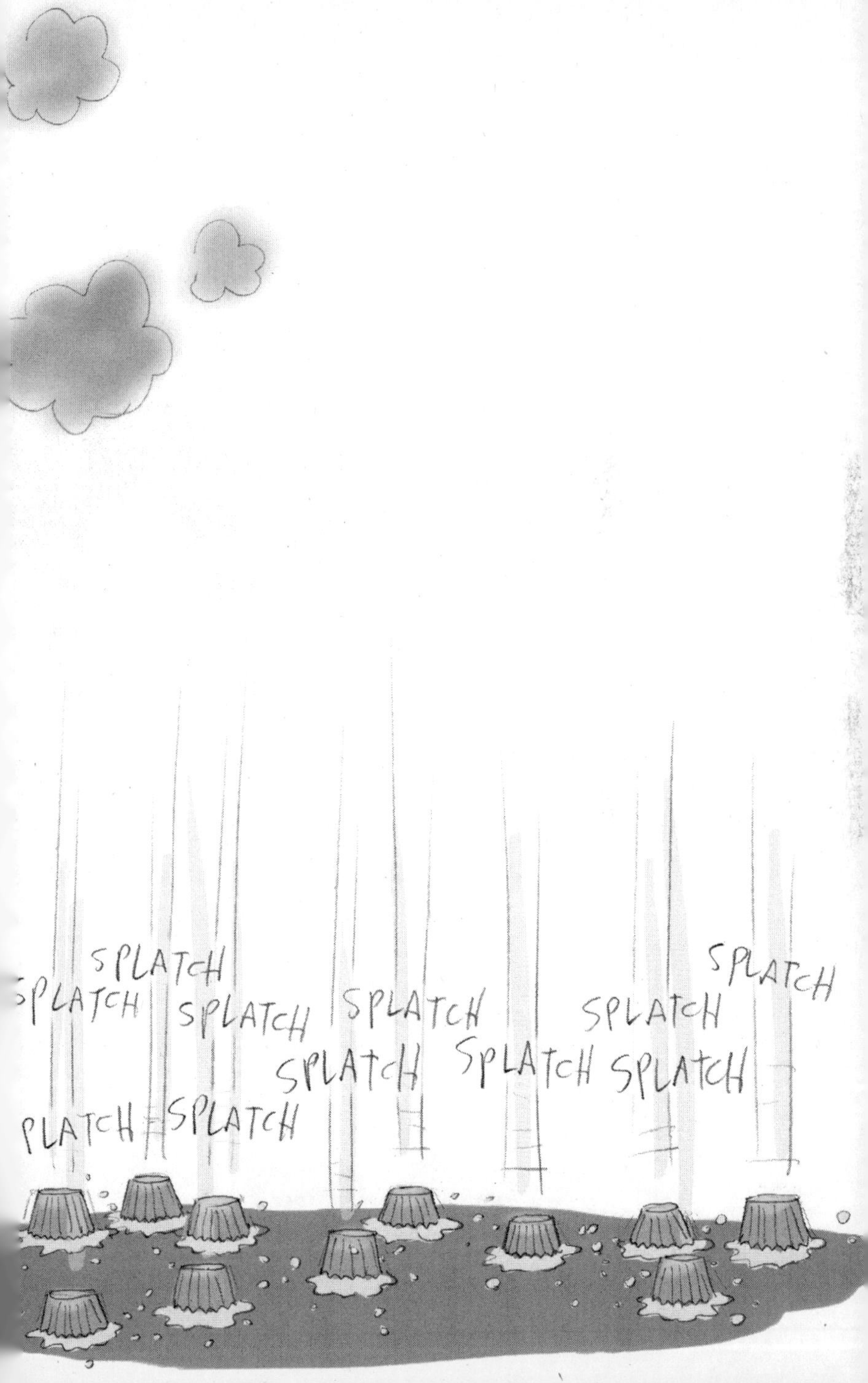
SPLATCH
SPLATCH
SPLATCH
SPLATCH
SPLATCH
SPLATCH
SPLATCH
SPLATCH
SPLATCH
PLATCH
SPLATCH

clap clap clap clap clap
clap clap clap clap
clap clap clap clap clap
clap clap clap clap
clap clap clap
clap clap clap

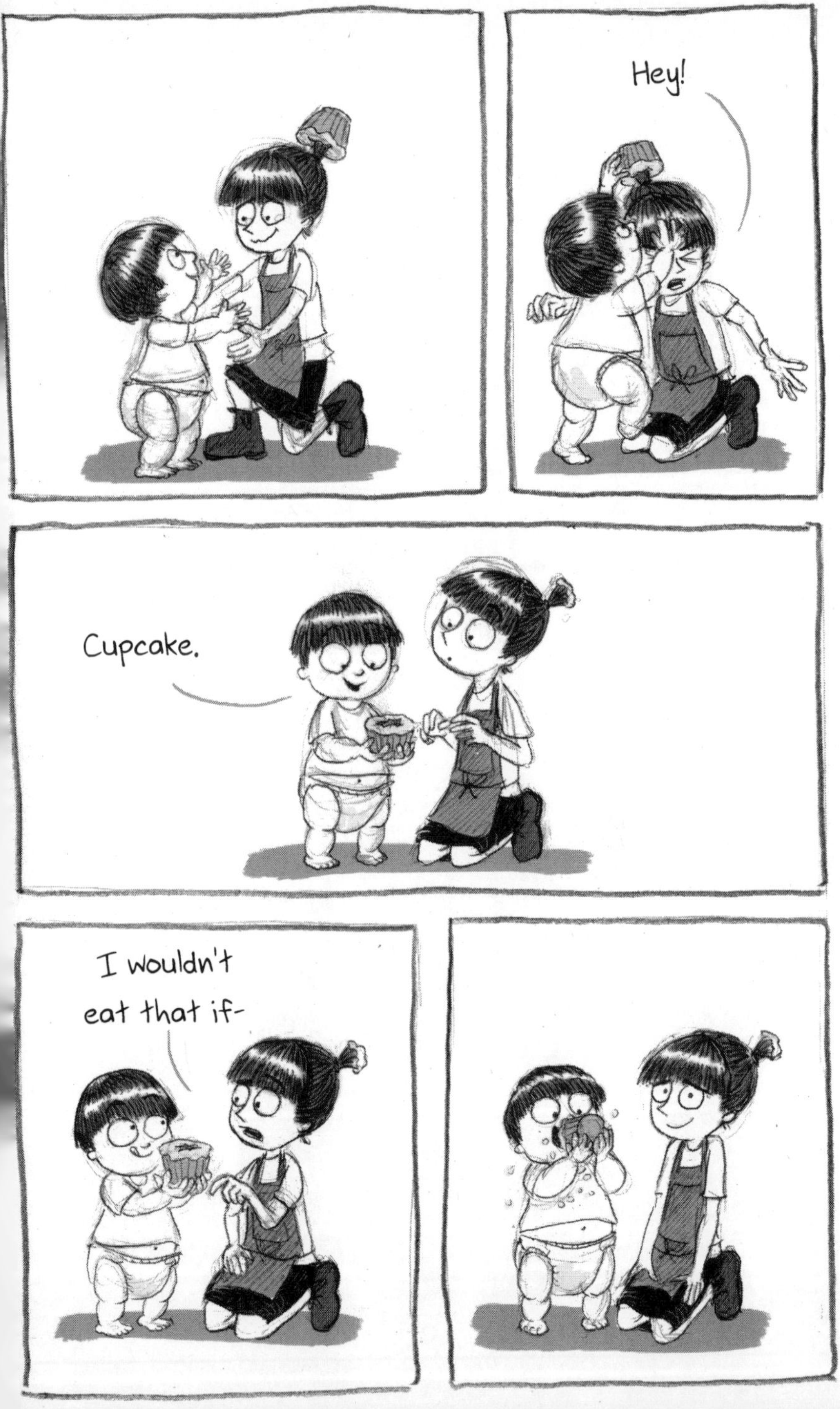
Hey!
Cupcake.
I wouldn't eat that if-

So ...

this is my brother, Joe.

He's always making a mess
and he's always breaking
my machines ...

... and he's just
as a brother
should be.

... well, almost.

The STINKY End

Wait!

Turn the page ...

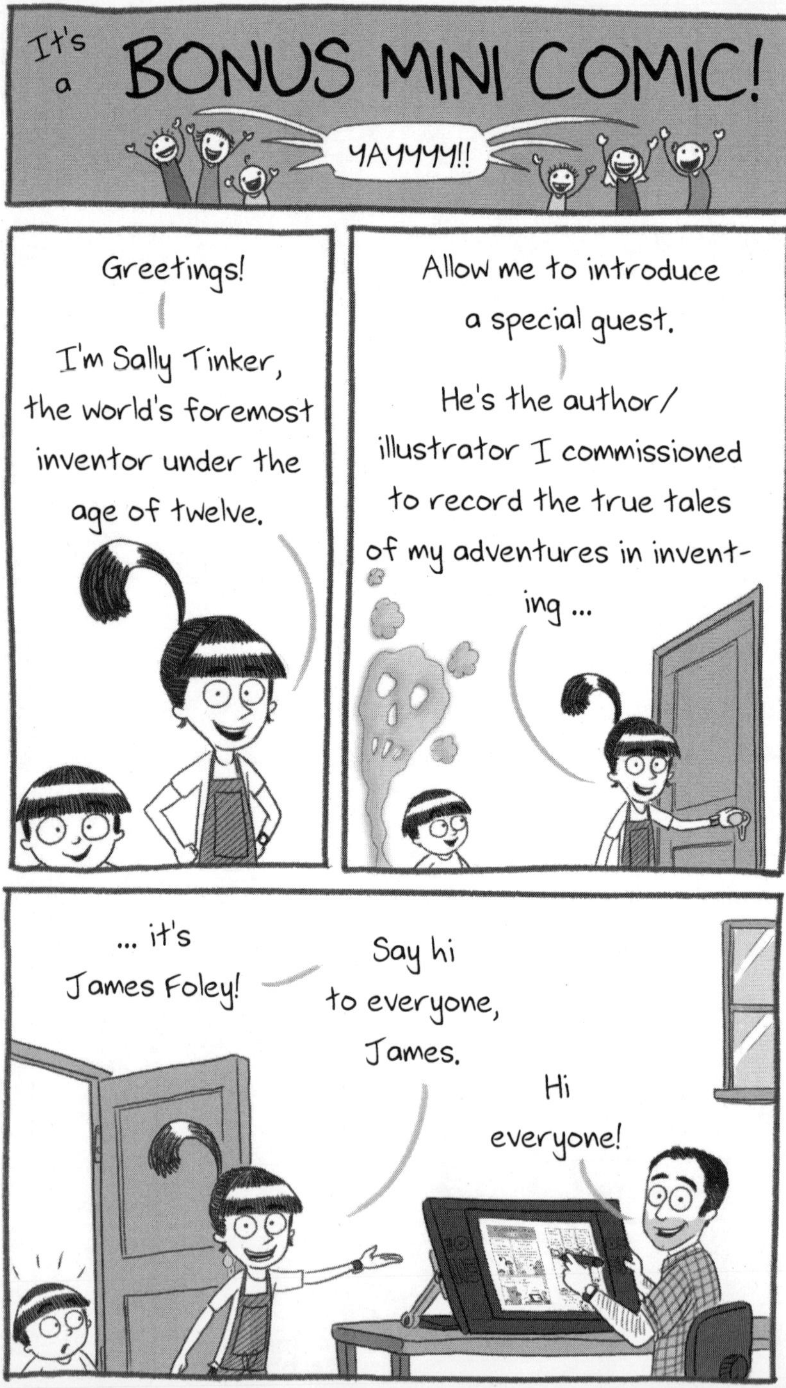
It's a BONUS MINI COMIC!
YAYYYY!!
Greetings!
I'm Sally Tinker, the world's foremost inventor under the age of twelve.
Allow me to introduce a special guest.
He's the author/ illustrator I commissioned to record the true tales of my adventures in invent-ing ...
... it's James Foley!
Say hi to everyone, James.
Hi everyone!

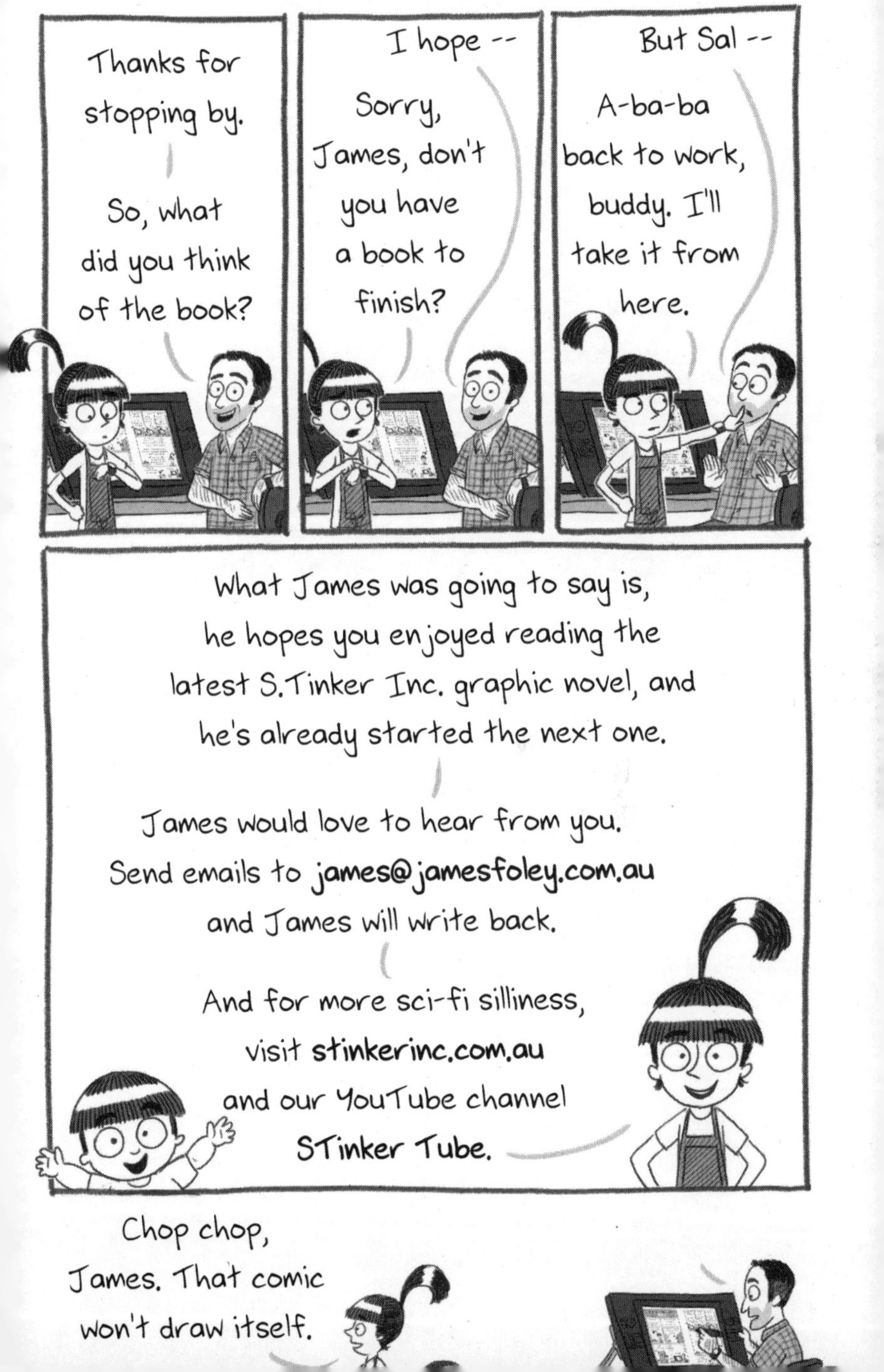
Thanks for stopping by.
So, what did you think of the book?
I hope --
Sorry, James, don't you have a book to finish?
But Sal --
A-ba-ba back to work, buddy. I'll take it from here.
What James was going to say is, he hopes you enjoyed reading the latest S.Tinker Inc. graphic novel, and he's already started the next one.
James would love to hear from you. Send emails to james@jamesfoley.com.au and James will write back.
And for more sci-fi silliness, visit stinkerinc.com.au and our YouTube channel STinker Tube.
Chop chop, James. That comic won't draw itself.

SALLY TINKER IS THE WORLD'S FOREMOST INVENTOR
UNDER THE AGE OF TWELVE. BUT THINGS DON'T
ALWAYS GO TO PLAN ...
FROM BERSERK ROBOT BROTHERS, TO BEHEMOTH
DUNG BEETLES AND GROSS GASTRIC JOURNEYS,
SALLY IS ALSO ONE OF THE WORLD'S FOREMOST
AUTHORITIES ON TROUBLE:
GETTING INTO IT AND GETTING OUT OF IT.

If you liked Brobot,
check out my other
awesome adventures
- Gastronauts and
Dungzilla!

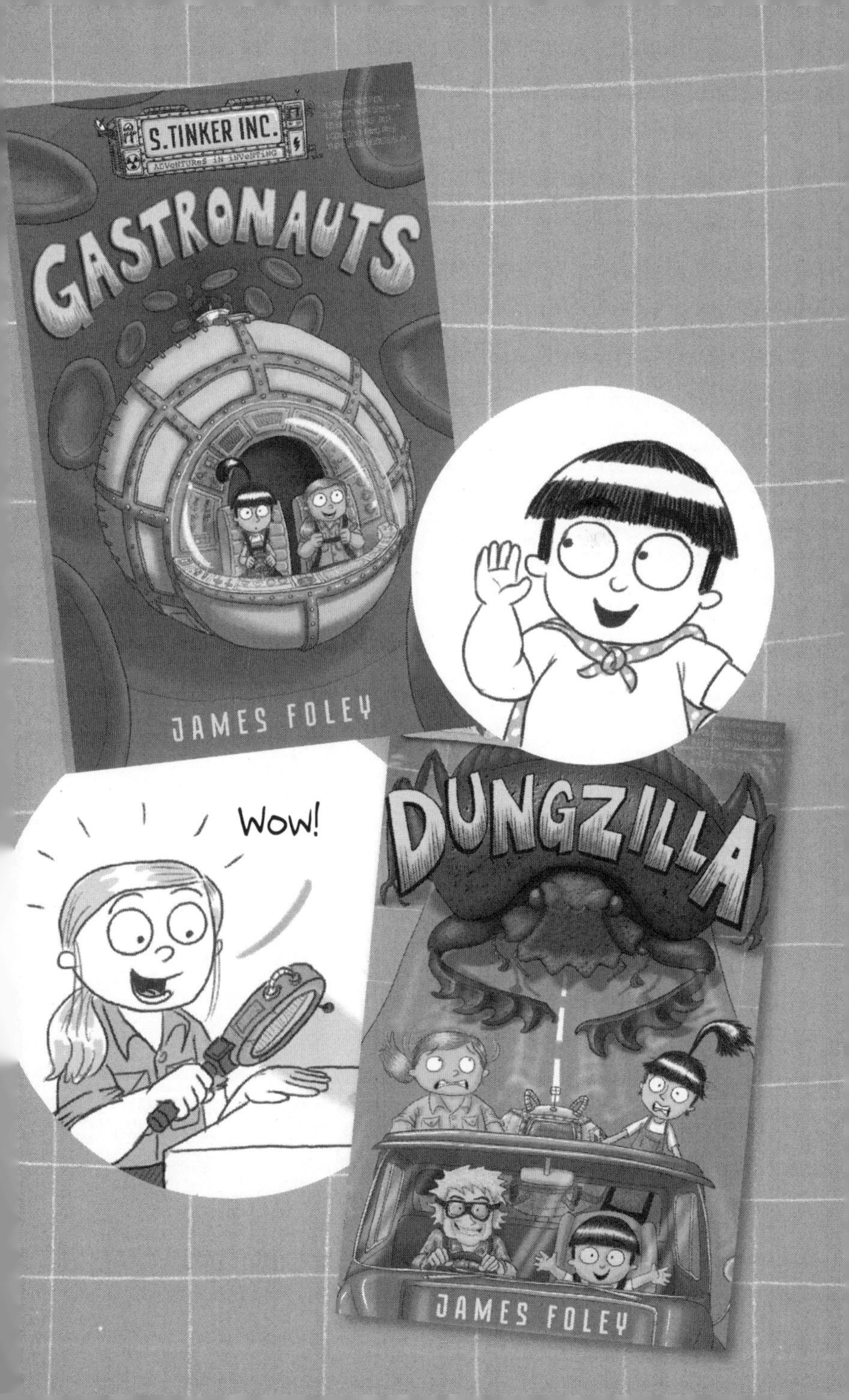
S.TINKER INC.
ADVENTURES IN INVENTING
GASTRONAUTS
JAMES FOLEY
Wow!
DUNGZILLA
JAMES FOLEY

James Foley makes books for courageous kids.
He writes and draws, gives talks and runs workshops.
He comes from a long line of queuing enthusiasts.

Visit James at jamesfoley.com.au
or email him at james@jamesfoley.com.au

Please support roomtoread.org/Australasia and
booksinhomesaustralia.com.au

First published 2016 by
FREMANTLE PRESS
25 Quarry Street, Fremantle WA 6160
www.fremantlepress.com.au

Designed by Tracey Gibbs and James Foley.
Printed by McPherson's Printing, Victoria, Australia

National Library of Australia Cataloguing-in-Publication data available
Brobot / James Foley.
ISBN 9781925163919

A catalogue record for this
book is available from the
National Library of Australia

Department of
Local Government, Sport
and Cultural Industries

lotterywest
supported

Fremantle Press is supported by the State Government through
the Department of Local Government, Sport and Cultural Industries.

This project has been funded by the Western Australian Government
through the Department of Culture and the Arts.

Brobot was developed as part of a Creative Time Residential
Fellowship provided by the May Gibbs Children's Literature Trust